ORPHAN CHRISTMAS MIRACLE

VICTORIAN ROMANCE

ROSIE SWAN

PUREREAD.COM

CONTENTS

Part V

OVERCOMING

PART I
OVERCAST

PROLOGUE

A *Bright Day in Spring*

Patterson Estate, Sheffield County, England

The church bells tolled continuously on that warm Saturday at the beginning of spring. The flowers were in full bloom around the estate and the small village chapel was filled with the scent of roses. Servants had filled every free space with vases of blooming white and red roses, hence the sweet scent. Villagers came out in droves and lined the road from the estate gate right to the small chapel in the middle of the square. Everyone was very eager to catch a glimpse of the procession that was slowly making its way from the large manor, down the road and to the chapel, for it was a very fancy sight indeed.

As patrons of the village, one of the gifts that the Patterson family had given to the small church was a medium sized second-hand organ, and melodious sounds were heard by those standing close to the chapel. It was clear that a skilled organist had been brought in, no doubt to make this day very special indeed, for none of the inhabitants of Patterson Village had ever heard such magnificent playing before. Clearly, Mr. Patterson had gone all out to make sure that this day would go down in the annals of Patterson Village history as the wedding of the century.

For on this bright Saturday morning, the spinster daughter of the lord of the manor was preparing to tie the knot. It wasn't that Patterson Village, named after the family that owned the estate, hadn't seen weddings before. If ever there was a village in Sheffield that boasted of its many nuptials in spring and summer, indeed Patterson was it.

This was a different kind of wedding, for the thirty-year-old spinster, never before known to be interested in matrimony, was wedding a much unexpected groom. This man was the estate's twenty-four-year-old gardener. Tongues wagged, and speculation was rife as to why the simple Edwin Cameron, son of the poor widow, Mrs. Grace Cameron, could have reached above his estate to consent to a wedding with a woman who was clearly his superior in every way. The rumour was that the young man would be dropping his own simple surname to take up the more prestigious one of his bride.

In the leading carriage of the procession, a middle-aged woman sat sobbing quietly in one corner, using the corner of her frayed shawl to wipe her face from time to time. The intended groom was the only other occupant of the carriage. Though his face was devoid of any expression, his gentle soul was bleeding because of his Mama's heart wrenching sobs.

"Ma, you've got to stop crying, for you'll make yourself ill," Edwin Cameron pleaded with his mother in a gentle voice. "You know that if there was any other way, I wouldn't be doing this."

"If only your father hadn't died and left us destitute and heavily in debt," Mrs. Cameron sniffed. "It breaks my heart to see my only son sacrificing his happiness just because his father was a heavy gambler."

"Mama, please don't distress yourself. Mr. Patterson said it's going to be a marriage in name only, and after two years have passed, Miss Elaine Patterson and I will go our separate ways. Then I can go and marry for love, after saving our home and name from ruin." He didn't tell his mother about the conversation he'd overheard between Mr. Patterson and his daughter, one in which an heir had been mentioned. Miss Elaine had brushed her father aside and told him that she had no desire to bear any child and was only getting married to fulfil the terms of her grandfather's will. The thought had troubled him for days because he couldn't imagine siring a child with the cold and hard Miss Elaine Patterson.

That she'd chosen him to be her husband had surprised even him, but then he'd decided to use the strange union to his advantage also. All his father's debts would be settled, and his mother would live as a free woman for the rest of her life. No price was too high to pay to ensure that his beloved mother never spent another sleepless night. Yet he made no mention of this to his distraught mother, instead seeking to reassure her. "Ma, all will be will, you'll see. Mr. Patterson is a man of his word."

But Mrs. Cameron was shaking her head. "Don't believe everything that those people tell you," she whispered urgently. "Right now, they hold our lives in their hands, and they can so easily change the terms of the agreement. I fear that you, my son, may be walking into a trap that you won't be able to extricate yourself from. There's more to all this than meets the eye, and my heart is full of fear, Son." She fell on her knees before him, and he quickly raised her back to the seat. "It's not too late to change your mind."

"Ma, I can't let you go to the debtors' prison or even the poor workhouse. This is the only way that I'll be able to keep you safe. It's a marriage of convenience, and besides, Miss Elaine doesn't even look at me. I'm merely a means to an end for her. Please," he wiped her tears, "Don't cry, Ma, you're breaking my heart." His voice cracked with emotion, and his face was quite pale.

Mrs. Cameron saw the distress on her son's face and quickly wiped her face. Her love for her son overshadowed the distress she was feeling. From the moment he was born, Edwin had been the light of her life, and seeing him this distraught nearly broke her heart. He'd always been a good and obedient son, and he shouldn't have to pay for the sins of his father. He always took too much upon his own shoulders. Whenever she had tried to stop him from overdoing things, he would tell her that as the man of the home, it was expected of him. Now he was shouldering yet another burden that wasn't of his making, that of ensuring that she didn't end up homeless or in a poor workhouse.

"See, I'm not crying anymore," she gave him a shaky smile. "I pray that all will be well with you in your new marriage, my son. But never let your guard down, not even for one moment. Always watch yourself around these people. Don't acquire a taste for their delicacies and never forget where you came from. You, my son, are a worthy man. Please don't trust these people too much. We come from different stations in life, and I want you to always know your place."

Though the young man knew that his mother spoke the truth, he was determined to go through with this wedding. He had no love for Miss Elaine Patterson, for she was an arrogant woman who had shunned many a suitor. Everyone said that her only true love was the estate that her ancestors had built up decades ago. The Pattersons' unquestionable and firm loyalty to the House of Hanover had seen them reaping vast benefits over many decades, and it was still as strong as ever. The only regret, the current Lord of the Manor was often heard to say, was that he had no male children to carry on his name.

Many felt that perhaps that was the reason that Miss Elaine Patterson strove to prove to her father that she was better than seven sons. The estate was the love of her life. She gave her all to it, and it prospered in her hands. It was therefore surprising that she had actually agreed to get married, and to a man who was considered to be a nobody, at that. But given that the man was going to change his name for her, it stood to reason that an heir was desired, a male one, who would continue carrying the Patterson name.

All these thoughts were in the minds of the villagers as they watched the wedding ceremony from afar. None of the villagers were invited to the fancy feast held at the manor afterwards, but it was piped abroad that the fare that was spread for the dozens of nobles and gentry who were invited, was enough to feed half of England for a full year. The festivities would go on for a full week!

Edwin watched as his bride walked down the aisle on her father's arm, and he felt nothing but deadness inside. This was the price he was willing to pay to keep his mother safe. There was nothing he wouldn't do for his mother. Miss Elaine Patterson looked radiant in her beautiful haute couture wedding gown, made especially for her by a Parisian designer. She carried a large bouquet of bright red roses from the garden that Edwin so carefully tended to, and this was the only gift he'd given her. He just wanted the day to be over so he could go back to his lovely roses that never judged or criticized him as his soon to be wife was doing even now with her cold grey eyes through the light veil that covered her face.

Same Day in Spring, Hundreds of Miles Away

Ravenscroft Village, Pembroke, Wales

The small village chapel was nearly empty, and only a handful of people sat in the old wooden pews. Some of the pews were even broken down, but it didn't matter, since there weren't enough souls in the chapel that day to fill them. There were no flowers and no choir lined up close to the ancient piano ready to sing the wedding march. There was not a carriage in sight, nor did the church bells toll on that warm Saturday morning in spring. To everyone around, it was just an ordinary Saturday morning, just like any other, but to two people, it was a very special day indeed.

Clive Chester slipped into the chapel through the side door and made his way to the altar where the cloaked vicar was waiting. The bridegroom smiled at his widowed father and waved to Mrs. Burns, who was his employer. Mrs. Burns was the village fishmonger's wife, and she'd taken over the fledgling business when her drunken husband broke his neck one evening after drinking heavily and climbing onto a scaffold to prove his prowess as a flying human being. The ground on which he'd landed proved victorious, and thus Mrs. Ethel Burns became a widow and the proprietor of Burns Fishmongers.

Clive's heart was beating very fast, and his eyes were glued to the main chapel door. His clothes were a size too large for him, but he wore the hand-me-down suit, a rare loan from his employer, with much pride, and he'd decked himself out best as he could. He still couldn't believe that Mrs. Burns, in a rare show of generosity, had decided to loan him one of her dead husband's Sunday suits, and even a pair of shoes, as well as the starched shirt and cravat. Everything Clive wore on his wedding day had once belonged to the late Mr. Burns.

A shadow fell over the door he was gazing at, and Clive's breath caught in his throat. For there at the doorway stood the most beautiful woman in the world to him.

"Ashley," he whispered, love shining on his face and making his eyes glow.

Ashley Reid raised her head and smiled, even though she couldn't see the face of her beloved through the thick veil that covered hers. It was discoloured with age, but she wore it with pride, as she did the unsightly gown that had been taken in too many times over the years, so much that it had lost its original shape. Many brides of her family had worn the dress that Cousin Morgan insisted had been given to its first wearer by Queen Victoria's grandmother herself. How true that legend was, no one could tell, but every bride that had come before Ashley had the dress altered to suit her as needed, and it was worn with pride.

Like the thick veil, also a gift from the Queen's grandmother, the gown was discoloured because of being washed too many times and from poor storage. The collar and edges of the sleeves were frayed, but Ashley, a good seamstress, had done her best to make it presentable. Perhaps its best features were the sparkling white flat pearl buttons that ran from the neck right down to the floor, and it had surprised Ashley that all the dress's original buttons were still intact.

As Ashley glided down the aisle to the man she had loved for so long, she purposed in her heart that all her daughters would wear the gown and the veil. For legend had it that every woman who wore it had a happy marriage, so she was very careful because the fabric was delicate. Yes, she would keep it safely until her own daughters wore it one day.

The moment she arrived at the altar, she heard Clive breathe in relief, and she knew that he'd been under a lot of tension leading to this day. It wasn't easy being the only son of a man who expected him to marry well, but Clive had chosen her and forsaken many others worthier than she was. This was special grace, and in that moment, as he held out his hand and she placed hers in it, she prayed that she would be a good wife to him.

Clive felt Ashley's hand trembling in his and he squeezed it gently, reminding her that he was by her side. He loved this woman with his whole heart, and even facing much opposition from his family hadn't moved him to change his mind about marrying her. Theirs was a large family and to all intents, the church should have been filled with his relatives, but because he'd refused to marry the daughter of the wealthiest man in their village, most of them had stayed away. They thought he was throwing his life away by marrying a woman who had no prospects in life and came from a very poor family. But she was the love of his life and nothing else mattered. After giving her hand another squeeze, he turned and faced the vicar, ready to say the vows that would bind him to Ashley Reid for the rest of his life.

"Dearly beloved...," the vicar's voice boomed in the near-empty chapel. The sermon was long and boring, and Clive was thankful that they had to stand through it because he was afraid that he might have fallen asleep had he been seated.

"And now you may face your bride," Clive felt Ashley nudging him and he blinked.

"What is it?" He whispered.

"My veil, remove it," she instructed from the side of her lips. Clive did as bidden, and when he looked into the eyes of the woman he loved above all else, it was as if time stood still. Ashley felt very shy at the intensity in Clive's eyes, but she couldn't look away from him either. Everything else faded away, and in that moment all that was left was just the two of them.

Whatever else the vicar said passed above the heads of the two lovers who were completely lost in their own world. As Cousin Morgan would say for years to come, it was the wedding of the century even if only a handful of friends and family attended it.

THE ROSE GARDEN

ive Years Later - Patterson Estate

F"I have fulfilled the terms of my grandfather's will," Elaine Patterson stood in her father's study. "So I want what is rightfully mine," she demanded. No one looking at the thirty-five-year-old woman could tell that she had just given birth early that morning. "I have provided this estate with the much yearned for heir, and as far as I'm concerned my duty in that respect is now over and done with forever. Now give me what belongs to me."

"Elaine, my child, what changed you from a sweet young woman to this bitter and manipulative creature standing before me right now?" Her father's brow was creased with concern. "Given what you've been through in the past few hours, shouldn't you be resting to regain strength? There's a time for everything, Child."

Elaine scowled at her father. "Papa, there's no need for emotional sentiments. Five years ago, you threatened that if I didn't get married then my inheritance would go to my imbecile cousin, Roger." She shuddered and grimaced with distaste as she thought about her cousin who was always hopeful of taking over the inheritance from her. Not if she could help it! She had sacrificed her life for this estate, and no one was going to snatch this victory from her. "So, I found a simpleton of a man who wouldn't be any trouble to me at all and married him. Then you said that I could only get the inheritance if I provided the estate with an heir. And much as it displeased me, I had to endure much unpleasantness to make that happen. I did what you asked and now it's time for you to fulfil your own end of the agreement."

"Won't you even at least let me go and take a look at my grandson," her elderly father slowly rose to his feet. "Please allow me to go and see my dear grandson. Then we can talk about anything else after that."

"Pa, the boy is a normal child. He has ten fingers and ten toes, if that's what you want to count. My simpleton of a husband named him Herbert, a weak name if you ask me, and I just hope that the child won't take after his worthless father."

Mr. Patterson shook his head at his daughter's words. Every father hoped to have a daughter who was gentle and tender hearted, but that wasn't the case with his only child. Though he loved Elaine very much, he often wondered if all her hardness stemmed from the fact that she'd grown up without a mother. He'd lost his beloved wife when Elaine was six, and his mother had taken over the role of parenting her. Many times, he was filled with regret that he hadn't stepped in occasionally to make sure that she was receiving the kind of care and upbringing suitable for a little girl. For he admitted that his own mother had been a tough woman, not known for her gentleness. Perhaps if his Rose hadn't died so young and so early, she might have steered their beautiful daughter in the right direction.

Now he blamed himself for his daughter turning out this way, a woman who had scoffed at numerous suitable suitors, men of class and worth, unlike the simpleton she'd married. But Mr. Patterson also admitted that he'd pushed his daughter into this situation by insisting that she get married and subsequently produce an heir if she ever wanted to inherit anything, according to her grandfather's will.

"I'm going to take a rest, but this conversation is far from over," Elaine said haughtily, but her father noticed the tired look and shadows under her eyes. Any other noble woman would be lying in bed and accepting all the fuss being made over her after giving birth, but not his Elaine. She had to prove that she was a strong woman, and he was afraid that her stubbornness would one day be her undoing. Still, he kept his thoughts to himself as he followed her out of the living room.

Expecting her to lead the way to her bedchamber, he was surprised when she headed in the opposite direction, towards the rooms reserved for their guests. Much as he wanted to say something to express his disapproval of the way she conducted her marital life, he decided that this wasn't the time. In any case, he had a grandson to welcome into the family.

"My son," Edwin touched his new-born baby's brow with a careful and gentle hand. "You're the future and I want the best for you," he murmured. Edwin was always very careful to stay out of his wife's way because he couldn't stand being humiliated any more than he already was. Even though he was happy that he now had a son, he felt sad because Elaine and her father had insisted that the child should be named Patterson, bearing his maternal surname. Then he reminded himself that he'd done the same when he'd married Elaine, and his own surname had been pushed out of the way.

Not for the first time Edwin told himself that he'd sold his soul to the devil, and all to keep his mother out of debtors' prison or the workhouse. He didn't once regret the sacrifices he made for his beloved mother, who had died as a free woman two years ago. She'd also died without knowing that he himself was Elaine's captive.

Even though his wife had settled his father's debts immediately after they married, she'd insisted on taking over ownership of their small cottage, and that was what she'd used to keep him subdued. Even after the two years stipulated in their marriage agreement had passed, Elaine had refused to let Edwin go free.

"I won't have you leaving me just so you can go and marry some village girl," she told him contemptuously when he begged for his freedom. "Never will it be said of me that I couldn't keep a husband. I won't be humiliated in that way after all that I've sacrificed," she'd hissed.

"We had an agreement," he protested, but his words fell on deaf ears. "We were to remain married for only two years and then go our separate ways."

"Yes, we did, but if you insist on gaining your freedom from me, then your mother will become homeless, and I'll have her committed to a workhouse."

Her words had shocked him., "Why would you be so cruel when I married you as we agreed? We were to remain in a marriage of convenience for only two years, then I would be free. Why would you go back on our arrangement?"

She'd given him a cold look, "The terms of my grandfather's will state that before I inherit fully, I must provide an heir for this estate, a boy child to take after my father."

"But what if we have a girl?" Edwin asked angrily. He realised that he should have listened to his mother's warning on his wedding day. She'd told him that these people weren't to be trusted but he hadn't listened. "Nothing was ever said about you and me having a child or children together/" He shuddered slightly.

Elaine's eyes narrowed at the expression on her husband's face. "You don't have to look at me with so much contempt and revulsion. Believe me, if there was any other way of having a child without putting up with all that it entails, I would do it. I wouldn't need you and you could then go on your merry way. But we're stuck with each other until I can get what I want. If we have a girl, then we'll have to keep trying until a boy comes along." She shuddered, "Would to God that the first child will be a boy so I have no need of any further torment of intimacy with you or any other man for that matter. But this estate is rightfully mine and I'll do anything to get it, even if it means putting myself through the horrors of childbirth right from the conception part."

That was three years ago, and Edwin recalled what his mother had told him. Her predictions had come true and now he was in a situation from which he couldn't extricate himself. Even though Elaine had promised to set him free after having a child, once again she changed her mind just this morning.

"The boy needs his father," was what she'd told him after the midwife had left. "The child cannot grow up without his father by his side. I know you want to go and marry some village girl. I won't have my son sharing his father with some halfwits birthed by a country bumpkin. No, Edwin, we'll stay married for the rest of our lives if you ever want to see this boy again. Try to leave me, and you'll never know any peace in your life. My son will not grow up being called a half sibling to some lowlife halfwits running around in this village. I won't have my son growing up knowing that his father is married to someone else."

That's when Edwin resigned himself to the reality that he was stuck in this marriage for the rest of his life. Much as it filled him with dismay, he drew comfort from the fact that this child was a boy, and he wouldn't have to endure any more false intimacy with his wife. He had a son whom he already loved deeply, and he was determined to be the buffer between his wife and the child. There was no way he was going to allow his child to become as cold and heartless as his mother.

Footsteps coming down the corridor alerted him to the fact that someone would soon be joining him, and he quickly rose to his feet, for he'd been kneeling beside his son's bassinet, and waited. Expecting it to be his wife, he was surprised that it was his father-in-law who entered the bed chamber. Not desiring to get into any conflict with his wife's father, Edwin prepared himself to leave the room.

"No, stay," he was told in a gentle voice. "I only came to see the child." Edwin was surprised that his father-in-law was even talking to him. In the five years that he and Elaine had been married, the two of them had barely exchanged more than a couple of words at a time.

Edwin knew that his father-in-law despised him and thought of him as nothing but an opportunist and a gold digger. He agreed within himself that he deserved all the scorn heaped upon his head. His wife said he was weak and spineless, and he'd never once refuted her claims upon his character. A stronger man would have walked away long time ago, indeed one full of strength would never have entered into an agreement such as he had.

He watched silently as his father-in-law slowly drew closer to the bassinet. It shocked him to see that the man was growing frailer with each passing day, and with each passing day, he seemed less formidable. It was as if the man knew that his end was nigh and so was making peace all around him.

"The child will grow up to be a very handsome boy," Mr Patterson said as he stood over the bassinet and looked down at his sleeping grandson. "I just pray that he becomes a man of strength and character too." The wistful tone surprised Edwin, but he said nothing. "If only there was time..." The man let his words trail away, and Edwin felt compassion within his heart. It was clear that Mr. Patterson didn't have many months to live.

"I'm sorry," the younger man found himself saying.

Mr. Patterson gave him a lopsided smile, probably the first since they'd known each other. "Don't be. You've done a fine thing, and I thank you."

Then, as if realising whom he was talking to, Mr. Patterson walked to the door and paused without turning around. "You know that you can never leave now," the man said in a soft voice. "Who else will guide this child into being the kind of man you want him to be, a man full of understanding but also compassion? It saddens me to say this, but if you left your son in the upkeep of his mother, you'll only ever have yourself to blame should he turn out to be as cold and manipulative as she is. Think about that." With those words, Mr. Patterson walked out of the room.

Edwin silently agreed, because he could never leave his son at the mercy of his cold wife. For as long as he lived, he would always be there to guide his son.

Ravenscroft Pembroke Wales

Their little cottage was a small stone building which had been part of a larger estate that was now nothing more than a ruin. Five years had gone by since their small but beautiful wedding, and their love for each other grew stronger with each passing day.

On this particular day, Clive and Ashley Chester sat on the old sofa, arms around each other. She was trembling and he held her close, feeling her pain and wanting to say something but lacking the words with which to comfort his distraught wife.

"Five years," Ashley was murmuring tearfully. "When will it be our turn to celebrate?" Her voice caught on a sob. "All our friends and family who got married after us have two and some even three children by now." She looked down at her hands. "My arms feel so empty."

The brokenness in her voice made Clive want to cry, but he had to be strong for her because she needed him. If he broke down now, then what would happen to his Ash? "My love, we'll have children, all in good time. The Lord will hear our cry and bless us with children."

"My arms long to hold a baby in them. Now the women in the village are calling me barren and dry wood, an empty vessel." She sniffed as the tears rolled down her cheeks. "Everyone refers to me as the woman who cannot have children for her husband, and I can't take it anymore," Ashley sobbed. "What good is a woman who can't bear children for her husband?"

Clive was angry that the people he'd grown up amongst could be this cruel to the one he loved. "Ignore them, for they know not what they say. Children are a gift from the Lord, and He'll give us ours in His own good time. I promise you that the children we have will be very special, and this wait will be worth it."

Ashley refused to be comforted, and she pulled away from her husband. "I would have remained silent and not complained about anything," she wiped her face. "But now your father has also started saying that he's sorry he allowed you and me to get married. Father Chester has always been on my side, but it seems as if even he is tired of waiting for a grandchild. You should put me aside and take a woman who will bear children for you. Father Chester says his lineage has to continue, and it seems as if I'm the one stopping that from happening. I can't have that on my conscience," She covered her face with her palms.

"Perish the thought," Clive said strongly. "Children are a blessing from the Lord, as I said, and He will give them to us in His own good time. I don't want you to think about any of the nasty things people are saying because I love you with or without children. I never married you for your childbearing abilities but because you were given to me by the Lord Himself. Ash, you and I are destined to be together for the rest of our lives, and nothing will ever make me leave you. My promise to you stands stronger today than it was on the day we first met. Nothing on earth will ever make me leave you, because I love you so much. You're my life, my heart, and my home, Ash. Please don't ever ask me to leave you, for you'll be breaking my heart."

Ashley smiled through her tears even though her heart was still heavy. She longed for a child but didn't want to cause distress to her husband with further talk on the matter. She knew that Clive loved her and would do anything to make her happy, including taking her side very strongly against those who spoke ill of her.

Yet their relatives wouldn't leave them alone. After two years of marriage with no issue in sight, they had started dropping subtle hints here and there which she'd chosen to ignore. But now five years later and they were openly and blatantly coming out to ask her when she would provide her husband with a child, but they did this, of course, whenever Clive wasn't present. All subtlety and diplomacy were gone, and whenever any of them got the chance, they asked her what she was still waiting for and why she wasn't a mother yet. They would then compare her to her peers who already had children. Things were now so bad that she'd started thinking of a way that she would leave Ravenscroft.

She loved Clive dearly, and the thought of leaving him was like a deep wound in her heart, but he was also suffering due to their childlessness, and he deserved better. Maybe if she left, then Clive would eventually be free to marry a woman who could give him children and carry on his family name. She was tired of being mocked and ridiculed and treated as a pariah. Even her own relatives had joined those who taunted and made unkind remarks. The only one who stood by her was

Cousin Morgan. Their mothers, both long dead, had been sisters, and even though there was an age gap of nearly ten years between the two cousins, they were very close.

Their friendship had been made stronger because it was through Cousin Morgan that Ashley had met Clive. He'd come to her house to clean her chimney. Ashley was visiting on that day and the rest had been history. Cousin Morgan had encouraged their relationship, and when they finally married, she'd even provided a room for them in her small cottage until they were able to find their own place. Over the years, it was Cousin Morgan who had held Ashley and comforted her when the unkind remarks became too much for her to bear.

That's why two days later when Clive left the house to go to work at the fish store Ashley made her way to her cousin's place. She shared her grief with her relative and friend, knowing that she would receive much needed comforting and she wasn't disappointed. It was close to lunch time, and as they prepared a simple meal of mashed potatoes and broth from boiled bones, Morgan shared words of comfort to her distraught cousin.

"The more you listen to all those tattlers, the more distressed you'll get," Cousin Morgan told her. She'd been married at the age of sixteen, but her husband died two years later, leaving her childless. She'd remained a widow and refused to remarry, even though she had a number of offers over the years, for she was still a beautiful woman even at the age of thirty-five. "When I refused to remarry after my Simon's death, the same people accused me of all manner of things. Woe unto me if I was ever caught standing with someone's husband or even just exchanging greetings with them. They called me all manner of names, but since I knew that I wasn't what they termed me to be, I simply chose to live my life and ignored them. Eventually they learnt to leave me alone, and now in my old age, nobody bothers about me again," she chuckled.

"Cousin Morgan, you're not at all old. There's still so much life left in you, and if I may say so, you'll probably outlive all of us. Even now I know that a few gentlemen wouldn't hesitate to take you as their wife, if you would only give them the chance."

"Why Ashley, you're so kind to say that," the older woman grinned. "That's why I'm telling you to shut your ears to what these people are saying. Ignore them and they'll soon learn to leave you alone. The more you show them that their words are hurtful and wounding you, the more they'll continue talking about you."

When Ashley left her cousin's house, her steps were lighter. She purposed to take Cousin Morgan's advice, and no matter how much ridicule she faced in the coming days, she never said a bad word about anybody.

She could see that her new attitude pleased her husband, for she no longer cried or gave in to bouts of depression. This went on for weeks, and Clive was happy that his wife was no longer the miserable and pathetic creature that people's unkind words had tried to turn her into.

Ashley took pleasure in her occupation as a seamstress, and when another of her many cousins decided to get married, she was called upon to adjust the family wedding gown. As she tucked in the delicate fabric, one of the pearl buttons came loose and fell off the dress. It rolled under the chair, and as she was trying to reach for it, Imogen arrived to pick the dress up.

"I'm afraid one of the buttons has fallen off," Ashley told Imogen. "It rolled under the chair, and I was just about to search for it when you arrived."

"Don't worry about it," Imogen said hurriedly, looking quite flustered. "Just give me the dress, and I'll bring it back once my wedding is over."

"Which reminds me, you haven't told me what I can do to help. Now that your wedding is in a month's time, how can I be of assistance to you?"

Imogen shrugged, "You might as well know because it will soon be all over the village." She was a pretty girl with wide brown eyes and thick dark hair. "I'm in the family way, so Henry said that we should go to Gretna Green because the old minister refused to wed us. We made a mistake." She looked miserable. "But I don't want my child born out of wedlock, so we'll go to Gretna Green and get married there. Henry is waiting for me, and I don't have time anymore. Just give me the dress."

Ashley packed the dress as best as she could, telling Imogen to be very careful because the fabric was now very delicate. It hadn't been used since Ashley's own wedding, because the other brides in the family had chosen to get newer ones, but her cousin wanted to get away as fast as she could and merely waved the caution aside. Once she was gone, Ashley sat down at her table and sighed. Even Imogen, five years younger than her, was already with child irrespective of the circumstances of conception. Would she ever hold a baby in her arms? Her hand went to her flat stomach, and she sighed once again.

"Dear Lord, You give children in Your own good time. Please grant my husband and me the blessing of a little one and take my shame away. Please, Lord."

When she heard the heavy tread on the doorstep, she knew that her husband was back. Quickly schooling her features into a smile, she bent down to search for the missing pearl button. She would put it on a string around her neck until Imogen returned the wedding gown and then she would sew it back. Finding it, she did just that as the door opened and her husband entered the house.

"What are you doing down on your knees on the cold floor?" He placed his satchel and a small package on the table.

"Cousin Imogen was just here." She told him everything. "I was searching for this button." She raised the string that was around her neck and on which the pearl button now rested. "I don't want to lose it, so I've made a necklace out of it. When Imogen returns the dress, I'll sew it back on. I just hope she doesn't tear that gown up in her haste."

"That lucky button is safely resting in the right place," her husband cheered. "Well, won't you give your tired husband his usual kiss to welcome him home?" The cheeky look in his eyes made her blush.

Ashley might have continued to persevere the ill treatment meted out by her relatives on both sides and also ignore unkind remarks tossed her way, but for something that happened to shake her to the roots of her heart.

Mrs. Burns' niece came to visit her, and the girl decided that she wanted Clive by any means necessary. Clive was a decent and morally upright man who loved his wife and respected his employer, but Stacy Brim was a spoilt young woman and a real troublemaker.

A few days after her arrival in Ravenscroft, Stacy came to the cottage when Clive was at the shop. Ashley had just finished cleaning the house when she heard a knock at the door. Even though their cottage was one of many still standing on the dilapidated estate, Ashley was always careful to keep her door locked securely especially when she was all alone in the house. Her nearest neighbour was just a few feet away, but Ash felt safer behind locked doors. The only time she ever left the door unlocked was when her husband was at home with her. The knock came again, and the person sounded rather impatient.

"Who is it?" she asked when the knocking persisted. She was sure that it wasn't Cousin Morgan, for her relative was visiting friends in Cardiff and wasn't expected back for another few days. Nor was it Clive, for he had his own key. "Who is it?" she asked again, not intending to open the door for any strangers.

"Mrs. Chester, my name is Stacy, and Mrs. Burns is my aunt. I've come to see you because I feel that we need to have a woman-to-woman discussion."

Ashley wondered why Mrs. Burns' niece was here and what she wanted. She barely knew the young lady, but out of curiosity she decided to open the door a fraction. She wasn't willing to let the other woman into her home because they weren't friends, and she didn't know what she wanted. And besides that, Ashley didn't have time for idle chatter and gossip because she was busy with her chores.

"I'm surprised that you would come to my house," she said, only part of her face visible to the visitor. "How may I help you?"

"Won't you let me in?" Stacy looked taken aback at the lack of welcome.

Ash shook her head. "You caught me in the middle of doing some thorough cleaning and I'm rather busy. I don't have time to spend chatting. My husband will soon be home, and I don't want him to find the house dirty and his dinner not prepared."

Stacy laughed, an unkind sound. "I just wanted to see for myself the kind of worthless woman that has refused to grant Clive his freedom. Do you know that he loves me?"

"You're lying." Ash didn't want to listen to anymore falsehoods because she knew that there was no way Clive could ever be unfaithful to her. He was too honourable a man to do that. She tried to shut the door, but Stacy put a foot in the doorway and blocked her attempt.

"Am I?" Stacy answered sassily. "When your husband gets home today, why don't you ask him where he was last evening? Didn't he come home very late?"

Ash frowned, wondering what the woman was getting at. Clive sometimes arrived home late when he was waiting to purchase fish from the trawlers. "I know that he was at the pier getting fish from the trawlers, just as he always does."

Stacy threw her head back and laughed, "Well if that's what you want to believe then so be it. But if I were you, I would insist on finding out where the man was, and you might be surprised at the answer."

With those words hanging in the air, Stacy turned her back and walked away, leaving Ash with many questions in her mind. She didn't want to believe that her husband could have been anywhere other than the place that he was supposed to be, but would Stacy Brim have made the journey to her house just to tell her false news? No, something must have happened for the woman to be so bold as to come out here and mock her. Ashley was determined that she would get to the truth, come what may!

THE CHRISTMAS MIRACLE

"Ash, you don't have to do this," Clive felt like bursting into tears when he saw what his wife was doing. He'd come back home from work and found her packing her few belongings in an old trunk, her intentions very clear. She was leaving him and all because of falsehoods spread by people close to him. "Ash, please give me a chance to prove to you that I would never betray your trust in me."

Ash was past the stage of reasoning any more. Just that morning, the village constable had come to their door with shattering news. Miss Stacy Brim was in the family way, and her aunt was claiming that Clive was responsible. It was being said that the two had fallen into a relationship, and now this had happened. Ash had seen how shocked her husband was at the news, and she followed him to Mrs. Burns' store, where his employer clearly stated that she'd seen Clive emerging from the window of her niece's bedchamber one night not many days ago. The woman had gone on to state that it wasn't the first time this had happened, either.

Ash felt like her heart was being squeezed. Stacy Brim was pregnant by her husband, and she was still childless. That told her that her time here was up and she needed to get away.

"You made your bed, Clive, and now you've got to lie in it." She looked at him and forced herself not to show him how much she was hurting. She noticed the sadness in his eyes and the tension around his mouth. His eyes were pleading with her, but she hardened her heart. No, she wasn't going to give in to her weakness for this man. She loved him very much, and she knew that for as long as she lived, no other man would ever be allowed into her life again, but there was no way she was going to continue living in Ravenscroft, not if he had put Stacy Brim in the family way.

"Ash," he said as he came closer and tried to take her hand, but she pulled away. He paled at the blatant rejection. She'd never once pulled away from him before. "Please, my darling," he pleaded. "You know that I would rather slit my throat than ever do anything to hurt you."

She stepped away from him and faced him, anger making her clench her fists by her sides. "Then what were you doing sneaking out of Stacy Brim's bedchamber? Mrs. Burns herself testified that she saw you on more than one occasion leaving her niece's bedchamber. You should never have been in that house in the first place, let alone Miss Brim's bedchamber."

"Ash," Clive's voice was rough. "I was never in Stacy Brim's bedchamber, and the last time I set foot inside Mrs. Burns' house was five years ago, a day after our wedding. That was when I returned her husband's suit and shoes that she'd lent me for the occasion. Never again have I entered her house, and certainly not since her niece came to live with her."

Ash heard the sincerity in her husband's voice, but she was feeling too raw. "But why would Mrs. Burns say that she'd seen you sneaking out of her niece's bedchamber?"

"To cause trouble between us, and from the way you're reacting, it seems that she's succeeded," Ash paled at the remark. "It's clear that mischief is intended for us, and I'm sure that some of my family members are behind all this. But you're the last person I ever expected to believe such a falsehood." He looked very weary as he left the bedroom and went to their small living room, sitting down heavily. The old couch creaked as he leaned his head back and closed his eyes.

Ash stopped packing and followed her husband to the living room, standing in the doorway and observing him. She wanted so much to believe in his innocence, but Mrs. Burns had insisted that she had seen Clive.

Even when the village constable seemed to express his doubts, the woman was firm in her convictions first because she'd seen Clive with her own two eyes, as she claimed, and then Stacy had confirmed that the man who'd been in her bedchamber twice was Clive.

"If you weren't in Stacy's bedchamber on those two nights as she claims, where were you then?"

"This is high season for fishing, and you know that the fishermen come in late with their trawlers overloaded with the catch. They never sell to anyone until they have offloaded their boats and counted out all the fish they have caught. On both those days, I was at the pier with the other fishmongers and traders."

"Mrs. Burns claims that on those two nights no one noticed you at the pier, and that is why she suspected and believed that you were the man in Stacy's chamber."

Suddenly Clive felt very tired. "I'm a Christian, and I take my faith in God and my vows to you very seriously. Have I ever given you any reason to doubt my love and fidelity to you, Ash?" She shook her head at the question he asked in a very quiet voice. She would rather that he'd have shouted at her, for his quiet demeanour was making her feel very guilty at having doubted him in the first place. "Then why would you allow the words of some ill-intentioned individuals make you doubt my faithfulness to you? Have you now lost all the respect you had for me and started thinking of me as a morally compromised person? Do you really believe that I would sneak into my employer's house and find my way to her niece's bedchamber?"

"But why would Mrs. Burns lie? What does she hope to achieve with her lies?" Ashley muttered.

Clive frowned wryly and shrugged. "You'd have to ask her that question, but like I said before, I believe that one or two of my relatives could be behind all this."

"To what end, and why do they hate me so much?" Ash suddenly felt cold and blinked rapidly, forcing herself not to burst into the tears that she could feel stinging behind her eyes. She couldn't believe that people could be so callous and unkind as to make up such terrible lies.

Clive leaned forward and placed his elbows on his thighs, then crossed his fingers and rested his chin on them. "From the moment that I met you and made my intentions to marry you quite clear, my family took up arms against our union. You know that they wanted me to marry Miranda Wells because her father is very wealthy, and my family wanted to benefit from that union." Ash nodded. "But I shut that down, and Miranda soon married someone else. I thought they would leave us alone. Now for some reason they believe that if they concoct such terrible lies, that you'll leave me," Ashley's face turned red, for she'd been in the process of doing just that. "And once you leave me," he went on as if not noticing how red her face was, "then I would be forced to take in Stacy Brim, who claims that the child she's carrying is mine. I don't know which of my family members is colluding with Mrs. Burns on this matter. But if I ever meant anything to you, Ash, please wait for a few days before you do anything rash. My only witnesses are the fishermen whom I was with on those two nights."

"Why didn't they come forward to defend you then?"

"Because they're out to sea and won't be back for a few days yet. Please give me just a few days, and the truth will be revealed. If there was a man in Stacy Brim's bedchamber, it certainly wasn't me. My God will vindicate me and silence all those wagging tongues."

Four days later, when the fishermen returned, there was an uproar when it emerged that the man who had been seen sneaking out of Stacy's bedchamber wasn't Clive, but one of the fishermen. The man had gone on and on about it while he was out to sea with his peers, and all his companions knew that he was about to become a father. Therefore, Clive was vindicated when Stacy was forced to admit that she'd lied to her aunt. The village constable wasn't kind to Mrs. Burns for claiming to have seen Clive leaving her niece's chamber.

"The person looked so much like Clive," the woman said defensively when she was cornered, her face white with shame. "I'm sorry that I framed an innocent man."

"It's a little too late for that." The constable wasn't mincing his words. "The reputation of a good man has been sullied, though I'm happy that he's been vindicated in the eyes of everyone who was interested in this matter. You should be thoroughly ashamed of yourself. And as for your niece, that girl is a piece of work, and if you're not careful she'll cause you a lot of trouble."

"I've sent her to go and live with the man responsible for her condition," Mrs. Burns said. "I won't have such a manipulative liar living with me again."

"That's your family's problem now, but next time be careful before accusing a person when you don't have all the facts right. Mr. Chester is a gentle man and has agreed to let things go. The next man might not be so kind, and you could then find yourself in a lot of trouble."

Ash was glad that she'd chosen to believe in her husband's innocence, albeit grudgingly. She felt very guilty when Clive didn't bring up the subject when they returned home. He was very quiet and barely said a word to her. When the silence became too much for her to bear, she knew that she had to make things right with her husband.

"I'm sorry," she blurted out. "Please forgive me for doubting you." Her fingers twisted nervously as she watched him.

"Come here," Clive said in his usual quiet way. He was seated on their threadbare couch, and Ash ran to him, wanting him to forgive her. He took her in his arms. "Ash, my word is my bond to you and to anyone else that I give it. I would never betray your love and trust in me." He took a deep breath. "That's the reason that, as of today, I'm no longer working for Mrs. Burns. She apologized profusely, and she even offered to double my wages, but I'm done. All trust is broken between us. I've worked for Mrs. Burns for five years, and never once did I give her any reason to think of me as an uncouth man, yet she chose to believe her niece and wanted to destroy our marriage. I can't live with that."

Ash almost felt sorry for Mrs. Burns for losing such an employee as Clive. He was an honest and hardworking man, and to lose him was definitely a big blow to the woman's business, but then she pushed those thoughts aside because the woman had betrayed her husband and nearly destroyed their marriage. Still, she was worried. If Clive was out of work, then how would they cope? Ravenscroft was a small village with limited employment opportunities. What would happen to them now?

It was as if Clive sensed her fears, for he pulled her closer, "You don't have to worry about a thing," he said, resting his chin on top of her head. "I've decided that it's time for me to move on and find something better for me, for us."

"What do you mean?"

"Ravenscroft is a small fishing village, and the opportunities for any kind of advancement in our lives is very limited. There are really no prospects of rising above what I am right now, so I have to leave."

Ashley felt as if the bottom had suddenly fallen from where she was standing. What if her actions had caused her husband to rethink their marriage? What if she had ruined any chances of them having a good marriage after all?

"The wise woman builds her house, but the foolish pulls it down with her hands." She remembered one of the scriptures that had been read to them on their wedding day five years ago. Had she foolishly allowed her insecurities to cloud her judgment such that she'd torn her own house down?

"I'm sorry," she felt like weeping. Fear filled her heart. "I'm sorry that I've driven you away and now you're leaving me behind."

Clive frowned then pulled back and rested his hands on Ash's shoulders. "Do you ever see anything like that happening to us? That I would go away from Ravenscroft and leave you behind?"

Tears of relief filled Ash's eyes and rolled down her cheeks. "I thought I had destroyed our marriage."

He chuckled softly even as he wiped her tears away. "Ash, every marriage has its challenges, and this one was ours. That doesn't mean that I would throw something this beautiful away. It won't ever happen. Would you come to London with me?" He looked into her eyes. "Life won't be a bed of roses or easy…"

"Yes," Ash dashed her tears away. "Yes, I'll come to London with you."

He laughed. "You didn't even let me finish what I was saying."

"I don't care what else you have to say because I'll follow you to the ends of the earth if need be."

Nine Months Later

Christmas Day Morning

The soft cries of a baby filled the house and Clive could barely contain himself for the happiness that he was feeling. He was a father. God had seen their pain, heard their weeping, and answered their prayers in a miraculous way.

Silently willing the midwife to finish attending to his wife and child, he paced outside his small cottage, waving at one or two of their neighbours. A plump woman waddled over to him. "Is it time?" she asked.

He nodded, "Yes, Mrs. Firth, it's all over, and I'm waiting for the midwife to be done so I can go in and see my wife and child."

"Well, we thank God for this," the woman said and walked away. He resumed his pacing.

At this point, he didn't even know if the baby was a boy or a girl. All he knew was that the Lord had remembered them and visited them with this miracle baby.

They'd left Ravenscroft nine months ago and refused to look back, and in that time, Clive had only visited his home once, to bury his father. He'd immediately returned to his wife in London.

London had welcomed them with a cold spell nine months ago, and with barely anything to their names but their old trunks, they'd been forced to spend the first few days at a homeless shelter. For the first time since they'd gotten married, husband and wife were forced to spend nights away from each other. This stirred Clive up to work harder to get a home for them, especially when each morning his wife would tearfully fall into his arms and tell him that she hadn't slept a wink for fear of being attacked in the night and having all her belongings stolen.

A chance remark by someone he met at the shelter made Clive decide to take his wife out of that place, and that was how they'd ended up in Brewer's Road, a slum dwelling in East London. It was a small community where the landlords gave out space to the inhabitants to build their own houses. Clive had jumped at the chance because the alternative slums were too crowded and dangerous for them.

It had taken them months of hard work because they'd decided to build a good home for themselves. Starting with one room, they painstakingly constructed it out of sod held together by pieces of wood and old pallets. After five months, their second room was ready, and that was when the two of them had discovered that the fatigue that had invaded Ash's body wasn't because they'd worked too hard. It was the signs of a little one on the way.

"It's a girl." The midwife emerged from the house. She was beaming. "Blessings to you on this Christmas Day."

Clive didn't wait a minute longer but burst into the house and to the second room when he found his wife lying on their narrow bed, their little new-born daughter in her arms. Ash looked so peaceful lying there. Clive approached and knelt reverently beside the bed. He put out a hand and touched his little girl. "She's so beautiful," he said in awestruck tones.

"What shall we name her?" Ash asked, tears in her eyes. She was a mother, and no one would ever laugh at her again.

"Mae, our little Christmas miracle," the besotted father said, never once taking his eyes off his new-born daughter. "Mae, our pearl," he repeated with tears in his eyes.

Patterson Village, Sheffield

It didn't take five-year-old Herbert Patterson long to know that his household was a strange one. He was a highly intelligent child who sensed that things weren't right between his parents right from that tender age. For one, they slept in rooms that were on opposite sides of the large manor, and his own bedchamber was on his Pa's side of the manor.

When he'd asked his father why his mother had to sleep so far away from them, he was informed that she snored and so she had to be well away from them. Also, Herbert noticed that none of the servants lived in their home. The servants would arrive very early in the morning and leave late at night, never once sleeping in the house, not even when there were guests to be attended to.

His grandfather had passed away the previous summer, just after his fourth birthday, and he sometimes found himself missing the old man. But with his father always there for him, it wasn't such a deep loss. He also loved spending time in the rose garden with his father.

On this particular day he decided that he would surprise his mother with a bunch of roses. "Pa, it's Mama's birthday today."

His father looked at him in surprise, "And how did you know that?"

"Because Grandpa told me before he died, and do you remember that we had cake then?" His father shook his head. "Pa," he said patiently, looking like a little old man, and his father's lips twitched with restrained mirth. "Last year, you remember when Grandpa bought that horse for Mama and said it was her birthday present."

"Oh yes, now I remember."

"Wasn't it a day like today?"

Edwin ruffled his son's hair. "Indeed it was," he said softly. Each time he looked into the face of his son, he saw a younger version of himself. And with each passing day he felt so humbled because his son was growing up with much tenderness in his heart. Edwin knew that his wife was irked that the child liked to spend a lot of time in the garden rather than in the study with her, being taught how to run the estate that would eventually be his one day.

"Pa, may I please have some flowers to take to Ma for her birthday?"

Father and son carefully selected twelve stems of red roses, and after removing all the thorns, Edwin carefully wrapped them in a piece of soft muslin cloth. "Now you can go and wish your mother a good day," the young boy was told, and proudly carrying his gift, he made way to the house.

There were no servants about the hallways even though it was early afternoon, and Herbert went on undisturbed. When he got to the study, he had to put the flowers on the floor so he could use both hands to turn the large knob. The door opened silently due to its well-oiled hinges, but before he could bend down to pick up the roses, he heard a strange sound coming from inside the study.

He was about to call out and see if his mother was alright, then he noticed that there was someone else with her in the study. His mother's back was turned towards him, but he could see that the man was one of his grandfather's friends. What shocked the boy was that his mother's back was completely bare and the dress she was wearing was bunched up at her waist. The man also didn't have his shirt on, and it formed a very disturbing picture in young Herbert's mind. The man had his arms around his Mama, and in that instant, he raised his eyes and met Herbert's disturbed ones. The man's face turned ugly, and he seemed to bare his teeth at the young boy, frightening him.

Without advancing further into the study, Herbert slowly pulled the door shut and then stood there staring at the flowers on the floor. Now what was he going to do with them? He couldn't very well leave them here because then his mother would find out that he'd been at the study door and seen her in the arms of another man. And he couldn't take them back to the garden for then his Pa would want to find out why he hadn't given them to his mother, and he didn't want to talk about what he'd seen.

So, he picked the flowers up and went to his bedchamber, where he placed them behind his desk. He didn't want to go back to his father because he didn't want to say anything about what he'd seen. But he couldn't very well stay in his chamber forever. At some point he would have to leave and meet with his father, but not right now.

NIGHT HAS FALLEN

L *ondon, Four Years Later*
When Clive walked into his house on Christmas Eve, he was met at the door by two very irate females. It was only six in the evening, but from the way they were both glaring at him, one would think that he'd been away the whole night instead of just an afternoon.

"I'm very sorry that I'm late," he said, careful not to let his eyes show his amusement. Mother and child, his beautiful wife and adorable daughter, had identical looks on their faces. They were both green eyed, and their thick dark hair fell down to their waist. Mae would be turning four the next day, and she mirrored the expression and stance that her mother had taken.

"You were supposed to return early," Ashley told her husband. "We've been waiting for you to take us to the market so we can do our own Christmas shopping and perhaps get Mae a present for her birthday as well."

"Oh, love!" Clive picked Mae up with one hand and pulled his wife close with the other. Then he kissed both their cheeks. "Please forgive me, but Mrs. Plume's chimney was worse than any other that I've ever cleaned before. Apparently, the last time it was cleaned was nearly two years ago. It took me a long time to finish what I was doing to her satisfaction, and I was waiting for her to pay me."

"You're forgiven for today," his wife told him with a loving smile, and the two females of his household hugged him. Clive felt the satisfaction that only one who knows true love does. He was loved and in return he loved and adored his wife and daughter. His only regret was that he was unable to give his family the kind of life they deserved.

He'd thought that moving to London would change their fortunes, but so far, they were still struggling, living from hand to mouth like everyone else in their neighbourhood.

Ashley never once complained, not even when he returned home empty handed after a long day of trying to find work. Many families were now hiring the services of very young chimney sweeps because they charged half of what the more experienced ones like Clive did. What those homeowners didn't know was that the small boys rarely did a good job, unless they were apprenticing for a more experienced chimney sweep. The city of London was now flooded with chimney sweeps, and it was getting harder by the day to secure a commission.

Still, he tried as best as he could for his family's sake.

He noticed his wife giving him an anxious look and smiled. "My bag please, Mother." He placed Mae back on her feet. His wife brought him the old satchel he carried everywhere with him. It contained the hankies that he carried to clean himself after tackling chimneys, and also an old tin box in which his wife packed his lunch every single day. No matter how little they had to eat, Ashley always made sure that something was left over from their supper for him to carry for his lunch the next day, but today the bag carried more than that. He pulled out a wrapped package and handed it over to his astounded wife.

"Mrs. Plume says happy birthday to Mae and Merry Christmas to us." He laughed as Mae rushed eagerly to her mother, and the two made short work of the wrapping.

There was half a pound of wheat flour, half a pound of sugar and meat, some butter, and even a fresh loaf of bread. There was also a folded piece of fabric, soft to touch, and it slipped through the fingers easily.

"Mrs. Plume's son returned from India and brought that muslin cloth. Now mother can make you a dress, Mae, my darling."

The next day, on her birthday, Mae woke up to find that her new dress was ready. She shrieked with excitement, and when they left for church after a heavy breakfast, the little girl made sure that all their neighbours knew that it was her birthday and that she had a new dress.

Everyone was worried about winter that year as the New Year began. Snow fell heavily and fireplaces were lit by day and night as the people of London strove to stay warm.

There was much work for chimney sweeps who braved the cold weather and trod through the snow to clean up yet another chimney.

"You need to clean our chimney." Mae woke up one morning to hear her mother talking to her father in low tones. "It's clogged and might cause us trouble. I tried to light a fire but so much smoke filled the house that I had to immediately put it out."

"I'll get to it as soon as I return home today," Clive promised as he picked up the tools of his trade. "I'll be quick and then return to clean our chimney, so please don't worry, my love."

Mae stood at the doorway for a few seconds, watching as her father walked out of the house and into the snow. Then her mother quickly shut the door to keep the cold out. Because of their clogged chimney, she wasn't able to light a fire in the grate and they had to stay warm by huddling under the blankets.

Mae was restless the whole day as she waited for her father to come back home. She didn't know why she was feeling the way she did, but she wanted her Papa back home with them. Her mother got no peace either, for the child kept snuggling up to her until at one point she got quite exasperated.

"Mae, will you please settle down and play with your toys? I have to finish embroidering this tablecloth for Mrs. Crane." Mae moved away and went to play with her toys, which were nothing but pieces of wood and a ragdoll that her mother had made for her from scraps of old cloth. She stacked the pieces of wood high and then crashed the tower and started all over again, but she was soon back at her mother's side.

"This child," Ashley muttered, then gently but firmly put Mae away from her. "If you don't want to play then go to the bedroom, get into your bed, and sleep."

Mae walked to the bedroom and stood at the doorway, then turned to look at her mother. Ashley felt her daughter's gaze on her and stopped sewing. She raised her head and was shocked by the expression on her child's face. It was filled with so much sadness.

"Mae, why are you looking at me like that?" But Mae said nothing, and instead, tears welled up in her eyes. "Come here." Ashley held out both hands and Mae ran into them. "You sometimes behave very strangely, my dear child."

Before they settled down for the night, Ashley turned to her husband.

"Have you noticed anything about Mae lately?" She asked him.

"No, why do you ask?" Clive murmured sleepily.

"It's just that for the past few days, our little girl has been acting very strangely, and it's worrying me."

Clive raised himself on one elbow, "What do you mean by saying Mae is behaving strangely? Is she ill, or has she come down with something? It's really cold out there and I know that Mae likes to play outside. Perhaps she could be catching cold."

Ashley sighed while shaking her head. "Mae's not sick, but there's something else troubling her. As you say, it could be that she's coming down with a cold but…" she let her words trail away and they were both silent for a little while. "My love, I've noticed that Mae has become very clingy and watches me all the time. Her eyes follow me everywhere, as if she's afraid that I'll go away and leave her. Even the neighbours have noticed her strange behaviour because she refuses to play with their children anymore, preferring to stay indoors all the time."

"That's why I've been telling you that we should pray for another baby. Being an only child isn't good for Mae. She loves people and enjoys being around them. It's very lonely for her, especially during this time when we have such poor weather, and she can't go outside to play with her friends anymore. Being cooped up must be the reason why you think she's behaving strangely."

"I haven't once stopped Mae from going to play outside unless it's very cold. Even on warm days, she doesn't leave the house. What do you make of that?"

Mae listened as her parents talked. They thought she was asleep, and she stayed very still. Mae fell asleep still trying to listen to what her parents were saying.

Then suddenly she was awake again and felt as if someone was holding a pillow over her head. She struggled a little before she realized that her eyes were stinging, and she cried out. Something smelled funny, and she was scared.

"Papa! Mama!" Her voice was weak, but her mother heard her.

"Clive! Clive, wake up!" Ashley cried out, jumping out of bed. It took a little while to wake her husband up because he was sleeping very deeply, no doubt exhausted after a hard day's work.

By the time Clive woke up, the curtain in their bedroom was on fire, and the flames leapt up, licking everything in sight. A glowing ember landed on Mae's bed, and she screamed as the blanket quickly caught fire.

"Get Mae," Clive called out, and her mother reached for her. He rushed to open the bedroom door and was driven back by a chug of smoke. Mae coughed painfully, her chest feeling as if it would explode. "We have to get to the door and go outside." Her father gasped for air.

They managed to get free and were soon outside, where they saw people gathering to look at their burning house. Mae was shivering.

"I need to get our money," Clive said. "It's under the mattress and is all we have."

"Clive, no," Ashley screamed, holding Mae close, but her husband darted back into the burning house. Mae felt her mother thrusting her into the arms of a neighbour and rushing into the burning house after her father. She started crying while the neighbour tried to soothe her.

"They'll be out soon," she was told as she was rocked from side to side. But somehow in her little heart, she knew that she would never see her parents again.

The front room was filled with thick, stinging smoke and Ashley fought to get to the other room so she could drag her husband out. Why had he risked his life and returned to the burning building just to save a few pounds? She was confused and couldn't see clearly as the flames roared in her ears. The heat was unbearable, but she needed to get to Clive. Then she started to cough and dimly heard someone calling out her name. Suddenly she felt strong arms grabbing her.

"We're trapped in here," Clive whispered as he sank to the floor. A flaming wooden beam had detached itself from the rafters and fallen across the door. "We won't get out of this, and I'm so sorry my love for risking your life in this manner. It's been good with you, and I'll never regret loving you. Ashley, I love you." His voice was fading away as the smoke overcame him. "Now and forever."

"Clive," Ashley coughed painfully and put her arms around her husband. This was the end for them, she just knew it. "My love, my life."

The last thought in the minds of the two lovers was their little girl, before the smoke overcame them completely and they shut their eyes, never to open them again.

DESPERATE TIMES

"We can't keep her," Mae heard Mrs. Pears whispering. "We can barely feed ourselves and our children, and having an extra mouth is too much for us to handle. What are we going to do?"

"I told you not to take the girl in, but you wouldn't listen," Mr. Pears' voice was rough. "It's very unfortunate what happened to her parents, but we're not the only neighbours around here. Someone else could have taken her in and so spared us all this confusion, but no, you just had to go and be the Good Samaritan, didn't you? Now here you are bemoaning the fact that we don't have enough food to keep us all well fed."

"Keep your voice down because we don't want the children to hear us," Mrs. Pears hissed. "What do you think we should do? We can't just kick the child out.

She's only four. What do you think will happen to her?"

There was silence, and Mae held her breath to hear what would be said next. She wanted to stay here where it was warm, but young as she was, she knew that Mr. Pears didn't like her being in his home. Mae had that inner instinct that always told her that something was wrong, and she felt it now. It was clear that the two adults were talking about her future, and she was afraid.

"I know," she heard Mr. Pears saying. "Let's take her to the hospital and leave her there."

"Can we do that?"

"Oh yes, children are left in hospitals all the time. We can say she is ill, and when the nurses take her for checking, we'll slip away and leave her in their care. They're bound to find her a home after that, and we can rest easy knowing that she'll end up in a good home."

"But what if the other neighbours ask us what happened to the child, what will we say? They've been helping us out because of Mae. What will they say when they find out what we've done?" Mrs. Pears sounded like she was crying. "They will hate and despise us."

"Mother, don't worry your head so much. I know how we'll do it, so the neighbours don't blame us. Just follow my lead always and never discuss our plans with anyone."

It was at this point that Mae fell asleep and had no idea of the plans that Mr. Pears and his wife made after that.

When they didn't mention anything in the coming days, Mae thought they had forgotten about their plans to get rid of her, and her small heart calmed down. She'd been living in fear, but it seemed as if her benefactors had changed their minds. Even Mr. Pears was being very kind when he was usually rough towards her on normal days. Maybe he would be her father and Mrs. Pears would be her Ma.

The other neighbours, though poor, brought clothes and food because they wanted to help as much as they could. So, the Pears children were also clothed and shod because of Mae being in their home. And Mrs. Pears called her 'the little miracle girl,' for the family's fortunes seemed to be changing even though it was at a very slow pace.

Mae missed her parents, but she had quickly realized that it upset Mrs. Pears if she asked about them or cried when she was feeling sad, which was most of the time. So, she would sneak out of the house and creep to the ruins that had been her home, sit in what used to be their loving home, and cry for as long as the tears would flow.

The child spent many hours hearing her mother's sweet voice singing to her and her father's deep laughter. And Papa had always carried a stick of liquorice for her in his pockets when he returned from work. It didn't matter if he'd made a single penny on that day or not, he always had liquorice for her. She missed all those times when her Pa would return home after a long day's work, scoop her up into his arms, and twirl her around. Once she'd seen Mr. Pears doing the same to his children, and when she'd excitedly run to him, he simply turned his back on her.

When days turned into weeks, Mae settled down in her new home and had no inkling that her life was about to change once more.

One Saturday morning, many months after her parents' burial, during which she had wept until she lost consciousness, Mrs. Pears woke all the children, including Mae, up.

"Wake up, wake up, children," she was smiling and even ruffled Mae's untidy hair. "Papa is taking us to town today."

"Why, Mama?" Sullen Todd Pears, the eldest child asked.

"Because it will soon be Christmas Day, and Papa wants to get us all new clothes."

At this announcement, all the children clapped their hands and danced around the small living room. But

Mae was puzzled, since it seemed as if they'd just celebrated Christmas a few weeks ago when her parents were still here. She couldn't believe that time had flown past so fast. It was midsummer, and even if she didn't yet know how to count the months, she felt that it was too soon to be Christmas Day. Then she shrugged. Perhaps she was mistaken about the months, for why then would Mr. Pears be taking them to get new clothes?

"Mae, I have to brush your hair and comb it out," Mrs. Pears said, and Mae sat through the woman's rough ministrations. Tears filled her eyes as she thought about how tender Mama's hands used to be whenever she was doing her hair. And whenever Mama brushed Mae's hair, she would sing her a song. The child longed to ask her benefactor to sing to her, but it wasn't the same. Nothing would ever be the same again.

"There, now you look very pretty," the woman said, ignoring the tears in the child's eyes.

Once everyone was ready, Mr. Pears brought around an old cart that neighbours often borrowed from the fishmonger, at a fee, of course. It smelled of rotting fish, but the children were too excited to care. It was the family's day out, and not even a foul-smelling cart could take their happiness away.

The cart rumbled down the uneven road, and the excited children sat at the back waving to the neighbours and shouting that they were going to town to get new clothes. Whenever the wheels hit a pothole, the cart jumped, and the children with it, screeching at the top of their voices.

It should have surprised Mae that the adults weren't shouting at them to stop making so much noise. Usually Mr. Pears took out his belt in order to silence the children, but today he was quiet, staring straight ahead.

Mrs. Pears kept casting furtive glances at Mae, but the child was too happy to realize that anything was amiss. This was a rare treat, and they were all set to have a wonderful day.

"We'll stop here," Mr. Pears announced when they got to Hyde Park. "Mother packed some sandwiches for us to eat, and then we'll go and get new clothes."

One by one, he helped the children down from the cart, and Mae was last. He held her for a second longer, and then with a deep sigh placed her on the ground next to the other children. Mae's eyes glowed as she saw all the fancily dressed people walking around. Her little mind recalled that Papa had once brought her and Ma here to see the Queen, and she had dreamed of the parade by the royal troops for a long time.

She was a beautiful child, and she made a lovely picture standing there gazing at those who were going in different directions. She could hear vendors calling out for people to buy their wares, and the smell of roasting corn and pies filled the air. The aromas made her hungry, but she knew that she would be fed shortly, for hadn't Mrs. Pears packed thick ham and cheese sandwiches for them?

The child was so lost in her surroundings that she didn't notice her benefactors gathering their children and placing them back on the cart. There were many beautiful horses to look at and so Mae didn't notice the old mule trudging slowly away through the throng. Her little eyes eagerly took in everything. It was a pleasant July day, and it seemed as if everyone had come out to enjoy the beautiful weather. From a distance, she could see ducks swimming down the river, and she found herself walking towards that direction. A hare that looked like it was about to speak made her giggle, and her childish laughter caused those around her to smile. It hopped off and disappeared into some bushes, and she was filled with regret. Maybe she'd scared it off with her laughter. She would be silent next time, she told herself.

Then a brightly coloured bird landed a few feet away from her and she clapped her small hands happily.

"Todd, Mary, look," she called out to her friends, but they were nowhere to be found. She shrugged her small shoulders and went on staring at the bird, which didn't seem frightened of her. Mary and Todd were probably playing on the other side of the park, where she could see many other children running around.

The bird hopped around, and Mae followed it, lost in her own world. Then it was disturbed by a raven and flew off, and she sighed in disappointment. Mae looked to see if she could spot Mrs. Pears, but the woman was nowhere to be seen. She was getting hungry and thought about finding her benefactor, but then something else caught her eye, and she was off again to see what other delights the park held for her.

Excited to be outside in the beautiful park, Mae had no time to be frightened, nor did she suspect that anything was amiss. Two small well-dressed boys ran towards her and then stopped right in front of her. They were older than Mae, but their bright and open expressions didn't intimidate her at all. They were also smartly dressed, not like the urchins who Mrs. Pears always told her and Mary to be wary of.

"You're pretty," one of the boys, the younger one said, and the older one giggled. "Do you want a banana?"

Mae nodded, and the boy gave her half of his banana.

"Do you want to play with us?" Again, Mae nodded. Surely Mrs. Pears wouldn't mind her playing with these good boys. In any case, Todd and Mary didn't seem to want to play with her, so she might as well find herself new playmates. With this in mind, the little girl followed the two boys, who were careful to walk slowly so she could keep up. She tripped and fell, and the boys were immediately at her side. Tears filled her eyes.

"I'm sorry," the older one took a clean hankie out of his pocket and wiped her tears, then tried his best to wipe the dust off her dress. He then took her hand while the younger one skipped beside her.

"Let's take you to Ma," the older boy said, and they walked for a short time. "Ma, look," the older boy approached a pretty woman who was seated alone on one of the benches, and there were two baskets on either side of her. "See what we found."

"Oh, Peter!" His exasperated mother looked at the beautiful child her son had brought. "What have you done now?" She looked around as if expecting to see the little girl's parents or whoever was taking care of her coming forward to claim her. But everyone around them was going about their business and barely spared them a glance.

"She was alone Mama," Peter said. "Simeon gave her half of his banana, and we brought her here. Mama, can we please keep her? She's so pretty, and she can be our little sister."

The woman's soft laughter reminded Mae of her mother, and she felt the ears in her eyes. "Peter, how many times have I told you that you can't just go around finding people's children and bringing them home? We can't just decide to keep her. Let me give you all some food and then when Papa comes back, we'll go and find her parents. She's too clean and well-dressed to be a stray child. Someone must be looking for her." Then she peered at Mae and saw the tears in her eyes. "Oh, you poor little thing." She noticed the smudge on her dress. "You must have fallen down. Are you hurt?" Mae shook her head. "Here, let me wash your hands."

"Ma, she fell," Peter announced unnecessarily, his eyes going to the basket which no doubt contained goodies.

"I can see that," his mother said. "Child, what's your name?"

"Mae Chester," she said, having learnt her name when she was only three years old. Her father would always ask her what her name was, because he said it was important in case she got lost and someone found her. In that way, Pa had said, someone would always bring her home. So, Mae learnt how to say her own name clearly.

After the kind woman had washed her hands and wiped them with a clean cloth, she picked Mae up and placed her next to her on the bench, then handed her a sandwich. Mae bit into the large sandwich. The bread was soft and fresh, as were the ham and cheese. The taste of her sandwich was like nothing she'd ever eaten before, and it seemed to melt on her tongue. It was soon gone, and she stared longingly at Peter's. He'd only taken a single bite out of his sandwich and then placed it back on the small plate his mother had handed him.

"Are you still hungry?" The mother asked, and Mae nodded. "Right then, here is a slice of cake and some milk."

Like the sandwich, the cake melted on her tongue. Mae hadn't eaten so much and so well in a long time. She remembered that the last time she'd had enough to eat was when her parents were still alive. The slice of cake did her in and she was soon dozing, a piece of it clasped tightly in her hand.

"Who is this delightful child?" A tall man joined them.

"Papa, her name is Mae," Simeon said. "We found her."

"And where are her parents?" He, too, looked around like his wife had done earlier. "Someone must be searching for her."

This was the quieter part of the park where there were no horses, and no one seemed interested in them.

Mae fell asleep, and the woman made her comfortable on the bench. She woke up after about an hour and cried out, thinking that she was alone. She'd been dreaming that Mrs. Pears had taken her to the market and left her there, and she was frightened.

"There, there," she was engulfed in a soft embrace. "You're safe, little one." The woman smelled of roses and Mae sighed. "We have to find your parents."

"Mrs. Pears," Mae said.

"Is that your Mama's name?" Mae shook her head. "Who then is Mrs. Pears?" The woman asked, looking at Mae and then her husband, who was observing them keenly.

"Todd and Mary's Mama," Mae said. She was swinging her little legs and smiling as she watched Peter and Simeon wrestling playfully on the ground.

"Where are your parents?" the man asked in a gentle voice, and Mae turned tear-filled eyes to him. She started sobbing and cried for a long time, and the couple got worried, but finally she calmed down and they all rose to their feet.

"The day is far gone, and I don't see anyone coming to look for you," the man said when he realised that Mae wasn't going to say anything more about her parents. "We'll take you home with us and then tomorrow we'll try and find Mrs. Pears." The little girl nodded, and a beautiful smile broke on her lips.

Life in the Ashton home was blissful, and Mae prayed that they wouldn't find Mrs. Pears, so she could live with these nice people. Their house was large, and she had her own bedroom, not like in Mrs. Pears' house where all the children slept on the floor in the small living room while the parents used the second room.

Mr. Ashton was kind, and his twinkling eyes reminded her of her Pa. He never shouted, even when the children were being loud and noisy. Sometimes he even joined in, and whenever he twirled the boys in the air, Mae also got her chance. And Mrs. Ashton was always singing, and when she brushed Mae's hair, her hands were gentle. Sometimes Mae would close her eyes and imagine that her Mama and Papa were back, and she would feel happy. But then she would remember that Todd Pears had told her that they would never come back because hadn't she seen them being put in a hole in the ground, and the sadness would return. Still, because of the way the two adults treated her with so much kindness, Mae dreamed that she was with her parents.

Every morning for nearly two weeks, Mr. and Mrs. Ashton took Mae to the police precinct to see if anyone had come forward to search for her.

"She might as well become ours," Mrs. Ashton told her husband one day when their quest had once again been unsuccessful. "It's clear that whoever was taking care of the child abandoned her at the park. There are so many people in London called Mrs. Pears that it will be impossible to find this woman, and especially since it seems as if she doesn't want to be found."

"We don't know that the child was abandoned, my darling," Mr. Ashton rebuked mildly. "She could have just strayed away from her minder."

"You really don't believe that now, do you? If someone had lost this child, wouldn't they have reported the matter to the police by now? There would also be a notice about the missing child," Mrs. Ashton said. "This child was put away like some old rug that no one had any more use for. But we'll not abandon her," her voice was fierce.

"You're right, Mother, and yes, it would be nice to have a little girl. She's so calm and the boys like her very much."

"Peter and Simeon have always wanted a little sister and now they have one."

"But we have to do it the right way. I'm a barrister and can't afford to do things in halves. We still don't know what happened to the child's parents. I'll get a detective on this issue right away. At least we know that her name is Mae Chester so it shouldn't be too hard for my person to get more information about her. One of the men at the Scotland Yard owes me a favour and I think it's about time that I collected."

That evening before the family went to bed, Mr. Ashton turned to Mae. "Mae are you happy living here with us?"

"Yes, sir."

"No," Mrs. Ashton laughed. "Please don't call Papa, sir. You can call him Papa and you can call me Mama."

"Mama?" Mae tried it out, a smile on her lips.

"Yes, my love." Mrs. Ashton looked at her husband, who gave her a slight nod. "We want you to live here with us and become our little girl. Then Peter and Simeon will be your brothers. Would you like that?"

Mae's smile grew wider, and she clapped her little hands. "Yes, yes, yes."

Peter and Simeon also cheered, and Mr. Ashton threw his head back and laughed.

"But we have to know where your parents are first. Will you please tell us what you can remember?"

"Yes, Mama." Mae was eager to please her new family. She had a new Mama and Papa and was not afraid anymore. She stayed silent for a brief moment. "The fire in the house."

Husband and wife looked at each other.

"Pa went inside, and Ma followed him." A sob broke out from the child. "The house fell and there was fire everywhere." She was now screaming in anguish, seeing the picture as it had happened on that fateful day. Mrs. Ashton quickly pulled her into her arms and held her until she fell asleep, still sobbing softly.

Mae was loved, and her nightmares began to decrease. Peter and Simeon had a governess who was kind and accepted Mae into the schoolroom. The lessons were fun filled and Mae was happy once again.

She was a fast learner, and her new family was very proud of her progress and achievements. In just six months, she could read and write as well as her two new brothers. Life was filled with love and laughter, and Mr. and Mrs. Ashton, now that they knew what had happened to Mae's parents, didn't waste any more time but started talking about adopting her.

Christmas Day that year was the first one she was spending without her parents, but Mae was so happy that it was just a tiny sad memory in her mind. Her new parents bought her a pretty rag doll and she carried it everywhere she went.

Then disaster struck in the New Year. Mrs. Ashton received a letter from her brother telling her that their mother was very ill and not expected to live long.

Mae was five years old now, and she sensed the sadness that engulfed the household.

Mr. Ashton called the children one morning not many days thereafter. For once, there was no singing nor laughter in the home. Mrs. Ashton had rarely left her bedchamber since receiving the letter from her brother two days before. Mae missed her new Mama's singing and smile, but she understood that it was a solemn moment for all of them. "Mother and I will be travelling to Bristol to see your grandmother. But Grandma Beth will be coming to stay here until we return. Be good for her, do you hear me?"

"Yes, Papa," all three children chorused.

"Miss Rover will also be here to help you. Study hard and when Mama and I return, we'll take you to the park to see the Queen."

"Yes, Papa."

From the moment Grandma Beth arrived in the household, Mae felt dread welling up within her. The woman had a hard and unsmiling face. Even Peter and Simeon seemed subdued in her presence. Mae wanted to cry and beg her new parents not to leave them behind, but the elderly woman's eyes silenced her.

Mr. and Mrs. Ashton left for Bristol on the same day that Grandma Beth arrived, and nothing was ever the same again. The children weren't allowed to play, and their lessons were longer since Grandma didn't allow Miss Rover to take them out to the garden to play, and Grandma Beth found fault with everything that Mae did, from how she sat to her eating habits.

"Children are there to be seen only when necessary, not heard," she told the three of them. "Now go to your rooms, and if I hear as much as a squeak from any of you, there'll be trouble."

For the next few days, the children stayed at the window of the living room with their little noses pressed against the panes, watching and hoping that their parents would return soon.

Then one morning Mae was woken up by Miss Rover, who was weeping.

"It's dreadful," the young woman said over and over again. "This is so terrible!" She dressed Mae in warm clothing and held her hand, taking her downstairs where Peter and Simeon were standing beside Grandma Beth. There were suitcases at the door.

"Where are we going, Grandma Beth?" Mae was excited and thought that perhaps their parents had sent for them. Papa had once taken them to the seaside, and they had stayed at a nice hotel and had so much fun. Maybe he'd sent for them.

"Don't ever call me that," the woman growled, and all laughter died from the child's lips. She shrank back, pressing herself against the governess's legs. "You're not related to us, and I'm glad to be well rid of you. My son was a fool for bringing a child picked off the streets. It seems as if you're a cursed child, for wherever you go disaster and bad luck follow you. You've brought nothing but bad luck to this family. If it was up to me, I'd have you burnt at the stake because you're clearly a witch."

Miss Rover gasped, and Grandma Beth turned her cold eyes to her. "Get rid of that child if you want to retain your position with me. My home can't receive vermin like this vagabond. My son and his wife are dead because of the curse that she brought to this family."

And so it was that Miss Rover, still sobbing, took Mae to the market and in the melee of people, released her hand. "I'm so sorry," the distraught woman said as she melted away into the crowd.

Mae started crying, looking around for her friend. "Miss Rover," she called out as she moved from stall to stall but to no avail. Her friend was gone, and she was frightened.

The large market was a very busy place, and she was pushed from side to side with some people hissing at her for being in their way. No one took notice of the crying child because they were busy with their own tasks. Shoppers purchased the items they needed, and the vendors supplied their customers with the best of whatever produce they had. No one noticed the crying child as she moved from one stall to the other. Finally, Mae found herself outside the market, tears running down her face. Her rag doll was clasped tightly in her hands where Miss Rover had shoved it hurriedly.

"Look, look," some dirty boys spotted Mae, and pointing in her direction, began to advance. No one seemed to care that they looked threatening, and Mae was terrified.

There were three of them, and Mae felt them grabbing at her beautiful coat. Next to go were her shoes, but she held on fast to her rag doll, screaming at the top of her voice. Only one or two people bothered to glance her way, and even then they shrugged and moved on. They probably thought it was market children playing a game and soon forgot the scene.

The boys were much bigger than Mae and started pushing her towards a large heap of rubbish.

"Stop that! Here! Stop that at once," and through tear filled eyes, Mae saw a large hand coming down hard and pulling two of the boys away from her, tossing them aside as if they weighed nothing. Then the hand once again reached and grabbed the third boy by the collar of his dirty torn shirt and shook him till Mae thought she heard his teeth rattling. He was then cast onto the rubbish heap. "If I catch you anywhere near my child, I'll beat the living daylights out of you. Do you hear?"

"Yes, Mrs. Brittle," the older boy said, terror on his face. He pulled his accomplices back to their feet and the three of them fled for their lives when the woman took a threatening step in their direction.

"Come." Gentle hands put the coat back on Mae's back and her shoes on her feet. "No one will hurt you because Mama is here."

Mae nodded tiredly. She longed for Mrs. Ashton's rosy scent but knew that her life was over once again in that respect. Mama and Papa Ashton were dead, for hadn't Grandma Beth told her that? And then it was clear that Grandma Beth didn't want her and had sent her away. But this woman, dirty looking and smelling terribly, was all she had. She had chased the bad boys away, and she didn't seem like she would abandon or hurt her.

"A little one like you should never wander the streets alone. This world is full of evil and wicked people. Come, let's go home."

Home was a roughly built structure made of old canvas and wood. It stood under the London Bridge, but Mae was too tired to complain. She was safe, and even if the woman looked funny and spoke to unseen people, she felt safe. Mae was grateful to be with a person who wouldn't let anyone hurt her.

"Eat this." Something was shoved into her little hands. It was a stale doughnut. "Eat it and then sleep little one."

And thus began Mae Chester's life under the London Bridge.

Two Years Later

Seven-year-old Mae sat on the bank of the River Thames with Mrs. Brittle and received a chunk of stale bread from her dirty hands. They didn't talk much, both watching the water as it flowed to the other end of the world as Mrs. Brittle liked to say. *"One day this river will take you to the other side of the world,"* Mrs. Brittle once told Mae. *"And when you get there, don't forget about me."*

"Here, drink," the half mad woman pushed a dirty bottle into the child's hands. Mae obediently received the bottle and drank whatever was offered. It tasted funny but quenched her thirst after chomping down the stale piece of bread. At least this time there had been a trace of cheese on the bread, a luxury for the two of them.

All around them, other homeless tramps like them scavenged for food from the heaps of rubbish that were dumped there late at night. Most hotels and households in London used this spot as a dumping ground, much to the joy of the homeless. The early birds, like Mrs. Brittle and Mae, often got the best food before it was trampled down by masses of the homeless in their mad haste to forage for something to eat.

Mae was so used to the squalor now that she barely noticed it anymore. In any case, her life was as comfortable as could be, given her situation in life. At least with Mrs. Brittle she felt safe, and none of the other street urchins bullied or teased her. Most of her days were filled with adventure as they roamed around the city doing nothing but scavenging for anything of value they could get their hands on. Sometimes they sold the trinkets they found to lower working-class people, and many times they kept the items for themselves.

On a good day, one could even find a nice pair of shoes, even if they didn't match most of the time. Clothes and utensils were also to be found, and Mrs. Brittle liked to say that they were going shopping on the days they visited other dumpsters. They would then carry their 'shopping' bags back to their house and the sorting would begin. It was interesting to Mae that even the things they discarded were picked up by other homeless people and turned into useful items for their use.

Once their paltry dinner was over, Mrs. Brittle rose to her feet and held out her hand to Mae, who placed her small one trustingly in it. They walked down the side of the river and emerged under the London Bridge itself, carrying whatever they had found in the dumping ground. Mae had a blanket wrapped around her shoulders, one of their offerings of the day.

All the London Bridge tramps had their own spots and if anyone wanted any trouble, all they had to do was take up another's place. When Mae and her 'Mama,' for that's what she called Mrs. Brittle, were a few yards from their home, Mae skipped ahead.

"Beautiful girl, come and visit me in my house," a rough looking young man shouted, and Mrs. Brittle hurled the now empty bottle at him. It struck him on the chest, then fell down and shattered into hundreds of pieces. "What did you do that for?" The man said in surly tones.

"Mind your manners and keep your eyes shut whenever you see my daughter," Mrs. Brittle snarled at him. "Or I'll pluck them out of your ugly face and feed them to the fishes in the river."

The terrified man scampered away, and Mrs. Brittle followed Mae into their house.

"Mae?"

"Yes, Mama?"

"Aah! I like it when you call me Mama," the woman said, and Mae beamed at her protector. "Listen to me. Don't ever walk alone. Do you hear me?" Mae nodded, her head bobbing up and down. "There be wicked creatures who can hurt you if you walk alone. I want you to promise me that you won't speak to other people unless I'm there with you."

"Yes, Mama."

"Now sleep, and I'll watch over you."

Mae curled up on the old smelly sacks and pulled her new blanket close. She didn't complain because her stomach was full and she was warm. Mrs. Brittle covered her with another old blanket with her rough but yet tender hands.

Mae was soon fast asleep, unaware that every single day her guardian never slept a wink, watching out for marauders who would attack the vulnerable. Mae had no idea that on one or two occasions, the woman had fought off wicked men who had tried to grab her.

The weary child slept the sleep of the innocent, and when it was dawn, she woke up and was handed another slice of stale bread.

"People are always generous at Christmas time," Mrs. Brittle told her. "So today we'll go around and beg for clothes. Then we'll go to the bathhouse and wash ourselves clean, so we'll look and smell nice on Christmas Day." The woman observed her with a critical eye. "You're growing up very fast and you need new clothes. Maybe we should go by the Salvation Army first and get you new clothes, a coat, and shoes. It will soon become very cold, and we don't want you getting sick."

"Yes, Mama."

"Mae, remember what I told you. Don't stray away from me. Stay close so that you won't get lost. London is full of people, and not all of them are good folk."

The trip to the Salvation Army store was made in companionable silence, for Mae had learnt that Mrs. Brittle didn't like talking when they were walking.

From time to time the child would look up at her 'parent' and smile, receiving one in return. Yes, her world was alright because Mrs. Brittle made it so.

The seven-year-old girl had no idea of how beautiful she was, and she never noticed the looks that many who saw her with her 'mother' exchanged as they passed by. But she'd noticed that lately Mrs. Brittle was overprotective of her and would snarl at anyone who came close to them.

They arrived at their destination without incident, and Mae got a new dress, a coat, and a pair of mismatched shoes from the old bins at the Salvation Army store. She loved her new coat and tucked her now old rag doll under her arm. Her feet had hurt from the old torn shoes she'd owned for about four months, but these new ones were comfortable. Mrs. Brittle even picked up two pairs of socks for her, and like her new shoes, they two were mismatched.

"There," the woman beamed at her. "Now you look very pretty."

And Mae felt pretty and happy in her new clothes. This was going to be a good Christmas, she thought. Last Christmas she'd been very ill with the flu, and they had stayed in their shack under the bridge. Mrs. Brittle never dared to leave the child alone, for she'd noticed that people liked looking at Mae. By the time Mae was well enough for them to make the trip to the Salvation Army, everything was gone save for a few tattered dresses. Still, Mrs. Brittle had taken those, for they were better than nothing.

But this year they were lucky, and even Mrs. Brittle got herself a new coat, shoes, and a dress. They happily walked down the street, but Mrs. Brittle was careful to stay away from trouble. Their visit to the dumpster behind the Savoy Hotel, one of their favourite spots, yielded a large piece of fruit cake. Even though it was mouldy on one side, that didn't matter to the pair, for this was a rare treat. Mrs. Brittle scraped the mouldy bits away and put the rest of the cake into their shopping basket. They also found some half-eaten sandwiches, which they added to their collection.

As they finished their excursion into the city, they passed through a quiet residential area on their way home. A few housewives allowed them to go through the rubbish barrels, and they found more titbits to add to their supper. Mae found a half-eaten apple which she offered first to Mrs. Brittle.

"You eat that one, and I'll catch the next," she was told, and the child munched happily on her loot. Today was a great day indeed, for they had so much food that for the next two to three days, they wouldn't leave home. The weather was changing drastically, and Mrs. Brittle even predicted much snow this year.

"Mae," the older woman called out to her.

"Yes, Mama?"

"Don't ruin your new coat, because I don't want you to catch cold this season." The child nodded and they walked on, ignoring those folks who jeered at them. Mae had learnt to turn her face aside from such insults because Mrs. Brittle had told her that she needed to learn to pick her battles wisely.

"Never spend time fighting when you know that you'll lose the battle," she'd been told time and time again. "Keep silent and be cautious. When you get into any fight, make sure that you'll emerge the victor, or else all your efforts will be in vain."

So, Mae walked on beside the woman who had taken her in and looked after her for the past two years, not saying a word when she was teased. She simply moved closer to her guardian and went on eating her apple.

It was while they were on their way back to their little house under the bridge that Mae started to get a funny feeling. She couldn't tell what had made her feel that they were in danger, but the prickly sensation at the back of her neck frightened her. As they walked, she kept looking over her shoulder and stumbled once or twice.

"What is it, Mae?" Mrs. Brittle noticed the child's agitated look.

"I think someone is following us." Her green eyes were wide with fear.

"Where?" Mrs. Brittle took Mae's hand before she stopped and looked around. Then seeing nothing unusual, she laughed softly. "My dear child, you must be seeing apparitions," she said. "But we need to hurry because it will soon be dark, and I don't want us caught out in this place and away from home."

Mae held onto Mrs. Brittle's hand, and they began walking quickly in the direction of the bridge. Then someone bumped roughly into Mrs. Brittle, causing the basket full of the goodies they had collected to fly out of her hand.

"Watch your step, you imbecile," the woman screamed, and a large stick descended on the back of her head, but she struggled to stay upright. She suddenly realised what was happening. The shove had been deliberate, and too late she realised that she should have been more cautious after Mae's warning. "Mae, run," she screamed as the stick descended once more, and she went down in a heap. Mae needed no second bidding when she saw her Mama lying still on the ground. She ran, but terror filled her heart when she heard heavy footsteps coming up fast behind her.

She could see the bridge looming close, and she knew that if she got there among her people, then she would be safe. Her Mama's friends would keep her safe until she came home. But then strong hands grabbed her, and she screamed, kicking and fighting her assailant with all her strength.

"Let me go," she screamed. "Help me."

"Calm down, Mae," the rough voice said close to her ear. "Nobody will hurt you."

"No, let me go."

"If you don't stop that racket, I'll be forced to subdue you, and you won't like that."

Mae found herself pushed into a waiting carriage. She moved to the corner, where she sat sobbing in terror. Who was this man, and what did he want with her?

"Mae, my name is Davenport. I'm a detective, and your uncle, Mr. John Lester, sent me to find you. He's been searching for you for over two years, ever since he heard that your mama had died. He promised your mama that he would take care of you should anything happen to you. Now sleep child, you have no need to fear."

The soft voice soothed Mae to sleep.

Herbert forced himself not to cry, and he presented a stoic face to his mother.

"This is for your own good," she was saying. "Herbert, I want you to grow up into a strong and stable man, not some weakling who will allow everyone to walk all over him." Her eyes darted to his father. "Remember that one day you'll inherit all this, and a good education will ensure that you become skilled in many things. Your grandfather and your ancestors before you built this estate from nothing. You're the next in line to inherit everything, and so I want you to stand out."

The twelve-year-old boy looked towards where his father was seated on a small couch in his mother's study. His Pa's head was bowed, and Herbert wondered what his father was thinking. Ever since his mother had declared that he would be going to Eton for the next few years, his Pa had seemed to shut himself inwardly. Herbert willed his father to fight for him and stop his mother from sending him away.

But he knew from experience that nothing his Pa said would be considered. The young boy had watched as time and again his mother shut down any suggestions that his Pa would make. Even if it was something worth considering, his mother never listened to his father. He turned to his mother, who was still talking.

"The tailor will be coming in tomorrow morning to take your measurements so he can prepare all the garments that you'll need for school. According to your new housemaster, all the formal school uniforms will be provided at the school, but we still have to get you a few other things." Elaine looked at her son, who stared blankly at her. "You could at least smile and say thank you," she hissed.

"Thank you," Herbert said, not because he was grateful, but because it was expected of him.

"Show some enthusiasm that you're going to one of the best schools in England. Do you know how hard I worked to get you into that school? Many boys such as yourself would give anything to get this chance. Yet here you stand like one who isn't willing to go to Eton."

Herbert wanted to tell his mother that he didn't want to go to Eton, but then he didn't want to earn her wrath.

His mother flicked her hand at him in dismissal. "Now leave me be," she said. "Both of you go and do whatever it is you do with all the idle time you have. I have work to do. Shut the door behind you."

The only reaction Herbert saw from his father after the scathing dismissal was a slight tightening of the lips. Herbert's eyes then turned to the fourth person in the study, one who had remained silent throughout his mother's one-sided conversation.

Mr. Gideon Smyth, his grandfather's close friend, had become a common fixture in their home. Now that Herbert was older, he understood whatever was going on.

For as long as he lived, he would never forget that day years ago when he'd brought flowers to his mother for her birthday and found her and Mr. Smyth standing in the study, their arms around each other and their upper bodies uncovered. From that time on, he'd stayed out of Mr. Smyth's way, and as he looked into the man's eyes, he saw something like triumph. Then he understood that his being sent away was because of this man.

Now that he was older, he knew that something was going on between his mother and Mr. Smyth. Many times, he'd wrestled within himself as to whether he should tell his father what he knew, mention his suspicions. But then he would toss the thought aside because he didn't want his gentle father to be distressed.

"Come," Edwin told his son as he rose to his feet after being dismissed by his wife. He no longer allowed her actions to get to him. He'd seen it all in the seventeen years that they'd been married, and nothing about her actions surprised him anymore. That she despised him was evident in her treatment of him, and he'd learnt never to show that her actions offended or affected him in any way.

He knew that Mr. Smyth, his father in law's old friend, was more than the personal financial advisor and solicitor his wife claimed him to be. Yet the fact didn't bother him at all, since this was a marriage of convenience, and any kind of intimacy between them had ended the moment she'd conceived Herbert. He was in this marriage solely because of his son, and nothing Elaine did bothered him at all. In truth, he was relieved that his cold and manipulative wife had other things, or rather another person, to keep her occupied.

Over the years since his father in law's death, Edwin had done all he could to protect his son from his wife's influence. With her being fully preoccupied with Mr. Smyth, Edwin got the freedom to nurture his son into a conscientious and kind-hearted person. Edwin's only prayer was that his son would never know about his mother's shameful acts that took place in their very home. Even though he'd never loved Elaine and had only married her to save his mother from shame, Edwin still felt that it was important for Herbert to always respect his mother.

"Pa!" Herbert's voice roused his father from his thoughts. Edwin looked around and realised that they'd reached the garden. This was his sanctuary, his place of refuge, and even Elaine didn't interfere with his roses. Just the previous year, he'd constructed a large greenhouse so he could grow roses all year round. Elaine loved having flowers in every corner of the house, and perhaps that was the reason she left him to his own devices, in as far as this garden went.

It was her indifference to his activities that had enabled him to have money of his own. Years ago, when they'd first been married, his father-in-law had given him an allowance. "My daughter's husband should dress well and not look like a vagabond," he'd been told.

"Carrying the Patterson name means dressing well and looking the part."

But as soon as his father-in-law had died, the allowance had stopped. Edwin refused to give his wife the satisfaction of having to ask her for money, so he'd started selling his roses. He had no idea if Elaine was aware that he provided flowers to many of the stately homes in Patterson Village, not that he even cared. She had her things to do, and he had his own.

In the past few years, he'd managed to build a nest egg for himself. He had a tidy sum saved up, because his needs were very few. The estate provided for all of his son's needs, and with no other dependants seeking his assistance, Edwin barely spent anything on himself. Also, with his father-in-law gone, they no longer entertained as much, and even when they did, his presence was never required.

One day, he always told himself, he would be free to walk away from this sham of a marriage, and he needed to prepare himself for that day, because he knew beyond a shadow of doubt that when he eventually walked away from Elaine and this marriage, he would be leaving with nothing.

All he was waiting for was for Herbert to turn eighteen. When that time came, he would sit his son down and explain to him why he and his mother had to go their separate ways.

"Pa!" Herbert sounded impatient as he looked up at his father.

"Yes, my son." Edwin smiled and pushed his thoughts aside so he could attend to his son.

"I don't want to go away to school." The young boy stood there and allowed his father to ruffle his hair.

"I also don't want you to go away, but this is for a good cause," Edwin told his son. "Eton is the best school in England, and more than anything, I want you to have a good education. With a good educational background, you'll be able to stand and be counted among men. I don't want you to end up like your Pa."

Herbert looked at his father's face and saw the sadness in his eyes. It was only recently that the intelligent young boy had discovered the reason why his father had insisted on sitting in on all his lessons as he was tutored by the schoolmaster hired by his mother. His Pa had never received any formal education while growing up, and it was during those lessons that he'd finally learned to read and write.

Edwin took his son by the shoulders and looked down into his face. Herbert was growing up very fast, and Edwin knew that in just a year or two, the boy would be taller than him. "Son, promise me that you'll give Eton a chance."

"But Pa…"

"Herbert, I want you to embrace this chance and do your best. Not for your mother nor for me, but for your own sake. If at the end of this school year you're not happy, then I'll prevail upon your Mama and have you stay here at home with us. But first you have to go out there and experience something different."

"What if I don't like Eton?" Herbert mumbled sullenly.

"And what if you go to Eton and end up loving school? Go and spend this school year at Eton, and we shall revisit this conversation when you return."

"Pa, will you be coming to visit me?"

Edwin smiled and once again ruffled his son's hair. "You can count on that. Nothing will keep me from coming to visit you from time to time."

Herbert sighed inwardly. "Pa, will you be alright on your own?"

"Why do you ask?"

"It's just that I've never seen you going anywhere. You spend all your time out here in the garden or with me in the schoolroom. Pa, don't you have any friends?"

"I have plenty of friends, and yes, I'll be alright."

IN THE QUEEN'S PARLOUR

"This will be your room," said the sour faced maid who had led Mae up the stairs to the first floor. After Mr. Davenport had deposited her at her uncle's place, he'd left without a backward glance. In as far as he was concerned, the job for which he'd been hired and paid was over. He'd shut his eyes and heart to the terror in the little girl's eyes as he'd delivered her to this hostile environment.

Mr. Davenport had been concerned when Mae slept through the transfer from the carriage and onto the train. He'd noticed people giving him strange looks as he'd carried the comatose child onto the train and had given them a sad smile. "My little niece, my dead sister's only child," he said. "She's been very ill since her mother's death and I'm taking her home so she can live with me and my family." He'd inwardly scoffed at their sympathetic looks. Folks were ready to believe anything as long as one said the right thing and made the right facial expressions. Being in a first-class compartment meant that he had the privacy he sought and didn't have to give anyone any explanations.

Mae had woken up halfway through their journey, and she'd asked him a lot of questions about her uncle. The little girl was very intelligent, and there was a bright light in her eyes as she talked nonstop, all fear gone now that she saw that he meant her no harm. He'd seen the hope in her eyes when he told her that her uncle, her mother's cousin, was expecting her. She had told him all about her parents and then another family of her brothers called Peter and Simeon. He thought she was a little mentally confused after living on the streets for two years with only a mad woman as her constant companion.

According to Mr. John Lester's words when he'd hired him to find Mae, his niece was probably mentally disturbed after her parents' deaths, given that she'd watched them burn in their home. Mr. Lester had searched for the girl as soon as news reached him that his cousin was dead, but the neighbours had told him that Mae had run away. That was when Mr. Lester had hired his services because he'd made a vow years ago to take care of Mae if her own mother wouldn't be there to do so, but only if she was still a minor.

"I know that you'll eventually find my niece," Mr. Lester had told him. "But I don't know in what state of mind she'll be.

I'm sure she's living on the streets, and you know what that does to a person. Don't be surprised if she shows signs of being mentally deranged because of the harsh life out there."

"If you feel that she's mentally unstable, why then are you bringing her to your home to live with your family? Wouldn't she be better off in an asylum?"

"I made a solemn promise which I intend to fulfil. Mae is still very young, and I promised Ashley that I would be her guardian until she turns eighteen."

"What if I never find her until she is all grown up?"

"My obligation will only last until she turns eighteen. If you don't find her in the years to come, then I'll assume that she died. But you've got to at least try for the sake of my conscience. My only fear is that I might be bringing a lunatic into my household," he shrugged. "In any case, I'll know what to do once she gets here."

But now that Mr. Davenport had found Mae he saw no signs of a mentally disturbed child, well except when she mentioned that she had two older brothers. Mr. Lester had told him that Mae was an only child after her parents had tried for nine years to have a child. Then he smiled, for children had such good imaginations. In her loneliness, the child had probably created a new family in her mind. Yes, that was it. And she surprised him when she talked of being happy that she was going to live with her uncle where she knew that she would be happy. He had his doubts about that but kept his thoughts to himself. If this child wanted to dream of roses and rainbows and happily ever after, who was he to disillusion her? Life would teach her not to be overly trusting of people and circumstances. But since he'd been paid to find and deliver her to her uncle, that was all he would do. He wasn't going to get involved in other folks' business.

Once he'd delivered her to her destination, it was the last time that Mr. Davenport would ever see Mae Chester, though once in a while, when he was in a reflective mood, he would wonder what had happened to her, and if things had turned out right for the child.

"You!" Mae was shaken out of her thoughts when the maid snapped at her. When Mr. Davenport had brought her to her uncle, she'd dreamed of a bedroom like the one she'd had at Peter and Simeon's house. She had also dreamed of her uncle waiting to receive her, a huge smile of welcome on his face. None of that had happened, however. Instead, it was this harsh person who had been tasked with showing her to her room, and not one of her cousins as she'd hoped. "I hope you're not here to cause me any trouble," the maid said, giving her an angry look. Mae shook her head, already dreading the days ahead.

The room into which she was shown was on the first floor at the end of the corridor next to the stairs that led up to the attic. What Mae didn't know was that it wasn't supposed to be a bedroom but a storage room of some kind. As soon as her uncle had received news that she'd been found, this room had been prepared for her. It was almost bare and had only a narrow bed with a thin mattress on it. The quilt was threadbare. Mae walked to the bed and then turned around to look at the servant who had brought her here.

All hopes of being in a loving home like she'd shared with her parents, the Ashtons and even Mrs. Brittle in her shack were gone. This was a hostile environment, but she had nowhere else to go. Fear filled her little heart and she wanted to cry, but then who would soothe her fears and comfort her if she did that?

Downstairs, she'd seen two older girls who had been introduced to her as her cousins, Bella and Ida. Far from being pleasant at her arrival, they had looked at her with cold, unwelcoming eyes. It was clear that she wouldn't find friends in them, and she sighed as she slowly sank to the floor and leaned her weary head on the bed. For the first time in two years, she found herself thinking about Peter and Simeon and their parents, Mr. and Mrs. Ashton.

After Mrs. Pears had left her in the park and she'd found the Ashtons, they had wanted her in their home and lives. In her innocence and hopes, Mae had expected that her uncle would receive her with wide open arms. Mr. Davenport had said that Uncle John was a good man. And after all, wasn't she his dead cousin's child? The Ashtons hadn't been related to her, but she'd spent six wonderful months in their home.

But the reality was much different from her daydreams. Weary and hungry, Mae put her head on her knees and wept. She felt so lonely and missed Mrs. Brittle very much.

"Stop crying," she was told in a cold voice, but she only wept the more. "If Mrs. Lester finds you bawling like a little baby then there'll be trouble for you."

Mae was woken up by the same maid who'd showed her to her room very early the next morning. She was hungry after only receiving scraps of food last evening. At dinner time, she hadn't been allowed to join the family at the table, but instead had been sent to the kitchen to wait for the leftovers. She had silently sat on a small stool next to the fireplace and obediently waited for her supper.

When the table was cleared, whatever leftovers returned to the kitchen were grabbed by the three older maids and shared amongst themselves. It was only when Mae had sneezed because of the smoke that they'd even remembered that she was present. By that time all the food was gone, and the plates were licked clean. One of the maids reached for the empty cooking pot and scraped the bottom, then brought Mae a plate of something she couldn't even put a name to and poured water on the mess, declaring it to be broth.

Too hungry to complain, Mae had fallen on the food and devoured it within no time, then followed the maid once again to her room, where she fell into a dead sleep.

"And who do we have here?" As soon as Mae entered the kitchen behind the older girl, she came face to face with a plump woman whose face was red. It was clear that she'd been stirring something in the large pot over the fire in the grate. "I'm Mrs. Brown," she said, and Mae was surprised when the woman held out a hand. She flinched, expecting a blow, and the woman paled. "You thought I was going to strike you?" Mae, in her innocence, nodded. "Oh child, I was only holding out my hand so I could shake yours."

"Her name is Mae." The sour faced maid of the previous day entered the kitchen carrying some plates. "Some gentleman brought her to the house yesterday, and I understand that she's supposed to be Mr. Lester's niece or something like that. I was instructed to put her to work immediately after breakfast."

"Come here, Mae." Mrs. Brown had kind eyes, and even though she was dressed nicely in as far as a cook could be, she still reminded Mae of Mrs. Brittle back in London. Tears brimmed in the child's eyes as she thought about the woman who had protected her on the streets and kept her safe. Was she alright, or had she died after that man had struck her? She should have remembered to ask Mr. Davenport if Mrs. Brittle was alright and begged him to check on her when he returned to London. Then she felt guilty because she'd forgotten the kind woman in her excitement after hearing that she was coming to live with her uncle.

"Don't cry." Mrs. Brown wiped Mae's tears away with the edge of her apron. "You must be very hungry."

"We gave her dinner last night," the sullen maid said, and her look dared Mae to contradict her words. But Mae was quickly learning that keeping her mouth shut helped her stay out of trouble.

Right after breakfast, which consisted of watery milk, bread, and cheese, the second maid beckoned to her. She learned their names while taking breakfast. The sour faced one was called Carol, the plump one was Sheila, and the one who had given her the terrible dinner last evening was Molly.

"Come with me," Sheila said. "I'll show you how to dust the furniture in the living room."

"Make sure she doesn't break anything," Mrs. Brown called out as they left the kitchen. "Show her what needs to be done while remembering that she's only a child."

"I know that," Sheila said.

Mae could hear voices on the other side of the door as they approached the living room. Sheila held her hand up in a motion for Mae to be quiet. Mae couldn't quite make out what was being said on the other side of the door, but she heard her name mentioned several times. The voices which belonged to her uncle, her aunt, and two cousins were really tense.

Sheila tiptoed away, and since she didn't ask Mae to follow her, the little girl stood there staring at the living room door. Suddenly it was thrown wide open, and her aunt appeared before her. She looked surprised to find Mae standing at the door and then her face changed.

"Listening outside doors is a bad habit." Mae's ear was pinched. "I'll not have a tattle tale in my home."

"Stop," Mae cried out, raising her small hands and trying to pull her ear away. The pain was excruciating, and it became too much to bear. With tears pouring down her face, she looked to her uncle for help. But he simply gave her a disinterested look, then picked up his newspaper and raised it high so that it covered his face. Through the tears, she heard her cousins giggling.

Still pulling her ear, her aunt dragged her to the kitchen.

"Mrs. Brown, teach this little rascal some manners. I caught her eavesdropping in on our conversation, which is terrible manners. I won't have an uncouth person living in my household. Teach her how to behave properly or so help me..." the woman bit her lower lip, and Mae was pushed forward so she stumbled across the kitchen.

Mrs. Brown waited for Mrs. Lester to leave the kitchen, then turned to Mae, who was weeping silently and rubbing her painful ear. "Were you listening in at the door?" Mae shook her head. "Wipe your face and stop crying. You have to learn how to cope with your new life in this house."

"I'll run away," Mae murmured, thinking of a way of leaving this unfriendly house. She would go in search of Mrs. Brittle, who had never once hurt her, even though Mae had heard it whispered that the woman was a raving lunatic.

"Don't let your uncle hear you saying that, or you'll receive a sound beating. Now come here and help me sweep this floor."

Herbert joined Eton at a time when significant changes had been made to the school in terms of granting the students better accommodation, giving them a wider curriculum and provision of better qualified staff. He found himself having a room to himself, contrary to his fear of sharing with some other boy who might turn out to be an unpleasant roommate.

Like him, there were about one hundred new boys, and most of them looked scared. It was clear that many of them had never been away from home for more than a day or two. But there were also the bigger boys, older in school, and who looked quite intimidating. They watched Herbert and his peers from the side-lines as they were taken around the school by some of the masters. They made frightening faces at the newcomers when none of the masters was looking, and Herbert felt afraid. He longed to go back home, but he'd made a promise to his father that he would bear it out for this school year. He didn't expect that he would want to return in the New Year, but for now, he just had to fit in like the other newcomers.

The house he was taken to was one of the newer ones, and he liked his room though it was much smaller than the one he had at home. It consisted of a narrow cot and a tall closet, a small table and chair. His room was on the first floor of the house, and the window looked out into the back courtyard. He could see crates of fresh produce being carried from an overloaded cart to the large kitchen. Even from this distance, he could hear the clattering in the kitchen and smell the aroma of a meal being prepared, for it was close to lunch time.

Like many of the other new boys, Herbert didn't enjoy his first meal in school. It consisted of a lump of mashed potatoes, with thick gravy over boiled cabbage, and some mutton which was generously served to them. There was also a banana beside his plate, and he chose to eat it rather than the mess that was on his plate. The young boy had no idea then that soon he would be devouring all the food placed before him and even wishing for more. But for now, his ignorance of the future was his protection.

That first night, after his father and mother had left and he was alone in his small room, he though he heard someone snivelling. The walls between the rooms were thin, and he could hear whatever was happening on the either side. He wanted to go and find out if the boy next door was alright, but he feared that the housemaster would catch and castigate him. Right from when he and fifty other boys had been brought into this particular house, Mr. Kenton, their housemaster, had let it be known that he wouldn't stand for any mischief, tardiness, or untidiness.

The last thing Herbert wanted was to draw any unnecessary attention to himself, especially since he'd promised his Pa that he would do his best and excel. He loved his tailcoat, the starched shirt, waistcoat, and striped trousers that were part of his school uniform. He'd also been outfitted with a top hat that he'd been told was to be worn only during special occasions.

"We all look like well suited soldiers going out to war," a voice commented dryly behind him the next morning when they were at parade. "If you ask me, we all look very funny. But at least we're not being made to wear those funny hats that make us look like we're carrying cooking pots on our heads."

Herbert bit back a grin as he turned to find out who the early morning jester was. He found himself looking into grey eyes, and the boy, younger than he was by a year or two, had such a very serious expression on his face that Herbert began to feel that he might have imagined the jokes. Then he saw the twinkle in the boy's eyes and grinned.

"Silence!" A voice roared from the front and Herbert hastily turned to face forward, his face turning red when he noticed one or two older boys standing a few feet away, giving him odd looks.

"And the master barks," the same boy murmured, and Herbert's lips twitched.

Once the assembly was over, Herbert turned to walk away but found his path blocked by the same two mean looking older boys who'd given him odd looks before. He felt fear and expected them to box his ears or slap him. The two boys did neither, and he wondered what they wanted with him.

"Why were you giggling like a deranged female?" one of the older boys asked.

Before Herbert could answer, a voice shot out. "Shouldn't you be picking on someone your size?" The question was posed. "Can't you see that you're standing before this one as an unfair match? Even in war, a king never goes to battle unless he's sure that he'll win the war. It's only a weak king who chooses a weaker foe to challenge. The two of you have out matched this poor fellow."

"Who are you to talk to us like that?"

"Someone you should be fearful of offending," the boy retorted back. "In any case, we have to report to our classrooms, and the tutors won't be too pleased if we're late. Now step aside and let us leave in peace, or name a time and place for a duel."

The two boys looked at each other and one of them made a rude sound as they walked away.

"Come," the brave boy told Herbert. "Let's get out of here before those two change their minds and come after us. We must be in the same class, and even if we're not, I'll make sure that we are." A third boy, younger than the first one, joined them, and they walked together to the classroom.

"The name is Peter Ashton, and this is my brother Simeon."

"Herbert Patterson," he offered, and so began a friendship that would last all their lives.

PART II
OVERLOOKED

THE LITTLE WALLS

Five Years Later

Mae was perched on top of a tree when she saw the tall, lanky boy trudging through the garden of the house next door. His shoulders were slumped, and the air of dejection that surrounded him made her tender heart constrict with compassion.

She'd overheard Uncle John and Aunt Naomi discussing the latest happenings in the neighbourhood. Apparently, Mr. Patterson, their immediate neighbour, had died after being ill for a few days, and his son had returned from Eton for the burial. She knew that his name was Herbert, for her cousins had spoken about him, often with stars in their eyes. Mae thought they sounded very foolish but never let her secret thoughts be known.

The tall, lanky boy must be the Herbert that Bella and Ida talked about. Her eyes followed him, but he was soon lost to her sight because of the tall flowering shrubs in the garden next door. A thick hedge separated the two homesteads, and though she'd never once visited the neighbours, she often wondered what their house was like inside. From her vantage point on top of the tree, she could see the large sprawling manor in the distance. It was a beautiful house, and she'd often heard her aunt speak about the inside of it in envious tones. Uncle John's house was much smaller than the manor.

Seeing an opportunity to find out what lay on the other side of the hedge, Mae climbed down and was careful not to let herself be seen, or there would be trouble. She knew that there was a small gate that connected the two properties, but she didn't dare use this, just in case anyone was about. Being small and agile, she soon found a rabbit hole in the hedge and slipped through it, dusting herself before going in search of her prey.

It was the sound of broken weeping that led her to the boy she'd been observing from on top of the tree. He had his head on his knees as he sat on the bench in the arbour. His shoulders were shaking, and Mae walked up to him and silently took the place beside him.

Herbert was so lost in his grief that it was a while before he realised that he was no longer alone. He'd come out here to be alone and didn't want to be disturbed, least of all by his mother. She was the one person that he had no desire to see or speak to, and as he turned, he had a harsh retort ready, till he saw that it was a total stranger. It was a girl of about twelve years, and she was observing him through serious green eyes, and he saw deep compassion in them. Something within him felt as if he was meeting a kindred spirit.

"Who are you?" Herbert asked as he wiped his face, feeling embarrassed at having been caught crying, and by a girl for that matter, so his voice came out all gruff. He cleared his throat when he saw the girl swallowing nervously. As far as he could tell, none of the servants in his mother's house had a child this young, and even if they did, it was highly unlikely that she would be allowed to walk freely around the manor. His mother was very firm on that point. The servants' families stayed in the cottages at the edge of the estate, never being allowed for any reason to leave the dwelling places allocated to them.

"Who are you, and how did you get here?" Herbert repeated his question but in a softer voice.

"My name is Mae Chester," the girl said. "And I live over there, in Cousin Bella's house." She pointed in the direction of the neighbour's house. Herbert rarely bothered about the neighbours because he was away at school for most of the year. It was only this time that he'd been allowed to come home early when his father became seriously ill. "Aunt Naomi and Uncle John said your Pa died. Is that why you're sad?"

Herbert nodded, unable to speak because of the emotions he was feeling. Pain at losing the one person he loved deeply, and also anger that his mother had left it too long, such that he'd only spent two days with his sick father before his death, threatened to choke him.

When he'd left for school at the beginning of this year, his father had been well, and not once had he suspected that he was ailing. Of course, Herbert had noticed that his father seemed thinner, but he hadn't put much thought into that. So, when he came home for an emergency break from school and found his father lying immobile in his bed, Herbert hadn't been able to hold his tears back.

"Don't weep too much, Son," his father had said in his usual soft voice, which was now raspy with pain. "You're a big boy now and soon will be all grown up. Take care of yourself and make me proud."

"Pa, I don't want you to die and leave me," Herbert sobbed as he lay on his father's chest. In the past five years, since joining Eton, he'd grown taller than both his parents, and his Pa had teased him about it. He didn't want to imagine that he was losing his best friend, apart from Peter and Simeon back in school. Throughout his life, the one person who'd always been there for him was his father. "Pa, how can you leave me alone?"

Edwin gently ruffled his son's hair with a trembling hand. He was dying and he was glad that for once his wife had done something that he'd requested her to do. She'd sent for their son so he could see him before he passed on.

"Sometimes there are things that are beyond our power," he told his son. "Death is never final for those who believe in the Lord," he said. "Herbert, I have to go this way, but my spirit will live on in you. Be good, be strong, and defend the weak at all times." He gently pushed his son away, so the boy sat up. "Look at me."

Herbert looked into his father's gentle eyes. They were filled with something that the young man on the threshold of adulthood had never noticed before. Strength! And that surprised him because he'd always thought of his father as being weak. Now that he'd been in Eton and had learnt a lot, he knew that his father was anything but weak. It pained him to see that he was only discovering this when his father was upon his death bed. How he had misjudged his father! The guilt made him weep the more.

"Don't cry," he was told. "I've made my peace with all this, and I'm glad that the Lord gave me these extra years to see you grow into a wonderful young man." At the stricken expression on Herbert's face, his father nodded. "Yes, I have been ill for a while but didn't want you to know about it because you were still too young. But my body fails me, and I have to accept the inevitable. The black lung disease that remained hidden in my body over the years has finally brought me to this bed. Before we came to Patterson Village, *we lived near the coal mines. That dust is what brought this on."*

"Oh, Pa!"

"Promise me this one thing."

"Anything, Pa."

"Herbert, I know that we've tried to give you the best kind of life, but you're also aware that things haven't been right between your mother and me." Herbert nodded. "Many years ago, before you were born, my father was a hardworking man and was able to support my Mama, your grandmother and me. But then he got injured when he was working in the coalmines, and life changed for all of us. Pa became bitter because he could no longer work and provide for us. He started drinking and gambling to escape from his pain. When the debts became too much for him, he gave up on life, and that's how your grandmother and I got to inherit all his debts. We would have been sent to the poor workhouse, and that would have killed your grandmother." Edwin was silent and Herbert wiped his eyes, listening to his father keenly. "I found employment as a gardener on this estate, and when your Mama approached me with a proposition that would get us out of trouble, I took it."

Herbert didn't need to be told what was coming next, but he listened anyway.

"A marriage of convenience is what it was supposed to have been, and it would have lasted for only two years. I needed money to get us out of debt and continue providing a roof for

my mother, while your Mama needed to come into her inheritance as per her grandfather's instructions in his will. We would meet each other's needs and walk away at the end of two years. But then there was another clause that we had to fulfil before we could be free." Edwin looked at his son. "There are many things that I regret in this life, but having you has never been one of them."

Herbert's face paled as he thought about the implications of his father's words. He'd been born out of a need for his mother to come into her inheritance.

"Don't be angry at your mother or me because of what we did. We love you, never doubt that at all."

"Why didn't you walk away from Ma once I was born?"

"There are many things you'll never understand, or at least not yet. But just know this, everything we've ever done has been because we love you and want the best for you. See how you didn't want to go to Eton five years ago, but now all you talk about is your school, your masters, and the friends you've made. Life is not simple, but neither is it as complex as we like to make it. But there's one thing that I want you to promise me."

Herbert nodded, "What is it, Pa?"

"You'll soon be an adult and will want to take a wife, marry, and have children. My son, promise me that whatever happens, you'll never marry a woman just because of convenience or desperation. I did it and nearly ruined all our lives. But now your mother can find happiness."

Herbert's lips tightened as he thought about Mr. Smyth. Even now the man was somewhere in this house with his mother.

"Herbert, don't think badly about us. Just find your own place in life and never let desperation push you into the wrong arms, for then you'll pay for it for the rest of your life. I have left some money in trust for you with my solicitor. It's nowhere near what you stand to inherit as your grandfather and mother's heir, but should you ever need it just know that it's all yours. Mr. Lowe will get in touch with you at the right time."

"Pa, I promise you," he said huskily. And it was a promise that he intended to keep, not just because of his father, but also for his own sake.

"Sir?" Herbert blinked, and Mae's face came into focus again. He'd drifted off and so missed a lot of what she'd been saying. "You don't have to be afraid to cry," she was saying. "Mrs. Brittle told me that it's alright to cry when I'm sad."

"Mrs. Brittle?" Herbert pulled a white hankie from his pocket and wiped his face.

Mae nodded. "She took care of me when I was in the other place. But then Uncle John brought me here." She looked sad, and his heart was moved. "I cried and cried when Mr. Davenport took me away from Mrs. Brittle, and I begged him to leave me with her, but he refused."

"Where were you before you came to live with your uncle?" She must be new because he couldn't recall ever seeing her. Of course, over the years he'd seen Bella and Ida Lester because once in a while his mother would entertain some guests, and their neighbours were usually invited to such functions. But he couldn't remember ever seeing Mae because she was unforgettable. Her green eyes would have ensured that he never forgot about her.

"In London, and I lived with Mrs. Brittle under the bridge." Herbert was shocked at the news. He'd seen plenty of homeless people but couldn't imagine that this child had once been one of them. Her uncle had probably saved her from a terrible life, but Mae didn't look like she was even ashamed of the life she'd lived out on the streets. "It was a smelly place," the child wrinkled her nose. "But Mrs. Brittle told me that we should always keep our house clean. We also had to hide from the bad people, but Mrs. Brittle kept me safe, and I miss her."

"Did you come to live with your uncle recently?"

Mae shook her head. "I've been here for five Christmases." She raised her small face to his. "Can I tell you a secret?"

"Yes, please do." Herbert found himself liking this little girl and wanted to know more about her.

"Christmas Day is also my birthday," she whispered. "Ma used to say that I was her special miracle." She blinked rapidly as the memories assailed her. "My Ma and Pa died when a fire burnt our house, and I was very sad. Then Mrs. Brittle found me, and I went to live with her. But then that man came and took me away. He hurt Mrs. Brittle, and I was sad."

Herbert was stunned to learn that this child had lived next door to him for the past five years and he hadn't known it. But then it was possible since he spent eleven months at school and only came home for the Christmas holidays, which lasted only three weeks. Still, it was odd because for the past five years the Lester family had been invited to the manor for New Year celebrations, and he was sure that if he'd ever seen Mae then he'd have remembered her. Or maybe she'd accompanied her uncle and his family but had been out of his sight.

Because his mother liked to entertain her friends during Christmas season, everyone was always kept very busy. Herbert, like his father, didn't care much for the fanfare and so would hide in the garden. Those were the best times of his life. He and his father had rarely interacted with their neighbours, and his mother never seemed to miss their presence. She liked to say that they were an embarrassment to her and so preferred that they remained out of sight. But of course, Mr. Smyth would stand beside her as if he owned the manor.

"I'm sorry that your parents are both dead," he finally told Mae, critically observing her. Though he didn't know much about their next-door neighbours, he was aware that they had to be wealthy to live around this neighbourhood. But yet Mae was dressed in an old frock that had a patch or two on it, and her shoes were torn, causing both big toes to peep out of them.

Though the sun was out on that late autumn morning, there was still a chill in the air, and he could see the goose bumps on her thin arms.

"Why aren't you wearing something warm?" he asked. "It's very cold out here today."

She shrugged. "I don't have many clothes," she told him as she looked down at her frock. "Cousin Bella gave me this dress, but it was torn so Mrs. Brown sewed this patch on it for me to hide the big hole."

Herbert didn't know what to say because the few times that he'd seen Bella and Ida, they were wearing pretty frocks, most of them new. But that wasn't his business, and he remembered that he had some liquorice in his pocket. "Would you like some candy?" Mae nodded. He brought out the few sticks of candy and they shared them, munching in silence.

"What's your name, Mister?" Mae asked in between bites. "I told you my name, but I still don't know what yours is."

He grinned at her, wondering that this little girl had caused him to momentarily forget his grief. She was so innocent and unpretentious. "My good name is Herbert."

"Mister Herbert," Mae murmured absentmindedly.

"No, don't put mister before my name. It's just simply Herbert."

"Can I call you Herb?" She asked with all innocence, her eyes bright and flashing with cheekiness.

He laughed softly, shaking his head, "I don't like being called Herb because that reminds me of plants, and as you can see, I'm not a plant."

"Very well then, I'll call you Herbert and you can call me Mae."

"May? That's the name of the fifth month of the year." He could equally be cheeky.

Mae rolled her eyes at him, "My name is Mae and not May."

"I can't tell the difference and they both sound the same to me."

Mae was about to argue, then she realised what he was doing and grinned at him. "My mama told me that Mae means miracle, but May is the fifth month. That's the difference."

Herbert was impressed at how articulate Mae was. "Do you have a governess who teaches you how to speak, read, and write?"

Mae shook her head. "Miss Grover doesn't let me into the schoolroom with Cousin Bella and Cousin Ida. But then when Mrs. Brown doesn't need me in the kitchen, I usually sit outside the schoolroom door and listen to the lessons. One day Aunt Naomi found me there and boxed my ear." She touched her right ear as if recalling the pain. "Then she told me that my place was under the stairs, and I should never go near the schoolroom again."

Herbert felt angry on behalf of the little girl and recalled what his father had told him. "... *always defend the weak...*" It was clear that, while Mae lived with her relatives, she was treated like one of the servants, maybe even worse. He noticed her short nails and bruised knuckles, which were clearly as a result of scrubbing floors and walls with strong lye and hard brushes. She was only a little girl.

He thought about telling his father, but then he remembered that he was gone, never to return. Once more deep sadness descended on him. Mae felt the shift in her new friend's emotions and felt sorry for him.

"Will you go away again?" she asked.

He nodded. "I will be going back to school in January."

"Will I ever see you again?" Mae asked in a small voice.

"Of course you will. I'll make sure that every time I come home, I will look for you."

"If you come to the house, Uncle John won't let you in."

"Why not?" Herbert's brow creased in a frown.

"Uncle John doesn't like visitors coming to the house. He told my cousins that if he ever finds their friends in the house again, then he'll whip them soundly. So please don't come to the house, or Uncle John will flog me."

"Does your uncle usually flog you?" Herbert found that his fists were clenched.

When Mae shook her head, he relaxed his stance. "No, but he shouts all the time when he gets angry. This is how he sounds." She mimicked her uncle as she waved her arms around. "His face gets very red and then spittle flies out of his mouth."

Herbert bent over with laughter. This little girl was hilarious.

"It's Aunt Naomi who boxes and pinches my ears all the time," Mae said solemnly. "I'm afraid of her." Then her face paled as she remembered something. "Oh no!"

Herbert stopped laughing when he saw the panic on his new friend's face.

"What is it, Mae?"

"Mrs. Brown sent me to the coop to get some eggs because she wants to bake a cake. But I saw an apple on the tree and climbed to get it, and that's when I saw you and came over." She jumped to her feet. "I have to go now." Before Herbert could put out a hand to stop her, she had fled. She returned a few moments later. "Thank you for the candy. It was very nice. My Pa used to buy me candy too." And once again she was gone before he could say a word.

Mae's heart was beating very fast as she approached the kitchen. Five of the twenty eggs that she'd collected from the coop were cracked and two were completely broken and oozed out of their shells. She knew that she was in trouble. She'd been so nervous as she collected the eggs that she'd knocked them in her haste.

"There you are." Mrs. Brown scowled when Mae finally entered the kitchen. "Mae, collecting eggs should only take you a few minutes. Where have you been all this while?" Mrs. Brown reached for the small pail, and the first thing she noticed were the broken eggs. "Mae, what have you done?"

"I'm sorry!" Mae raised her little hands to fend off the blows she was sure would be landing in quick succession. She waited for a while and then dropped her hands. Mrs. Brown's face was twisted with shock.

"Mae, I wasn't going to strike you. I've never hit you before so why would you think I would do that, and just because of two miserly broken eggs?"

Mae hung her head. "I'm sorry for breaking the eggs," she said in a small voice.

"Be more careful next time. Do you hear me?"

"Yes, Mrs. Brown."

"Now go over to the sink and wash your face thoroughly. You've spread liquorice all over your face, and if your aunt sees you looking like that, she'll think you stole Bella and Ida's candy. Or did you take what doesn't belong to you?" The woman's gaze was stern. "I've told you time and again that I don't like little girls who steal other people's properties."

"I didn't steal it." Mae tone was full of indignation, causing Mrs. Brown to hide a smile. "My new friend gave it to me."

"And who is this new friend that gave you liquorice?"

"His name is Herbert, and he told me not to call him Mister. His father died, and I saw him crying, so I went to tell him that I was sorry about that, and he gave me the candy."

Mrs. Brown's eyes nearly popped out of their sockets. "You went over to Mrs. Patterson's house?" Mae nodded innocently. "Child, you're going to get yourself into a lot of trouble. That woman doesn't like people going to her house, least of all those who look like little scallywags, such as you do. If she finds you near her manor and comes to complain to your aunt and uncle about you, I shudder to think how much trouble you'll be in."

"But I didn't go to the house. I was in the garden with Herbert. The roses there smell so nice, and they're so pretty. Next time I'll ask Herbert to give me one red and one white rose."

"Listen to me, little girl," Mrs. Brown bent until her face was close to Mae's. "If you know what's good for you, then you'll stay on our side of the hedge. Don't ever let me catch you going over to Mrs. Patterson's home. Now go and wash your face."

"Yes, Ma'am," Mae whispered then quickly washed her face just in time because her aunt entered the kitchen a few minutes later. Mae was cleaning the sink, and the woman cast a suspicious glance at her.

"Mae I've been calling for you for the last hour, where were you?"

"Pardon me, Mrs. Lester." Mrs. Brown moved so she was standing between Mae and her employer. "It's all my fault because I sent Mae to clean the chicken coop and collect eggs because I want to bake a cake for Bella."

Mae's heart was pounding because she knew that her aunt always looked for any reason to strike her.

"Bella needs you to clean her room," the woman said at last. "And be fast about it because she needs to lie down and take her afternoon nap. If you'd done this earlier then I wouldn't have had to come looking for you."

"Mrs. Lester, Mae already cleaned the rooms upstairs and downstairs." Mrs. Brown came to her defence.

"I want her to do it again." The woman's voice was forceful. "Everything in Bella's room is dusty, and you have to clean the floor again."

"Yes, Ma'am, I'll go and do it right away." Mae walked to the closet under the stairs and pulled out a pail and broom as well as the cleaning rag. After filling the pail with water from a large barrel outside the kitchen, she picked up the other cleaning materials and trudged up the stairs to the first floor. When she got to Bella's door, she carefully knocked.

"Who is it?" She heard Cousin Bella calling out.

"It's Mae, and I'm here to clean your room again." The door was flung wide open, and Mae kept her face down. Her two cousins were both in the room and she stood at the door, waiting to be bid to enter.

"Does her Majesty Mae, Queen of the Kitchen, want me to curtsey before she enters my bedchamber?" Bella mocked.

"I'm sorry," Mae said, for that's what she'd learnt over the years. Each time her cousins made scathing remarks or hurled insults, she had to apologize to them. She cautiously stepped into the room and placed her supplies on the floor. The room was clean because she'd dusted and mopped it that morning, but she never dared to disobey any orders given by her aunt. Whatever she was ordered to do, no matter how unreasonable, Mae went ahead and did it.

As she cleaned, she heard her cousins giggling behind her back, but she chose to ignore them. All she had to do was finish cleaning the room and leave. Then she heard a splash behind and quickly turned even as Ida opened her mouth and screamed.

"Ma, come and see," the girl was shouting as Mae stared in horror at the sight before her eyes. Ida's pretty fur scarf was in the soiled water in the pail. "Ma, Mae has ruined the scarf that Pa bought for me."

Mrs. Lester was at the door in seconds. "What's all the shouting all about, Ida? Why are you making such a racket?"

"Ma," Ida was sobbing, "Mae snatched my scarf from Bella's bed and threw it into the dirty pail."

"I did no such thing!" Mae was shocked at the malice in both of her cousins' eyes.

"But you did it, and I saw you with my own eyes," Bella said forcefully. She turned to her mother. "Mama, I told you and Papa long time ago when you brought this vagabond to our house that she would be nothing but trouble, but you refused to send her away. She's always spoiling our things, but you still let her stay. Why do you keep her in this house?" And saying this, Bella walked over to the pail and pulled out the scarf, which was dripping with water. "See what she did, Ma."

Mrs. Lester frowned as she grabbed the dripping scarf from her daughter's hand and slapped Mae across the face with it. "You wanted my child's scarf so you ruined it, and it can no longer be used. There, you can have it."

Mae burst into tears at the unfair treatment, but her aunt wasn't done with her. "See that you clean this room and then get out and never set foot here again. Do you hear me?"

"Yes, Ma'am." Mae sobbed as she cleaned the water that had splashed all over the walls and floor. Then her aunt pushed her out of the room and tossed the cleaning items after her and slammed the door.

Mrs. Brown took one look at Mae when she entered the kitchen, the dripping scarf still around her neck and the woman's lips tightened. Would there be no end to this child's mistreatment in this house?

When she'd first come to work for Mr. and Mrs. Lester years ago, she'd thought that they were genteel people. But in the past few years, specifically ever since Mae came to live with them, she had seen the ugly side of them and always wondered how seemingly genteel folk could be so cruel.

THE JUDAS SMILE

"Have you heard?" Bella rushed into the kitchen where Mae was helping Mrs. Brown to prepare lunch.

"Careful there," Mrs. Brown scolded when Ida also rushed into the kitchen, and the two girls bumped into the table, rattling the plates. "What has your feathers all puckered up?" The woman asked.

"Herbert is back from school," Bella announced excitedly. "And Pa has invited him and his mother to our house for lunch on Christmas Day." Her eyes were dancing with merriment.

Mae bowed her head and pretended to be busy polishing the cutlery, though she was aware of Mrs. Brown's furtive glance.

"He's grown so tall and handsome now." Ida's eyes were dreamy.

"Don't you go making cows' eyes at him," Bella lashed out angrily at her sister. "It's a known fact that Herbert is mine. I was promised to him years ago, and he's just been waiting for to come of age, and then he'll propose, and we'll get engaged," Mae heard her sixteen-year-old cousin saying. "Oh, I can't wait to be Mrs. Bella Patterson, Mistress of Patterson Manor and Estate," she giggled. "I'll have many servants waiting on me, and then I'll be able to buy all the frocks and jewellery that my heart desires." She ignored her sister, who was giving her a sullen look, and danced around the kitchen. "Every December, I'll make sure we hold a Christmas Ball such has never been seen in this county. And my wedding dress..." Bella clapped her hands. "Mama told me that Mrs. Patterson promised that a couture designer would be brought in from Paris to make a special gown for me. Ida, you'll be my best maid, and just think, one of Herbert's handsome friends will fall in love with you." Her words cheered her sister up. "Ours will be the wedding of the year."

Mrs. Brown rolled her eyes and snorted softly, so it was only Mae who heard her.

"Come, Ida, let's go and find Ma so we can tell her that we need new frocks for Christmas Day's luncheon. After all, I can't appear before my betrothed in the rags of yester year."

Once again, with a flurry, the girls were gone.

"In my day I've seen a few retards, but your cousin Bella takes the cake," Mrs. Brown said as laughter bubbled from her lips. "That girl is delusional if she thinks Master Herbert will ever spare her a single glance. That young man is of a very serious nature and deserves a mature young woman who has her head on straight, not some hoity toity miss with stars in her eyes and emptiness in the place where the good Lord intended for her to have a brain."

"Cousin Bella is very beautiful," Mae said. "I'm sure Master Herbert will soon fall in love with her. And she comes from a good family too."

Once again, Mrs. Brown snorted derisively. "Beauty that is only skin deep is no beauty at all, but just an illusion. Master Herbert has his head on straight, and I doubt that your empty-headed cousin will ever win his heart." Her eyes grew serious as they focused on Mae. "Now if the young gentleman were to set his cap at you…"

"Please don't ever say that," Mae interrupted her and cast a fearful look towards the door through which her cousins had recently exited the kitchen. "You never know who might be listening, and then there'll be trouble for both of us for sure. Besides, I'm turning fourteen on Christmas Day, and such thoughts shouldn't even be in my head."

"In my day, we got betrothed at the age of twelve, were engaged by the time we were fourteen, and married at sixteen. I know what I'm saying." But when they heard footsteps coming down the corridor, they both shut up and bent down to continue with their chores. A few seconds later, Mrs. Lester entered into the kitchen.

"You're here twiddling your lazy thumbs, and the table hasn't been set yet," she snarled at Mae.

"I was just finishing polishing the silver, Ma'am."

"Don't speak back at me, you insolent and deranged child, or I'll box your ears until they're black and blue."

"I'm sorry," Mae mumbled, picking up the silver tray and hurrying out of the kitchen before her aunt could make good on her threat.

As usual, she had her lunch in the kitchen with Mrs. Brown and the other two maids. When she'd done the dishes and cleaned the kitchen, Mrs. Brown told her to go to her room and rest.

But Mae had other plans. If Herbert was home from Eton, then there wasn't a moment to spare. She knew that he would be in the rose garden, and she couldn't wait to see him and tell him all about her life while he'd been gone. After his father's burial two years ago, he'd been very reserved, and Mae hadn't seen him again until the day he was leaving for Eton. On the pretext of coming to look for her cousin, he'd told Mae that he was going back to school and that she shouldn't forget him. Then last year he hadn't come for holidays, and Bella had announced that he was doing his final exams at school. Mae had hoped that after he was done with his schooling, he would come and settle down in Patterson Village. But the year had gone by without her seeing her dear friend, whom she never forgot.

Now he was back, and she'd missed her friend very much. Mae had grown taller in the two years that Herbert had been away. She felt that she was lanky and not at all graceful like Bella and Ida were. Often she found herself envying her cousins, because they always got new clothes, hats, and shoes, while she received their old and discarded ones. It was her aunt's nature to find the most frayed garments, which she would then hand over to Mae.

While some of the clothes could be patched up and made to look presentable, most were usually beyond repair. These she ripped up and made small hankies or used as patches for other dresses. She never complained, even though she sometimes wished that her uncle would buy her a new dress.

On this day, she was wearing a green frock that had a large blue patch on the left side. It had been very new when Ida burnt it one evening. She was in the parlour with her parents and got too close to the fireplace. A spark flew from the fireplace and set the dress on fire. The damage was so extensive because the dress was made from silk material. Mae's joy was that the accident had happened in the presence of her aunt and uncle. Otherwise, she knew that her cousin would have blamed her for the misfortune since the dress had cost a pretty sum. As usual, it was tossed to her, and she'd ripped it up and sewed in the large piece from yet another old frock.

Mae waited until the house settled into silence, for she knew that her aunt and uncle, as well as her cousins, would retire to their chambers for their afternoon naps. No one would stir until around four, by which time she expected to be back. So, she had at least two hours to find Herbert.

It was very cold outside, and the overcast skies promised snow later in the evening. Pulling the thin shawl tightly around herself, Mae slipped out of the warm kitchen and immediately started shivering from the cold. She ran towards the chicken coop, for she'd discovered another concealed hole in the hedge through which she could pass and enter Herbert's garden, for that's how she referred to it.

Just as she'd expected, Herbert was in the greenhouse. He was standing with his back to her, and her heart skipped a beat when he slowly turned around after sensing her presence. He was now eighteen years old and looked very dashing. Mae felt her legs becoming weak when he gave her a dashing smile.

"I was wondering when you would appear," he said as he walked towards her. "Come, let's get out of the cold, and you can tell me all that you've been up to in the past two years since I've been away."

He held out a large hand and Mae placed hers in it, following meekly as he drew her forward. He took her into the greenhouse where it was warmer, and she breathed in the lovely scent of roses. Herbert reached out and plucked a red rose, got rid of the thorns and tucked it in her hair. "There now, you look really pretty."

"Thank you," she whispered breathlessly.

Herbert led her to a bench at one end of the greenhouse, and they both sat down. "Oh Mae, I've missed you so much. Can you believe that I've been counting days until I could be back here with you?"

Mae felt very shy in the presence of her friend and wondered what could be happening to her. Hitherto, she'd always been very chatty around him, but not today. It felt as if she was tongue-tied.

"Don't you have anything to say to me?" Herbert asked while still holding onto her hand. He intertwined his fingers with hers and gently squeezed them. "I hope you're not feeling ill."

"No," the word came out all breathless. "Welcome home, Herbert."

"Did you miss me?"

She nodded. "Very much," Herbert was pleased at her honest and truthful answer. If there was something that irritated him, it was pretended coyness in a woman.

Mae had no such vices, and her answers had always been honest. He just wondered if much had changed for her in the past two years. Over the months while he'd been away, he'd wished that his father was still alive, for then there would have been someone looking out for Mae. He'd worried about her, and seeing her dressed in yet another patched up dress made his lips tighten.

Mae noticed the expression on Herbert's face and thought that she had offended him. "I'm sorry," she whispered.

"Why are you apologizing when you haven't done anything wrong?"

"You looked like you were angry with me."

Herbert shook his head. "I am angry but not with you, never with you Mae." He touched her cheek gently. "I have something for you," he said as he reached into the inner pocket of his trench coat and brought out a small package. "This is for you. Happy birthday in advance, and may you always be joyous, Mae."

"Thank you." Mae received the gift, and tears filled her eyes.

"Open it."

Mae's fingers felt like thumbs as she fumbled with the knot on the string around her present, but at last she opened it and then gasped. It was a beautiful locket in the shape of a heart, and though there was a loop where a chain should be, there was none. Even though she didn't know much about jewellery and its pricing, she could guess that this particular item had cost a pretty penny.

"I can't accept this." She looked at Herbert with stricken eyes. "If my aunt or uncle or my cousins see this locket, they will say that I've stolen it." She held the gift out to Herbert, but he shook his head, refusing to reach for it.

"That's the reason I chose this particular obscure gift for you, Mae. It comes with a chain, but I removed that piece so you can get an old piece of string and tie it around your neck. That will keep it hidden under your clothes from prying eyes. I doubt that anyone will want to bother about a piece of string tied around your neck. Besides, I've noticed that you already have a string," he pointed at her dainty neck. "What do you have hanging on that piece of string anyway?" He asked, quite puzzled.

Mae's hand went to the said string and gently tagged at it. "It's an old pearl button," she said. "It belonged to my Mama. Uncle John once saw it and mocked me, saying that I was living in the distant past because this button came from Mama's wedding dress that got lost years ago, before I was born."

"Then how did you get this button?" Herbert reached out a hand and touched the small pearl button. It was old but still shiny.

Mae shrugged. "As far as I can recall, I've always had a string and this pearl on it around my neck. I had it after my parents were killed, and so it means that maybe Ma was the one who gave it to me. When the string gets old and breaks, I replace it with another."

"You see," Herbert beamed. "Now you can carry this pendant with you. Place it next to the button, or better still, place the button inside the empty space and carry me with you in your heart, or rather close to your heart."

Mae smiled and opened the locket. She found a small piece of folded paper inside the locket and looked at Herbert curiously. "What is this?"

"Unfold the paper and see." She noticed that he'd stopped smiling.

She unfolded the paper, and there were the writings '*M and H together forever*' inscribed on it. "What does M and H mean?"

"Can't you guess?" His gaze was unnerving, and then something suddenly clicked in her brain.

"Oh!" She blushed.

"Yes, that's what it means. Now even when I'm not here with you, you can touch the locket and feel my presence going with you everywhere."

"Thank you." Mae pulled the string over her head, untied the knot, and removed the small pearl, then slid it into the locket with the piece of paper.

"The locket has its own gold chain," Herbert said and undid the top button of his shirt. "Here it is." He passed a finger round the chain. "I'll wear it always and keep it safely for you until I can reunite the two and place them both around your neck. I didn't want you to get into trouble with your people, but I had to give you a present that would make you think about me always. Happy birthday in advance and Merry Christmas too."

"I'm so happy." Mae slipped the string over her head and hid it under her clothes.

"Now you can carry me close to your heart always."

"I promise that I'll take very good care of this lovely gift."

Herbert glanced at the young girl as she played with her fingers. He sighed inwardly, knowing that she was still too young to understand the implications of his words. In a few years, she would be a beauty, though one couldn't tell by looking at her right now. She was passing through her teenage years with a spotted face. Unlike her cousin Bella, who was a raving beauty, Mae looked quite ordinary, and to the normal eye, not even warranting a second glance. Yet Herbert felt very protective of her, and he knew that the feelings he carried in his heart for her would only frighten her should he reveal them. It was too early, and she was still very young. There would be enough time later for all that, but for now he would be her friend and confidante, because he knew that she needed one.

"I have to return to the house before anyone wakes up from their nap and finds me missing." Mae rose to her feet. "Cousin Bella said that you would be coming to their house on Christmas Day." Even though Mae had lived with her uncle for the past seven years, not once had she ever referred to his house as her home. She felt like a stranger there.

Herbert nodded. "Mama told me that your aunt and uncle had sent us an invitation to lunch on Christmas Day, so yes." He touched her cheek. "My dearest friend Mae, I'll be there on that day to celebrate your birthday."

Mae grimaced wryly. "No one ever celebrates my birthday because they don't remember."

Herbert wanted to tell his young friend that he was sure everyone in the household knew that her birthday was on Christmas Day, but they chose to ignore the fact.

"Well, don't you worry about a thing, because even if everyone else in the world forgets, God and I will always remember your birthday. I'm sorry that I wasn't here last year to celebrate your birthday with you. And since we weren't invited to your uncle's house, I couldn't come and give you the felicitations of the day." Then he remembered something and reached into his pocket once again. "I almost forgot, some candy for you." He gave her a small bag. Even without opening it, she knew that it was stuffed with liquorice.

"Oh!" Mae's eyes glowed as she received her second present that day. "I'll have to hide my candy from my cousins." As she fumbled with her pockets, she blushed when she noticed that Herbert was looking at her with raised eyebrows. "If Bella and Ida see my treats, they'll take them away. Thank you." She reached forward and gave him a quick kiss on the cheek. Before he could say anything, she had slipped away. She remembered to get rid of the rose that Herbert had placed in her hair because she didn't want too many questions asked about it. With a sigh of regret, she tossed it into the shrubs before dashing back to her uncle's house.

Christmas Day was very busy, and Mae was exhausted when lunch time came around. She hadn't been allowed to go to church with the family that morning because she was kept busy preparing for the luncheon.

Apart from Herbert and his mother, two other families had been invited. From Ida and Bella's excited chattering, Mae knew that the young sons of both families would be present.

Mae had no new dress, but at least her aunt had given her one of Bella's better-looking frocks this year. Even though it was old, it was more presentable than any of the others she owned. In any case, she was to wear a white apron over the dress because she would be serving the guests when they arrived. No mingling with the guests, she'd been warned, not that she even wanted to.

Herbert found the occasion quite tedious because of his pretentious hosts. Even though Lester House had a large living room, the place was crowded, and he was bored. He wished Mae was present, as he always found conversations with her very enjoyable because there was no pretentiousness or guile in her. While she clearly wasn't educated, for he doubted that her relatives were inclined in any way to help her acquire knowledge, she was naturally very intelligent.

There was buzzing all around him, and he wished this would all end so he could go back to his father's garden. Since his death and Herbert's absence, the greenhouse had been neglected because his mother didn't think it was a worthy cause. But one of the servants had been doing his best, though secretly, lest he incur the wrath of the Lady of the Manor.

Bella was talking loudly, no doubt to attract the attention of those present, yet her conversation was all about the things she wanted to buy come the new year. Herbert wanted to roll his eyes in boredom. As he stood apart from everyone else, his lips tightened again, for Mr. Smyth was present at this dinner. He'd expected that his mother would marry the man in the two years since his father's death, but so far not a whisper of such plans had reached his ears.

Herbert also noticed two other young men, general acquaintances of his, who seemed to be hanging onto Bella's every word. They reminded him of little puppies gazing adoringly at a sumptuous plate of delicacies, and he hid a smile while pretending to cough. All eyes turned to him.

"I'm sorry," he said, "I got something stuck in my throat."

"Mae," her aunt called out sharply. "Our guests need more drinks."

"Yes, Ma'am," Mae's voice was soft, and Herbert watched as she walked towards him carrying a tray. She offered him a glass of water, which he took, and murmured his thanks. Mae nodded slightly but kept her head down.

"Bring me some water too." Ida's voice was a snap of complaint. "I'm thirsty, and there you are wasting time doing nothing. You look like an old woman who can't even walk. Come on and bring me that glass of water and stop shuffling your feet." There were a few snickers and Herbert frowned. He couldn't believe that these people were enjoying Mae's discomfiture.

Herbert saw the colour creeping into Mae's face as embarrassment overcame her.

"I – I'm very sorry," she mumbled as she moved towards her cousin. The tray was crowded with brimming glasses, and he noticed it wobbling in her hands.

As Mae approached her cousin, Herbert stared in horror and anger as one of the young men quickly shot out a leg, tripping her. Instinctively Herbert rushed forward to help but it was too late. The glass of lemonade nearest the edge of the tray pitched forward and emptied its contents all over Ida's dress.

There was a resounding smack. "You imbecile," Ida's shrill voice cried out. "You've ruined my new dress."

A look of terror spread all over Mae's face. Herbert was close enough to grab the unbalanced tray before more damage could be done to anyone else.

"It was an accident," he told Ida, as he placed the tray on a small stool. He turned around to find Mae holding a hand to her smitten cheek.

"I'm sorry," she said tearfully, looking at her aunt, her eyes begging the older woman to understand.

"Get out," Ida screamed. "You've ruined my dress because you're jealous that you don't have anything. I could just slap you so hard," and she raised her hand to do this, but Herbert was faster, and he gripped her raised hand.

"You need to calm down because this was just an accident."

Herbert waited to see if anyone would come to Mae's defence, for he was sure that he wasn't the only one who'd seen the young man tripping her. But all eyes, especially Bella's, glistened with malice. When she noticed him observing her, she pretended to look concerned, but he'd already seen what was hidden in her dark heart.

"Miss Ida," he turned to the still fuming woman, "If you can dab a wet cloth on your beautiful gown, it will dry out and leave no stains. But you have to do it immediately."

"This imbecile thinks that she can ruin my dress so that I'll give it to her," she hissed. "I'd rather burn it to ashes than see someone so shapeless wearing it."

Mae was immediately banished to the kitchen by her aunt, and Herbert watched with fury in his heart as she walked away looking like a broken reed. He waited until she was gone and had shut the door, then he drew closer to the young man who had tripped her.

"I saw what you did," he said in a voice that was only audible to the offender. "And just know that one day when you least expect it, I'll get vengeance for that poor girl you just humiliated. Don't let your current high station in life make you to despise those you consider to be beneath you. The Lord will fight their battles and one day you'll face worse humiliation."

"But…" The young man paled. But Herbert was done with him and moved away. The whole day was ruined for him, and he wished he could just walk out and go home.

He didn't see Mae for the rest of the afternoon, and as soon as it was socially acceptable, he excused himself and went home, leaving his mother staring after him. Once he got there, for he used the shorter route, which meant passing through the Lesters' backyard, he used the small gate that separated the two estates. He didn't want to talk to anyone so made his way to the greenhouse.

To his surprise, he found Mae seated in the arbour. She was weeping softly into her apron.

"Oh, Mae." He sat down beside her. "Don't take your cousin's ugly words to heart."

"It was an accident," she sniffed, wiping her nose on the sleeve of her shapeless frock. "I never meant to ruin Cousin Ida's beautiful dress."

"I know that because I saw that Percival fellow tripping you."

"She was so angry, and I'm afraid that my aunt will flog me because of this."

"No one will flog you."

Mae shook her head and continued weeping. Herbert didn't know what went on in her uncle's house, and his coming to her defence had only made matters worse.

Then she thought she saw something in the bushes and was startled. "What's wrong, Mae?"

"I think there's someone in the bushes."

"Really?" Herbert rose to his feet and walked around, then returned and sat down once again beside her. "It might have been a little rat, nothing else."

"Very well then," Mae said, but she felt uneasy. "I have to go back to the house now."

"I'll find a way to see you again before I leave."

"What was all that about?" Herbert turned when he heard his mother's harsh voice. He was standing in front of the window in the living room, gazing outside. There was snow everywhere, and he found himself wishing that his father was still here. "Herbert, I asked you a question."

"Mother, if I could understand what it is you're asking me then I would give you the answer you want to hear."

"Why did you humiliate Miss Ida like that?"

Herbert's eyebrows shot up. "Now you're saying that I humiliated Miss Lester."

"Yes, that stupid girl poured lemonade all over her pretty dress, and you stood there defending her. What kind of a man are you becoming?"

"One who defends the helpless," Herbert answered.

"I won't have you embarrassing my friends or their children. You should have been paying more attention to Miss Bella, but instead there you were, minding the business of a servant."

"For your information, Mother, Mae isn't a servant in that house. She's Mr. Lester's niece but is treated like a slave."

"There you go again, defending someone so worthless."

Herbert's hands clenched into fists, but then he told himself not to get angry. His mother was clearly goading him, but he wasn't going to take the bait.

"Anyway, that aside." She sat on one of the large couches. "I wanted to talk about your joining the university. Cambridge or Oxford are good choices for you. Mr. Smyth says …"

"Stop right there, Mother." His eyes flashed at her. "Since when did you take it upon yourself to start discussing my affairs with strangers?"

"Mr. Smyth isn't a stranger to this family. He's your grandfather's friend and has always been here whenever we needed him."

Herbert threw his head back and laughed. "Oh he's been around alright, but because you were the one who needed him. Pa never wanted him here, and neither did I."

He saw his mother shifting uncomfortably on the couch. There were footfalls, and Mr. Smyth appeared in the doorway. "With all due respect to you, Mr. Smyth, this is a personal family matter, so would you excuse us," he told the older man and saw his face flushing.

"Herbert, that is rude."

"Mother, Mr. Smyth isn't a member of this family, so I don't see why he's even here."

"I'll go," the man mumbled and shuffled out of the living room.

"That was totally uncalled for."

Herbert narrowed his eyes at his mother. "There's one thing I'd like you to remember, Mother. I'm not my father so you won't handle me in the same way that you did Pa. I'll fight you every step of the way should I feel that you're trying to infringe on my personal desires."

"What's gotten into you? Are you getting too big for your breeches now?"

Herbert shrugged. "I'm only letting you know that I won't allow you to push me around like you did to my father. He wasn't a weak man like you always said, but he was meek. Pa could have walked out on you years ago, but he stayed because of me. It takes a strong man to set his own plans and pride aside and put up with all manner of humiliation."

"How dare you speak to me like that?"

"I dare because you've made me lose respect for you." He saw her pale, and his heart was struck but the anger within him wouldn't rest. "You think I didn't know about you and Mr. Smyth?" She gasped, and he gave her a cold smile. "I was only five and begged Pa to prepare a bouquet for your birthday. You were in the study when I brought the flowers, and I saw you and Mr. Smyth together, and both of you were half naked." His mother gave a soft moan. "I carried that secret with me for years because I didn't want to hurt my father. My joy is knowing that he went to his grave without ever finding out the despicable things you were doing right under his nose."

"Herbert…" she held out a hand, which he ignored.

"I won't be going to university, and certainly not one that Mr. Smyth had approved of."

"You don't have to cut your nose off to spite your face."

"That's not what I'm doing, because I've decided to find my own path in life without your help. For my father's sake, I will continue to show you respect as my mother, but please don't push me anymore. Let it never be said of my father's son that he is weak." With those words, he walked out and left his mother, who looked shrivelled against the thick cushions.

SOMETHING AMISS

The moment Mae left Herbert and returned to the house, she knew something was wrong. And it wasn't because of whatever had happened earlier with Ida's dress. No, this was something else. For one, it wasn't her aunt who was waiting in the kitchen, as she'd expected. It was Uncle John, and he looked enraged.

"Where have you been?" He asked in a cold voice.

"Out in the garden," she stammered, wondering what her uncle was doing in the kitchen. Mrs. Brown and the other two maids had left immediately after Christmas Day lunch had been served so they could celebrate the rest of the day with their families. Mae looked at the pile of plates and pots that were waiting for her to wash. This was her duty, and she wouldn't be allowed to go to bed until the kitchen was once again spic and span.

Uncle John never set foot in the kitchen, at least not since Mae had come to live with them, which was why she knew that things were really bad.

"What were you doing in the garden, and who were you with?"

Mae noticed Bella standing behind her father, and the look on her face made her heart sink. Out there in the arbour, she'd been sure that she'd seen something, or someone, lurking in the bushes, and she had mentioned the fact to Herbert. To put her mind at rest. he'd gone to check and when he found no one, dismissed her fears with a laugh. The feeling of uneasiness hadn't left her, and she now knew why. It had been Bella out there in the bushes, spying on them.

"I won't have you shaming this family with your careless ways. Do you hear me?"

"But..."

"Have I given you permission to answer me back?" He growled, and she moved behind the kitchen counter, out of his reach. Her uncle had never once struck her because he left all forms of punishment meted out to her to his wife. But right now, he looked angry enough to hit her, and she became very frightened. There was no one to save her should he choose to lash out.

"Bella told me that you were shamelessly throwing yourself at Master Herbert, her betrothed. Is there no end to your shamelessness, you insolent girl? Wasn't it enough that you humiliated my daughter in front of all our guests, now here you are making a nuisance of yourself over a man who has no interest in you? I rue the day I made a promise to your mother that I would take care of you in the event of her death." He looked very forbidding, and Mae was terrified. "I'm a good and religious man, or else I would toss you out on your ear this very moment. Were you even sixteen now I would have marched you out of this house right this instant. But I know just what to do to a vagabond I like you."

Herbert was troubled because the holidays were over, and he hadn't seen Mae since Christmas Day. Every day he went out to the greenhouse hoping to find her there, but she never came. He hoped she was alright, and many times he wanted to go to her uncle's house and ask about her, but the thought of running into Bella made him stay away. For the remainder of his holiday, he spent his time in the greenhouse pruning and taking care of his father's roses.

Like his father had done for years, Herbert also made sure that he plucked fresh roses every few days and filled the house with them. He and his mother weren't speaking, but at least Mr. Smyth was gone from the house. They shared mealtimes and exchanged a few words here and there, but that was the sum of their interaction. He missed his father greatly, and tending to his plants gave him some comfort.

What his mother didn't know was that he'd already enlisted himself in the army and would be leaving to join his fellow cadets at the Royal Military Academy at Woolwich, where he hoped to become a royal engineer. Peter and Simeon had also enlisted, and they were to serve in the same regiment. He knew that if his mother ever got wind of his joining the army, she would do everything within her power to ensure that his appointment was rescinded.

It was with a heavy heart that he left home, not sure if he would ever return alive because service in the army was filled with uncertainties. He prayed that Mae would be alright, and if God willed it, he would return and take her way from this wretched life.

Mae found out the hard way the kind of punishment her uncle had planned for her. After marching her up to the attic, he locked her inside with a dire warning. "This is where you'll remain until sense enters that demented mind of yours."

For the next five days, she wasn't let out of the room nor were any meals, not even water, brought to her. By the fifth day, her room stank because the chamber pot was full, and she could barely stand because she was weak with hunger and thirst. She wished for death each evening, and when morning came, she wept bitterly because she was still alive.

"Why won't You just end my life and let me have peace," the young girl wept. "This pain is too much for me to bear."

Meanwhile, downstairs, Mrs. Brown had returned from the brief holiday with her family. It was New Year's Eve, and the house was quiet because, unlike the previous years, there was no celebration being held this year because the family had been invited over by friends of theirs.

At first when the woman didn't see Mae for a day or two, she thought nothing about it. But then she became troubled when the third day came and there was still no sign of Mae. No one was mentioning Mae's name, not even the two loud mouthed servants who were terrible gossips, and that made her very suspicious and afraid. Something must have happened to Mae while she was gone, and she felt guilty that she'd left her behind and very vulnerable.

"You look troubled," Sandy, the new scullery maid, commented. She'd joined the household on the twenty sixth of December and was still learning her way around the kitchen. "Is there any problem, Mrs. Brown?"

Mrs. Brown nodded. "Yes, I'm troubled and puzzled at the same time. There used to be a young girl, about fourteen years old, who lived in this house. I left her here on Christmas Day when I took leave to be with my family. At the time, no one told me that she would be leaving this household." She looked at Sandy keenly. "When you got here, did you see such a girl? Or has anyone mentioned what might have happened to her?" Sandy shook her head. "Her name is Mae Chester." Sandy shook her head again.

"Mrs. Brown, perhaps Mae went to spend Christmas and the holidays with her family. When I got here on the twenty sixth, I didn't find her here, or any of the family members. The only people here were Molly and Carol. The other maid left early on the twenty sixth, and that's the reason I was given this position so quickly."

Mrs. Brown made an impatient sound. "Mae has no family. The poor girl is an orphan, and Mr. Lester is supposedly her uncle, but I've never seen one treating his niece so badly. I don't think she left this house, and my fear is that something bad must have happened to her. Where are Carol and Molly? Weren't they here when I arrived?"

Sandy shrugged. "They mentioned that they had only returned to pick up their properties and leave again, for they don't want to work here anymore. They were already on their way out when you arrived."

"Is that right?" Mrs. Brown wasn't sorry to see the two gossips leave. She didn't like the two maids because they spied for the mistress of the house, and often against Mae. "Good riddance," she muttered. But she was still troubled about Mae's absence.

"Well, I best be getting upstairs to dust the rooms before Mrs. Lester comes back home and finds that nothing has been done. I just wish the woman wouldn't shout too much when giving people instructions," Sandy mumbled, and Mrs. Brown frowned at her.

"Be careful of your words in this house, Sandy. Walls have ears, and you could get into a lot of trouble."

Sandy walked up the stairs and was humming to herself as she cleaned Bella's bedchamber and tidied it. She was disgusted at the state she found the room in, and as Sandy cleaned everything and collected the dirty laundry for washing, she wondered why a well-groomed and smart young woman like Miss Bella would let her room look like a pig style. Didn't her mama teach her that a nice young lady, who was hoping to one day get married, had to learn how to keep her house well? Then Sandy shrugged. She would probably get married to a wealthy man like her father and employ many servants to do all the work for her. As soon as she was done, she moved to Miss Ida's room, which was even worse. What was wrong with these genteel women, she wondered.

It was while Sandy was cleaning Ida's room that she thought she heard a sound, so she stopped moving around the room and listened. She heard it again, and it sounded like a low moan. Her heart began to beat very fast, and she looked around her in fright. Was this house haunted? In as far as she knew, she and Mrs. Brown were the only ones in the house. Molly and Carol were long gone by now, and she doubted that any of them could have returned.

Mr. Lester and his family, who had left on the twenty sixth, after her arrival, would be spending the next few days in the home of their family friends some five miles away. There was a celebration to usher in the New Year, and it had been rumoured that a representative of His Royal Highness Prince Albert Edward, Queen Victoria's heir, would be in attendance. Sandy had heard all this from Miss Bella as she packed suitable attire for the young mistress. It surprised Sandy that for a weekend getaway the girls needed over ten outfits. Well, she was only a servant, and she did as bid. She groaned when she thought about all the laundry that she would have to do when her masters returned.

The moan came again, and Sandy dropped the damp cleaning cloth and fled from the room. She burst into the kitchen, panting hard and startling Mrs. Brown.

"Why do you look like the hounds from hell are pursuing you?" Mrs. Brown placed a hand over her heart. "Child, you startled me, and my heart nearly stopped beating. Don't ever do that again if you know what's good for you, or I'll take this ladle to your knuckles," and she waved the item in her other hand.

"Mrs. Brown, this house is haunted." Sandy was shaking. "There's a phantom in the house."

Mrs. Brown gave the girl an exasperated look. "What's wrong with your head? Have you suddenly run mad? I've lived in this house for nearly twenty years and never have I even heard of such a preposterous tale. You're just a lazy girl who doesn't want to work, so you're coming up with all manner of excuses to stay down here in the kitchen. You just wait until Mrs. Lester gets here and finds that you haven't cleaned the rooms as she asked. You'll get a good beating."

"But I'm not lying," Sandy cried. "I was cleaning Miss Ida's chamber when I heard a sound coming from the room above me. I think it's the attic. It frightened ten years off my life, I tell you, Mrs. Brown."

Mrs. Brown frowned slightly; the girl looked too shaken to be telling empty tales.

"Show me," she demanded, and Sandy led the way to Ida's room. The two of them stood for a while but there was no sound, and Mrs. Brown turned to Sandy. "Next time you hear the wind in the willows, just shut the windows and carry on with your chores. It's a good thing the family isn't at home, so I don't have to prepare anything elaborate for dinner. But you've wasted my time, and next time you try to trick me like this I'll be the one to box your ears. You've done nothing but waste my time." The angry woman turned to leave.

"Listen," Sandy whispered, clutching at Mrs. Brown's arm. The older woman stopped and cocked her ears, then she too heard the low moan and looked up at the ceiling.

"There's something in the attic," she said. "Let's go and get to the bottom of all this mystery. I'll soon show you that there's no phantom in this house. It may be a stray cat or something," she told the frightened girl.

Sandy shook her head and moved away from Mrs. Brown. "You go and check, and I'll wait for you down here where it's safe."

Mrs. Brown chuckled as she shook her head. "If there's something in the attic and it eats me up, don't you think you'll be next?"

"No!" Sandy looked around her wildly, as if seeking a way of escape.

Mrs. Brown made a clicking sound with her tongue, walked out of the chamber, and took the narrow stairs that led to the attic. She found the door bolted from the outside and drew it back. The foul stench that hit her nostrils made her gag. The attic was dark even though it was just early afternoon. The small window didn't bring in much light, and all she saw were the outlines of old furniture that had been stored in the attic for years.

"Sandy," she shouted.

"Yes, Mrs. Brown?"

"Quick, get me a candle, and hurry."

"What is it?"

"Stop asking questions and just do as I say. Be quick about it." Mrs. Brown had to stand back on the stairs, for the stench was too much. Sandy soon brought a candle, and the sight that met their eyes caused them to look at each other in horror. The sight of the still form on the floor shocked the two women.

"Oh, my goodness!" the buxom woman exclaimed as she pushed her bulky frame into the small space.

"Who is this?"

"Sandy, go downstairs and immediately bring me some milk. Also bring a pail of warm water and some lye soap. This is such a disgrace that I think I might be sick."

Mae heard the voices as if coming from a distance. Then gentle hands raised her, and a cup was pressed to her lips.

"Drink," she was told in a firm voice. She obediently opened her mouth and felt the warm milk on her tongue. She began to gulp greedily. "No, drink slowly or the milk will choke you." Her lips kept moving as she silently begged for more milk. "I'll have to give it to you in small sips so that you won't throw up."

Once her stomach was full, Mae fell into a deep sleep, unaware that Mrs. Brown and Sandy continued to watch over her. The older woman had washed her while Sandy took the chamber pot outside and emptied it. They then swept the whole attic and brought an old mattress from one of the servants' rooms downstairs and laid her on it.

Mae slept on even when her two rescuers left her in the attic and once again locked her inside. But Mrs. Brown's conscience refused to let her rest.

"We can't just leave Mae up there like a prisoner," she told Sandy.

"What would you have us do, Mrs. Brown?"

"I think we need to bring her downstairs so we can take good care of her. If you never met her before today, it means that she's been locked up in that room for the past five days, since Christmas Day. That was the last time I saw her when we were preparing lunch together."

"Carol and Molly didn't mention her when the three of us were left here as the family went visiting."

"This is a disgrace, and we need to bring Mae downstairs."

"Won't we get into trouble? Someone locked her up in the attic for a reason." Sandy put a hand to her heart, "Or maybe she ran mad, and Mrs. Lester locked her up there so she wouldn't hurt herself or anyone else."

Mrs. Brown gave Sandy such a look that she felt ashamed. "You're the mad person," she hissed. "Now let's go and bring Mae down here at once, and don't give me any of your silly excuses. Once we do that, you can go back to cleaning the rest of the house before Mrs. Lester and the family return."

DOWN THE MEAN STREETS

H erbert sat at the edge of his seat in the train carriage. He wished it would go faster and get him quickly to his destination.

Ravenscroft, Pembroke in Wales is where he was headed, and he wondered what Mae would think of his new captain's uniform. He was one of the youngest captains in the British Army at the age of twenty-one. While many thought he'd earned his promotion because of his family's money, he and his men knew otherwise.

When he'd joined the army right out of Eton two years ago, he'd been eager to go overseas and fight alongside his peers. The Berlin Conference had come up with ways that the European powers were to divide Africa amongst themselves, and Britain also had to look out for her interests abroad. So, after six months of intense training Herbert's unit was dispatched to Africa.

As soon as they got to Egypt, which was his first posting overseas, his whole unit of twenty-four men came down with severe malaria. He was the only one who didn't fall ill, and so he had to take care of his men. They were stationed at Asyut, close to the River Nile, a dangerous area indeed. The place was swampy, and apart from the dangers of marauding crocodiles that smelled blood, they also had to contend with swarms of mosquitoes and tsetse flies.

With his whole unit indisposed, it had fallen on Herbert's shoulders to ensure that they were safe until help come to them. Having befriended a young Egyptian man, he sent a message to the sergeant in Cairo. When Abdul Bashir didn't return for many days, nor any help came to them, Herbert deduced that the poor fellow had been killed and so hadn't delivered the urgent message to his superiors in Cairo

In the next few days, their captain and six other soldiers succumbed to the terrible malaria, but Herbert refused to give up hope. In his time alone, as he watched over the remaining men, he remembered what his father would always tell him in the past.

"Son, just know that God is always closer than we think and nearer than we expect."

"And how can you tell, Pa?"

His father had ruffled his hair and smiled down at him. "Because God says so in His holy word. Psalm forty-six and verse one reassures us that God is our refuge and strength and a very present help in time of need."

So, morning, noon and night, the young man spoke the words of that verse over and over again as he paced along the shores, watching out for the crocodiles and snakes. He held onto the promise in the verse when things looked bleak indeed. His men were weak because of continuous purging, and he risked his life and health to ensure that he provided fresh and clean water for them to drink. One by one the men began to get better.

In all that time, it didn't occur to Herbert that they were in hostile territory, nor did it enter his mind that they might be attacked by the local tribes.

Four weeks later, as he was on the shores of the Nile fishing for tilapia to prepare for his patients, he saw a steamboat. He knew that shouting wouldn't get the attention of those on board, so he quickly lit a fire, and as the smoke rose to heaven, he sent up a prayer with it.

Within a few hours, they were rescued, and all the bodies of the dead which he'd buried in a large shallow grave to prevent wild animals from desecrating them, were carried on board the steamer in a solemn ceremony. Soon the steamer was headed back to Cairo. Herbert had lost none of his men, for even the dead were all accounted for.

It was only when they got to Cairo that Herbert learnt that Abdul Bashir had faithfully delivered the message, but the writing was all smudged due to his being rained on along the way. As soon as he'd handed the note over to the sergeant, the young man had collapsed because of malaria, which had caused him to become severely dehydrated. He became delirious and told of the unit being in trouble, but his words were all garbled up and it sounded as if he was saying they were in Asmara.

Abdul had died before he could fully recover and give the unit's exact location. The rescue ship had been dispatched and had spent many days searching for the missing men along the shores of the Nile in Asmara. They had given up hope of finding anyone alive after four weeks and had been on their way back to Cairo when they'd seen the smoke signal.

The train pulling into Ravenscroft Halt is what roused Herbert from his deep thoughts. It was a small nondescript station consisting of only one street on which were two grocery stores and a tavern.

The first store owner was an unfriendly fellow who was of no help at all to Herbert. The answers he gave were indecipherable because all he did was grunt, so Herbert had no idea if the answers to his questions were ayes or nays. So, he decided to visit the tavern since the second store was shut by the time he was done with the first man.

Since it was midday, the tavern was empty, and as soon as Herbert entered the dimly lit room and sat at a table, a tired looking woman walked towards him.

"What's yer poison?" she asked from between blackened teeth. She was chewing tobacco and spat on the side, and Herbert could barely contain his disgust at the uncouth action.

"Daisy May," the man behind the counter shouted. "You know the rules. No spitting on the floor. Take your uncouth manners outside."

The woman mumbled something, then turned back to Herbert. "Well, Soldier, what will ye have?"

"Ginger ale if you have it, and I'll also pay for some information."

Daisy May grinned and pulled out a chair and sat down at the same table. Her body odour was sickening, and it took all his strength not to retch at the stench of stale sweat, alcohol, and tobacco emitting from her.

"How much?"

Herbert reached into his pocket and pulled out his wallet. Then he extracted a pound note and placed it on the table. The woman's eyes lit up greedily and she reached for it.

"Not so fast." Herbert pulled the note out of her reach. "Information first."

"Go ahead and ask." She sat back and looked at him through weary eyes, and he felt deep compassion for her. She couldn't have been more than twenty-five years old but looked twice her age. It was clear that life had dealt her hard blows, and she'd resigned herself to whatever came her way.

"I'm looking for a certain young woman…"

The woman snorted. "All the men who come in here are looking for some young woman, but all the wenches left this miserable place to try their luck in the cities. It's just me and Gad over there who are left." She looked around the tavern. "Business is terrible and so you won't find any young girls here."

Herbert shook his head. "The woman I seek came from Sheffield about two years ago. Her name is Mae Chester, and she lived with her uncle then. His name is Mr. John Lester, and he lives in Patterson Village in Sheffield. Mae, the young woman I seek, has an aunt out here and came to live with her. Would you be knowing her?"

The woman scowled then rose to her feet. She walked to the counter and whispered something to the man behind it. They kept casting strange looks at Herbert and he was immediately alert. Then after a while both of them walked over to him. It was the man who spoke.

"I hear that you've been asking about John Lester." Like Daisy May, he, too, was chewing tobacco.

"No, I'm not asking about Mr. Lester. I came to find his niece. Her name is Mae Chester. She moved here from Sheffield to be with her relative, an aunt, but I don't know her name."

The man grunted. "There's only one relative of that Lester fellow left in Ravenscroft. He abandoned the poor woman years ago and has never been back since." The barman turned to Daisy May. "Take the counter and I'll show this soldier the way to Old Morgan's home. But no hanky panky now, do you hear me?"

"My payment?" She held out a hand to Herbert, and he placed the pound on her palm. She immediately folded and then tucked it into her bosom. "Thank you."

Herbert smiled at her. "You're a good person, Daisy May," he told her. "Thank you, and I wish for you a good life."

He followed the barman outside, and he didn't see the speculative look in Daisy May's eyes as she watched them depart.

Herbert was careful as he followed the Gad tavern man down the deserted road. This looked like a small community, though he could see buildings in the distance. As a town, it was really tiny, and he wondered if any business could thrive in this place. Even the store he'd visited had many empty shelves. He was being very cautious not to fall into a trap. The man didn't speak until they got to a cottage at the edge of the small town.

"This is where Mrs. Morgan Baller lives," he said. "She's been a widow all her life, and she's quite old, so she may not be of much help to you."

Herbert frowned slightly, surprised that the man hadn't once mentioned anything to do with Mae. Then he shrugged and parted with another pound, then watched as the man walked away. He turned to look at the cottage and approached the small gate, which squeaked as he opened it. Then he found himself in a small, unkempt garden, which further surprised him. He doubted that Mae had ever lived here because he couldn't imagine her leaving the garden to look this untidy. The cottage that stood before him was old but in decent shape, and he walked up to the front door and knocked.

"Come in." A frail voice bid him enter. He turned the knob and pushed the door open, stepping into a small parlour. It was brightly lit, and he could see a woman lying on a narrow cot by the window. She didn't raise her head, and even from this distance, he could see that she was ill. "Heather, is that you?"

"No, Ma'am," Herbert took his beret off and tucked it in his back trouser pocket. "My name is Herbert Patterson. Are you Aunt Morgan?"

The woman raised herself slowly and sat up. She observed him through jaded green eyes. "You sound like a Londoner." She coughed and beat her chest. "What brings you all this way, Soldier?"

"I came to find Mae Chester, my friend."

The woman looked at him as if he'd taken leave of his senses. "Are you sure that you've come to the right place, Son?"

"I certainly hope so. Mr. John Lester is our neighbour back in Sheffield, and Mae lived with him for years after her parents were killed. Mae and I became very good friends and I cared about her. But I had to go to military academy, and two years ago when I was on brief furlough before reporting to my duty station, I went back home to see her, but I was informed that she had returned to Ravenscroft to live with her relatives. Since I didn't have many days of leave, I wasn't able to make the journey up here then."

"Was that what Cousin John told you?"

"Yes, Ma'am."

She waved a feeble hand at him. "Sit and tell me all about Mae." Herbert spent the next hour telling the woman about Mae and her mistreatment at the hands of her uncle and his family. By the time he was done, she was weeping brokenly, and he was really concerned.

"I'm sorry. I didn't mean to distress you," he said, regretting why he'd allowed his emotions to get the better of him. But he was worried about Mae, and he couldn't help himself.

"But I thank you for telling me everything." She wiped her face with the edge of the sheet and blew her nose. "John and Ashley and I are cousins," she started. "Ash was Mae's mother, and she married Clive Chester, a local boy. The two were so much in love, but his family tormented my cousin because they couldn't have children. They blamed Ashley for their childless condition." She frowned. "Clive couldn't take it anymore when some of his relatives colluded with the woman he was working with, to frame him for putting her niece in the family way. Ash had decided to leave him, but he managed to convince her to stay, and they moved to London. After a few years, Ash wrote to tell me that they had been blessed with a beautiful baby girl.," Mrs. Baller smiled, a faraway look in her eyes. "Little Mae was born on Christmas Day, and her parents were overjoyed. She was the light of their lives because they had tried for nine years and never stopped praying." She turned her eyes to Herbert. "They gave the child the name Mae, meaning their little miracle. Ashley and Clive brought the baby here for the family to see, and the naysayers were silenced forever. Cousin John had also come to visit on account of his Mama's illness. At the time, he was a humble man who worked for one of the lords down in London as a personal aide. He was full of stories of having met a woman whose father was a local landowner in Sheffield, and they were married and had two daughters who were both older than Mae. Bella and Ida, yes, those are the names of Cousin John's daughters. Everyone was happy for Ash and John. We were such a close family at the time."

Herbert hated to see the woman looking so distraught and wished there was something he could do to comfort her. But he also needed to find out more because it might lead him to where Mae was.

Cousin Morgan raised her head and fixed her eyes on Herbert. "It was during that time that Ash made John promise that if anything ever happened to her and Clive, if Mae was still a child, that he would take her in." She shook her head. "When we got the news that Cousin Ash and her husband had died in a fire, we all believed that Little Mae had perished too, because no one spoke about her."

"Mae survived the fire," Herbert said softly.

"I know that now. Cousin John came around to bury his mother about six years ago, but he never said anything about finding Mae." She frowned again. "And now I know the reason why."

"So, when was the last time you saw Mae?"

"That one visit when Cousin Ash and her husband brought the child here was the first and last time that I set my eyes on Mae. You say that she's no longer living with Cousin John?"

"Two years ago was the last time I saw her. When I returned home and asked her cousins about her whereabouts, they informed me that Mae had returned to Ravenscroft. I was then posted abroad and couldn't come at the time. That's why I'm here today."

Cousin Morgan started crying again. "Why didn't John bring the child to me if he didn't want her? How could he be so cruel? I lost my cousin and her husband, and now little Mae is gone too," she sobbed. "This pain is too much for me."

Two weeks later, as Herbert was returning to London, he sat lost in his thoughts. Though he was sad that he hadn't found Mae, at least something good had come out of his visit. Aunt Morgan, for that's what she'd insisted on him calling her, was back on her feet again and well on her way to full recovery from the bad cough that had assailed her for a while.

He'd repaired her house, all four rooms of it, and fixed all the broken-down furniture. He'd replaced the worn-out items in the house with new ones. He had cleared the garden and planted flowers in the front and peas and turnips at the back of the house. He'd even purchased two dairy goats so Aunt Morgan would have plenty of milk for her personal use, and she could sell the surplus to live on.

When her neighbours found out why he was in Ravenscroft, many of them didn't have any kind words to say about Mr. Lester. And as he was leaving this morning, it seemed as if the whole village had come out to the station to see him off. Perhaps what had surprised him more than anything was when Daisy May had turned up with a serious looking fellow by her side.

"Soldier, thank you," she told him.

"Why?"

"You were the first man in a long time to treat me with respect." She was clean, and even though her teeth were still black from years of chewing tobacco, she was no longer smelly, and he saw the beauty of her face. *"You treated me with kindness, and after you left it got me thinking."* She turned to the man beside her. *"This is Tobias Raider. He's been asking me for years to marry him, but I didn't think he was serious. What woman would think a man was serious about marriage when they met in a tavern?"* She winked, and the poor fellow blushed. *"But after you left, I went home and asked him if he still wanted to marry me."* She was grinning. *"We got married, and I'm going to be a respectable woman now. Thank you for helping me restore my life."*

"Daisy May, you've always been a respectable woman." He smiled at her. *"And I wish the both of you much happiness in your new lives together. One day I'll be back, and I hope to meet your children then."* He gave her five pounds. *"Find something good to use this money for."*

Herbert sighed when he thought about the promise Aunt Morgan had exacted from him. "Find my Mae and bring her to me."

"I promise you that I'll find Mae and bring her to you, Aunt Morgan."

And it was a promise he intended to keep, no matter what it cost him.

It was late afternoon when Herbert got to London, and he immediately found himself lodgings on Oxford Street. He slept soundly but was up at the crack of dawn. He was here in London on a mission to find Mae, regardless of whatever state she would be in.

Recalling the many stories she'd told him about Mrs. Brittle and how they'd lived under the bridge together, that was the first place he started early the next morning. He wondered if the old woman was even still alive and if she would remember Mae. Twelve years was a long time, but he was hopeful.

To his disappointment, he found that the spot under the London Bridge where Mae had mentioned was devoid of any shanty dwellings. It was clean swept, and it was clear that this had been done a while ago, so he had no idea where to begin searching for any of the homeless people who had once lived there.

Having not found Mae in Ravenscroft, he'd thought that she might have returned to London. She must be out on the streets somewhere as a beggar or maybe even worse. He closed his eyes in pain, not wanting to imagine that life could have caused her to sink so low and go to the other dark side. But even if she was living the dark life, he would rescue her. Daisy May was proof that even the most jaded women of the night could reform and change. He would find his beloved Mae and rescue her from whatever terrible life she might be living. Even if she belonged to a ringer house, he was prepared to pay whatever amount the Madame demanded to secure her release.

Having come to that decision, he decided to begin his search with the most commonly known ringer houses. As he was walking along the Old London Road, he spotted a young woman ahead of him. His heard skipped a beat because her disposition, size, and thick dark hair reminded him of Mae.

"Mae," he called out, and hurried after her. She looked back once, but she was too far away for him to see her face clearly. Determined not to let her out of his sight, he hurried after her. In his haste to follow the young woman, Herbert didn't realise that he'd entered the part of London where even the bravest fear to tread. His thoughts were set on getting to Mae and taking her out of the streets.

Then the girl suddenly stopped. He rushed forward, and when she turned around and he saw that it wasn't Mae, he wanted to weep with frustration. He'd lost hours following the wrong person.

"I'm sorry." He shook his head. "I thought you were someone else."

"Why were you following me?" She demanded in a tone of voice that made Herbert take a step backwards. "You've been following me all over London. What kind of a person are you?"

"From the back, you looked like someone I know. I'm sorry for scaring you." He realised where he was and knew that he had to be very careful about how he handled the situation. This was her domain, and he was an intruder here and so at the mercy of this young woman and her kind.

"That's what you perverts all say when you want to pounce on an unsuspecting woman." She put two fingers in her mouth and whistled, a shrill sound that told Herbert he was in serious trouble.

Three rough looking young men emerged from nowhere and approached Herbert menacingly. He raised his hands in surrender and forced himself to remain calm, even though he was really afraid. Such people almost always carried wicked looking blades, and they wouldn't hesitate to make short work of him, leaving him to die on the filthy streets.

"Sirs, I don't want any trouble," he said, trying to make it so that none of them went around to his back and suddenly attacked him. As long as he had them in his view, he could defend himself. "I'm sorry that I mistook your sister for someone else and followed her. Please forgive me."

"You were following our young sister so you could attack her," the oldest of the young men said.

Herbert shook his head, but the men kept advancing. He retreated slowly, praying that someone would come to his aid, or he would find an open alley through which he could escape. The men realised what he was trying to do and rushed him all at once. One of them grabbed his hands and restrained him from the back while the other two quickly frisked him, relieving him of everything, including his beret. The oldest man reached for the beret and placed it on his head.

"Now I, too, look like a soldier!" They all laughed, including the girl.

He was tackled and was soon on the ground. "Lizzie, hit the pervert." Herbert felt a blow to the side of his head and another on his face that split his lip. Then one of the others pulled out a wicked looking knife that glistened in the pale sunlight.

Herbert closed his eyes, believing that his end was near. "Dear Lord, please help me." He didn't want to die, because then what would become of Mae? "For Mae's sake, please spare my life so I can find and rescue her," he prayed silently, even as he felt the blows raining on his back.

Then the knife was plunged into his left thigh and sliced downwards, and the pain was excruciating, forcing him to scream. As he put out his hand to stop a second knife attack, he felt the sharp blade cutting through his sleeve and once again he felt a sharp pain, this time on his hand.

"Not so brave now, soldier," the girl jeered. Just when he was sure that the end had come, a shrill whistle split the air.

"The Bobbies are coming," the girl shouted. "Let's get out of here." The girl stood over him and spat on his face. Then they all melted away into the shadows taking his wallet, shoes, watch, and beret with them.

Herbert couldn't believe that he was still alive and struggled not to lose consciousness. He tried to crawl, but it felt as if thousands of needles were pricking him all over his body.

"Don't try to move because you've been badly wounded," he heard someone yell and prayed that it wasn't more trouble. He knew that his body couldn't handle another spate of beatings.

"He's a soldier," the same voice shouted, and even as he felt himself fading away, Herbert was glad that he'd thought to wear his uniform. "A foolish soldier to have dared to venture into this dangerous alley, but he's still alive."

It was at that point that Herbert lost consciousness.

Herbert woke up in the emergency room at St. Bartholomew's Hospital, and he managed to whisper his full name to the doctor who was attending to him.

"Do you have any relatives we can reach out to?" He whispered the name and address of his friends and then once again slipped into darkness.

When he next woke up, he found his two dear friends Peter and Simeon standing beside his bed and looking down at him.

"Captain, we thought you wouldn't ever wake up," Peter said solemnly. "The doctor said you'd lost a lot of blood and the wound in your leg was very deep. What happened to you?"

Herbert didn't want to tell his friends about his search for Mae. His whole face felt swollen, and his injured leg throbbed.

"Don't make him talk. Can't you see that his lips are swollen?" Simeon rebuked his brother.

"Sorry, Captain." Peter gave him a sheepish grin. "We want to know who did this to you so we can make them pay."

Herbert shook his head slowly, feeling as if there was dynamite exploding inside his skull. Even if he could talk, he had no hope that his assailants would ever be found. They were long gone and hiding in the shadows, like all criminals did. He prayed that they would soon be arrested before they hurt anyone else. As he drifted in and out of consciousness, Herbert listened to the light banter between the brothers. His last thought before he slept was a prayer that no one would tell his mother. He didn't want her showing up here and creating a fuss.

But his silent prayer wasn't answered, because the next day he awoke to a commotion outside his private room. Peter and Simeon were long gone, and he was alone, though they'd promised to return later in the day to check on him.

"If my son is dying, then I have a right to know." He heard his mother's voice and prepared himself for the inevitable. As usual, his mother's voice was cold. His Ma never shouted but her voice caused even strong men to quake in their shoes. "If you don't let me see my son in this instance, there will be trouble for all of you. Do you know who I am? Admiral David Patterson was my grandfather, and if you don't want me to shut this hospital down, then you better step out of my way for I'm going in to see my son."

"Oh no!" Herbert muttered in dismay. His mother was very skilled in running roughshod over anyone she considered to be inferior to her, and she often caused a lot of trouble.

"I'm sorry, Mrs. Patterson, but the patient is resting. He received extensive injuries and the doctor said he shouldn't be disturbed."

"That patient is my son, and I'm going in there to see him." His mother's voice was firm. "Believe me, I'll do it even if I have to crash through you to get into that room."

The door was forcefully pushed open, and his mother strode in as if she owned the place. Herbert's swollen lips twitched when he saw the nurses fluttering nervously around her.

"Stay back," she barked, and they shrank back, huddling together in the doorway. She walked over to the bed and stood looking down at him. Then she reached out a hand and gripped his chin firmly, turning his head from side to side.

"You were lucky," she said, showing no emotions at all on her face. "Who did this to you? I'll have them hanging in Newgate before sunset today. How dare they lay their hands on you?"

Herbert was glad that he hadn't mentioned Mae to his friends, because he was sure that it was Peter and Simeon who had sent for his mother, believing that it was the right thing to do.

"I'll find out in any way that I can who did this to you," his mother continued. "And they'll be sorry that they were ever born into this world by the time I'm done with them."

"Ma," Herbert's voice sounded tired.

"Sleep now, my son." She gently stroked his brow. "I'll be right here when you wake up."

"Thank you," he whispered, and he allowed himself the relief of oblivion once again.

PART III
OVERWHELMED

THE GIRL IN THE CAGE

Mae the gripped the edge of the windowsill and fought back her tears. She refused to turn around and beg for freedom like her cousin expected. She'd lived in this house for the past eight years and gotten to know all her relatives very well. No one was to be trusted, least of all her cousins.

Two years ago, when she'd been confined to this room, it was because of Bella who had reported her to Uncle John, and of that she was sure. And even as her uncle had been meting out the harsh sentence of full isolation, Mae had seen something in her elder cousin's eyes. Fear and jealousy! That brought a smile to her face as she loosened her grip on the windowsill. Bella was actually afraid of her, and this gave her some power, though she knew that if her cousin found out that she wasn't intimidated by her, there could be no telling what she might do.

"I'm telling you, fall on your knees before me and beg for mercy, and I'll tell Papa not to keep you locked up anymore," Bella told Mae, who still refused to turn around. "You don't have to be so stubborn and remain a prisoner in this tiny room. Turn around and kneel down before me, and I'll save your life. Aren't you tired of being locked up for the past two years?"

Mae signed and finally turned around. She didn't speak a word but simply looked at her cousin.

"You'll die in here," Bella hissed, "and the rats will feast on your rotting body." She gave Mae an angry look. "I have your life in my hands, and all you have to do is kneel down before me. You think my father is cruel? You're about to see a side of me that you never imagined. You will call for help but no one will answer you. There will be no more food for you until you submit yourself to me. Let's see how stubborn you'll be after spending many days without food and water."

To further rattle her cousin, Mae merely shrugged and then turned her back to her. She smiled when Bella made an angry sound of frustration. "See if I care if you die," and she stomped to the door, opened it, then slammed it hard and bolted it from the outside.

Bella left just in time. During the horrible confrontation with her cousin, Mae had felt her breath being squeezed in her chest and threatening to burst out of her like a geyser. She held on until she heard Bella walking down the stairs, thundering like an angry elephant, then she crumpled to the floor and bent her head, gasping for air. She felt like her throat was about to burst open with the stress of keeping the screaming inside.

Mae was terrified, even if she'd given Cousin Bella the impression that she wasn't. Her uncle and his family intended ill towards her and locking her up in this airless attic was their way of showing her that they were in full of control of her life. She was not just a prisoner physiologically, but mentally and emotionally too.

Keeping her locked up meant that for two years she hadn't smelled the sweet scent of flowers from the garden beyond their fence. She hadn't been allowed to go outside without strict supervision, and even when she did it was late at night or very early in the morning. For two years, Mae had only seen the sun through the small attic window.

Something moved in one corner. She bit back a scream and quickly fled to the other side of the attic. She was terrified of the dark and of rats. Apart from the maid who had rescued her, no one else came up to attic for any good. Her aunt and cousins would visit her from time to time, but only to mock at her.

The young girl whimpered as she crawled towards the window. It had been barricaded from the outside, and no matter how hard she'd tried to get it to open, it had stuck fast. It was during times of despair like this that she thought about Herbert. Hadn't he missed her at all in two years? He had promised to be there for her, but she hadn't heard a single word about him from her cousins these past two years. Had he forgotten about her?

Refusing to give up hope, Mae got to the window and scrambled to her feet. She once again tried to push it open, like she'd done for months. But like before, it was still stuck firmly and wouldn't budge. Once again, she collapsed on the floor and started sobbing in anguish. Was this how her life would end? She fell asleep on the cold floor and didn't hear when the door was opened or the person who walked in and stood over her with a satisfied look on their face.

The sound of a bird singing outside her window awakened Mae. She opened her eyes to the dawning of day and recalled the events of the previous day when her cousin had come to taunt her. But she wouldn't break, no matter what they did to her.

Mae hadn't expected to fall asleep after crying for a long time. No one had brought her any lunch or dinner, and she doubted that breakfast would be coming either. Hadn't Cousin Bella threatened to let her starve? Her stomach rumbled with hunger, and she sat up, leaning her back against the wall.

Mae thought of going to the door and banging on it to plead for her freedom, and she even crawled a few steps in that direction then stopped. No, she wouldn't beg for her freedom, nor would she ask them for food, because she would only be humiliated. If this is how they wanted to end her life, then so be it, but she would never beg again, since all that happened when she did was more humiliation.

Over the years, her cousins had done the same thing to her many times. They would cause trouble and then report her to their mother. Aunt Naomi would lock her in her small bedroom as she went in search of whatever she needed to use to flog Mae. As soon as she was gone, Bella and Ida would appear and make Mae beg them for her freedom.

"We'll beg Mama not to punish you, but you have to kneel down and plead for mercy." Mae would do so. She had fallen for their cunning tricks time and again, only to have them laugh hilariously at her submission while rejoicing when their mother had taken the whip to her back. But they had never reported her to Uncle John until Christmas Day two years ago. And now here she was. This showed her that she could expect worse humiliation than before.

"I'll stay and die in here," Mae whispered, "before I let them humiliate me again."

She recalled how Mrs. Brown had saved her from starving in the past, but her rescuer was gone forever. On Christmas Day, after her uncle had locked her in, the family had left to visit their friends. Mrs. Brown and the other servants were all gone, so Mae was left alone in the house for five days. But then Mrs. Brown had returned and rescued her, carrying her back downstairs where she and the new maid, Sandy, had taken care of her until she recovered. Mae had expected that once her uncle returned, he would show remorse for having locked her up and left her to starve. But she was wrong. As soon as he returned and found out that she was free, he'd marched her up the stairs again and back to the attic, a whip in his hands, though he hadn't struck her, not even once.

Her only regret then was that she'd put Mrs. Brown in trouble. Even as she stared at the door, she wondered if this was how it would all end. The last time her uncle had starved her for five days, and maybe this time it would be for longer. Mae put her head on her raised knees and wept. She wished for death because it would be better than this pain she had to endure.

THE CANDLE GOES OUT

The only person Mae saw in the coming days was the new maid, the one who together with Mrs. Brown had saved her from starvation the first time she was locked up. And at the time she'd been dismayed to learn that Mrs. Brown had been asked to leave the house after the incident. It was hard to believe that many months had passed since that incident, and she'd stopped counting the days altogether.

Perhaps fear of explaining Mae's death was what scared her uncle and his family into providing meals for her again. After being left hungry for two days, Mae started receiving one meal each morning. It was cold and unappetizing, but the hunger pangs made her ignore the terrible food. It sustained her, but barely..

Even while she was kept locked up, she had to continue with the chores that could be done while in isolation.

She had to darn her uncle's socks, repair her cousin's dresses, and mend the curtains. When she wasn't attending to the family's clothing, she was busy polishing all the silver and cutlery. Mae knew that her aunt was frustrated that she wasn't able to put her to work downstairs as before, because the whole idea was to keep her locked up. They clearly didn't want anyone to know that Mae was a prisoner in the house, and many times the young woman wondered what was going on in the world. No one told her anything at all.

Then an idea came to her one evening when she was mending one of Bella's pretty frocks. It had caught on a nail, and there was a small hole, which she skilfully repaired. Years ago, Mrs. Brown had taught her how to carefully sew the seams of a dress to reduce its size, and she'd had enough practice with Aunt Naomi's garments. Her aunt was plump, and her clothes were large, nearly twice her size. When these were now brought to Mae in the attic, she began to carefully undo the seams, and then using a rusty pair of scissors that she had found in one of the trunks, Mae trimmed off bits of cloth and lace from her aunt's dresses. She couldn't do the same to her cousins' clothes because these were always made to fit. Then she sewed her aunt's dresses back together again very neatly. If Aunt Naomi ever felt that her clothes were slightly smaller than before, she never said a word.

Mae then used the pieces of material to make handkerchiefs, and she adorned them with the lace.

She kept these hidden in a small hole in the floor which she had created from prising loose one of the wooden tiles. That was where she also hid the pair of scissors, because she knew that if relatives found out that she had such an implement, they would take it away from her just out of spite.

One morning many days after, Sandy brought in her day's ration. Mae had one of her hankies in her hand because she felt a cold coming on, and Sandy saw it.

"That's so pretty," the young woman said. "Where did it come from?" Mae was about to open her mouth when the girl went on. "Oh, I know, it looks like one of Mrs. Lester's dresses, so it must have dropped from her pocket when you were repairing the garment. Let me take it to her."

"No, it's mine," Mae said. "I've been making them. Please don't tell my aunt or my cousins about this." She knew that she was taking a great risk revealing something like this to the maid, but she was hoping that the girl would become a friend and help her in the days to come. "Please don't get me into trouble."

"Don't worry." Sandy made a face. "I don't like it that you're locked up in this place, and if I had a choice, I would never work for such cruel people. But they pay me fair wages, better than I would get anywhere else. I'm only here because of my Ma. Pa only drinks all his money, so I have to work to take care of my mother, else I would leave this place and never return."

"I'm sorry for getting you and Mrs. Brown into trouble two years ago. I was afraid that your services would be terminated."

"It's true that I nearly lost my position, but since there was no one else to work in the house after all the other servants had left, Mrs. Lester chose to keep me."

They heard footsteps, and Sandy hurried out of the attic, bolting the door. Mae heard Bella's voice and wondered what she was telling the maid. Maybe she was scolding her for bringing food for her. After a while, there was silence, and Mae looked down at the congealed mess on the plate and wrinkled her nose in disgust. Today, for some reason, her stomach rebelled at the food and she pushed the plate aside.

Mae sat on the floor and stared at the door, wondering if she would ever be free. Two years ago, after her uncle had brought her back into the attic, Mae had hoped that Mrs. Brown would at least tell someone whatever was going on so she would be freed. And she'd been hopeful when Sandy told her that Mrs. Brown had threatened to report her relatives for keeping her as a prisoner.

"Well, as soon as Mr. Lester gave Mrs. Brown her marching orders, the woman had some choice words to say to him and his wife," Sandy giggled. "I thought their eyes would pop out of their heads. Mrs. Brown said she was going to report your uncle, and he would go to prison for keeping you locked up like a slave."

Mae's heart fluttered with hope. If Mrs. Brown reported her uncle to the village constable, then she would soon be free.

"Did she report my uncle to the constable?" Mae held her breath.

Sandy sighed. "She did, and the village constable came by. Mrs. Lester then accused Mrs. Brown of stealing her jewellery and crystal ware. The poor woman denied it but when some silver and crystal ware were found in her house, the constable refused to believe any other word that she said. She and her family were then thrown off the estate in shame."

Mae's heart fell. She knew that Mrs. Brown was not a thief. Those items must have been placed in her house by one of the other servants who were loyal to Mrs. Lester.

In the coming days, Mae noticed that Sandy spent a longer time in the attic with her than before. While she welcomed the maid's friendly chatter, she knew that if it was ever discovered that Sandy was being kind to her, the maid would lose her position. Mae doubted that anyone else would show her mercy as Sandy did.

"You shouldn't be found here talking to me," Mae told Sandy one morning. "I wouldn't want you to get into any more trouble, and you need the money for your mother. But if there's any way that you can get a message to someone for me, I would be most grateful."

"Who?"

"Master Herbert Patterson. He lives next door." Mae was surprised when Sandy seemed to shrink back as if she'd been struck. "What's wrong?"

Sandy shot to her feet. "I have to go now."

"Wait…" Mae called out, wondering at the maid's strange reaction to her request. Then she began to fear that she's been too hasty in trusting the new girl. What if she reported her to Uncle John, or worse, Aunt Naomi? All day long, Mae waited with fear for one of her adult relatives or even Cousin Bella to burst into the attic and punish her. But nothing of the sort happened, and when it was Ida who came to take her out for her evening visit to the outhouse, Mae feared the worst. Maybe someone had found out about Sandy's friendliness, and she no longer worked at the house, but she saw the maid in the kitchen, even though the girl pretended not to notice her. At least Ida didn't make mention of anything that Mae had discussed with Sandy, which could only mean that she hadn't betrayed her. Of course, Ida taunted Mae as usual, but nothing was said about her request to Sandy.

The next day Sandy didn't bring her the day's ration in the morning as she usually did, and Mae began to feel that perhaps this was the punishment she would get for opening her mouth and confiding in her. But in the evening, just before she retired to bed, she heard the door being opened and quickly sat up, wondering who her late night visitor was. Sandy brought her some food, though her face was closed to Mae. It was as if she regretted trying to make friends with Mae.

"Thank you for not abandoning me," Mae whispered when Sandy had dropped the plate of food on the floor. The maid didn't speak a word but simply walked out of the door.

Mae reached for her food with a sigh and was surprised to find that it was different today. She'd been served some chicken, and the food was still warm enough for her to enjoy it. Also, there was more than usual, and she wondered what was going on. For a brief moment, she felt that it might be a trap of some sort. She kept expecting someone to burst into the room and snatch the plate away from her. She eventually ate the food, and for the first time in many days, was replete.

Over the next few days, Sandy brought Mae food in the evening. It was enough and also well prepared, so she knew that it came from her uncle's table. She longed to ask Sandy why she was being this nice to her, and yet the girl never spoke a single word to her, but then she decided that she wasn't going to look a gift horse in the mouth.

One afternoon, Mae sat in the attic, feeling very bored and restless. For once, there wasn't anything for her to do because she'd done all repairs and polished all the silver in the house, and she wished she had some chores to undertake.

She had pushed all thoughts of Herbert to the back of her mind and forced herself never to think about him. The chores she did kept her mind occupied, but without them the thoughts pushed their way back, and she was forced to think about him.

It was hard for her to believe that Herbert had forgotten all about her and hadn't tried to find out whatever was happening to her. Even if he'd returned to London, surely he could have at least come to the house to inquire about her.

Mae touched the string around her neck and started to bring out the locket. When she heard footsteps on the stairs and the bolt being drawn back, she quickly put it out of sight again.

Sandy walked into the room carrying a covered dish. For some reason her stomach looked slightly bigger than usual. Before Mae could ask her if she was ill, Sandy sighed, "Look, Mae, I can help you in every other way, but please don't ever mention that man's name to me."

Mae wanted to ask Sandy the reason for her comment, but since she needed an ally in this dark season of her life, she simply nodded and received her food. "I'm sorry if I made things difficult for you. I won't ever mention that name to you again."

"I know you're wondering why I've been bringing you food in the evenings," the girl continued. "I didn't like it when I had to bring you cold meals with congealed grease, which was food from the previous day. I've been making sure that there's nothing left over from the evening meal, so you won't have to eat cold food in the morning," Sandy said.

"Thank you for your kindness," Mae said.

Sandy walked around the attic, touching some things and moving others. "If you tell anyone that I brought this thing to you, I'll deny it." She reached under her large apron and brought out a kitten, and Mae realised why the maid's stomach had looked slightly bigger than usual. "At least it will help keep rats out of your room."

Mae smiled as she received the unexpected gift. It was a ginger kitten, and as soon as Mae held it, the animal snuggled close to her chest. Tears filled her eyes. "Bless you," she told Sandy.

"I also brought you some candles, so you won't continue sitting in the dark, and a box of matches. But you have to be careful not to light a candle while the people downstairs are still awake. Make sure no one finds out that I've been bringing you these extra things."

Sandy continued walking around the attic after handing Mae two candles. "What's in these trunks?" she asked.

Mae shrugged, feeding the kitten whatever was left over from her meal. Sandy bent down, opened one of the trunks, and immediately began coughing because of the dust and musty smell. She quickly shut it and moved to the next one.

"Have you ever seen these?" The excitement in her voice made Mae look up quickly. "I can't believe that you've been in here and never checked inside these trunks. See?" She held up a frock. "It's old but the material is good."

"They belong to my cousins, and I never touch anything that isn't mine," Mae said.

Sandy turned the garment from side to side and noticed that it was ripped up in many places. She picked up another and it had the same problem. "Mae, these dresses are torn, but see the lace on them?" She brought one closer to Mae. "Why don't you remove the lace and use it for those pretty hankies you make?" Mae rose to her feet, dropping the kitten so it could explore the attic, and joined Sandy. As the girl said, the frocks were old and torn, but the lace was still good.

"What will I do with so many hankies? As it is, I have over twenty of them now, and I can't use them all."

Sandy smiled at her. "Do you remember the one you gave me?" Mae nodded. "I sold it for a shilling to someone in church. Another lady saw it and asked if I could get her some more. You can make hankies, and I'll sell them. Then when you have enough money, you can run away from this horrible place. Nobody deserves this kind of treatment, and if there's anything I can do to help you get out of here, I'll do it."

Mae wiped her face. "I don't ever want to get you into trouble. I still feel so guilty about Mrs. Brown and how she must be suffering."

"The woman is a saint, and God rewarded her goodness to you. The other day when I was at church, I met one of Mrs. Brown's friends. She told me that Mrs. Brown found work on another estate on the other side of Sheffield and seems to be doing very well."

"I still feel guilty that I got her into trouble, and that's why I don't want the same thing to happen to you."

"If we're careful, we'll never be caught. Hide whatever you're doing during the day when those people are up and about and work only at night. I'll make sure that you never run out of candles, but be careful that you don't burn down the house."

"Thank you."

Seasons came and went, but Mae didn't notice or dwell too much on the passing of time. Now that she had meaningful labour, she didn't think so much about running away from her uncle's house. Apart from the insults and taunts from her cousins almost on a daily basis, being locked up in the attic wasn't all that bad.

The beatings by her aunt had ceased, and though she was still getting only one meal a day, Sandy ensured that it was hot and plentiful.

"I'm surprised that no one has stopped you from bringing me so much food," she commented one day.

"They really have no idea that I'm doing it." Sandy grinned cheekily. "Every day when the new cook asks me to serve the food in the dishes to be taken to the dining table, I make sure that I serve one extra and hide it in one of the pails in the broom closet. As soon as the family sits down to dinner, I then make it as if I'm coming upstairs to clean Bella and Ida's bedchambers," the girl grimaced. "You know how dirty and untidy your cousins are, and that their rooms have to be cleaned two or three times a day. That's the excuse I use. And when dinner is over, I usually collect the leftovers as if I'm bringing them to you, but then I carry the remains to the chicken coop instead."

Mae was grateful for the maid's kindness, even though she knew the girl was taking a great risk. "Please don't get into trouble on my account. I would never forgive myself if you suffered because of me."

"Don't worry. I'm always careful."

Sandy continued to sell the hankies Mae made, and whatever money she brought back was shared equally between the two of them. Mae also realised that she could only survive in the world out there if she had money of her own. She dreamed of one day leaving this house and going to start a small business or finding work in one of the clothing factories. But she knew that she would need to rent a room to live in, and that could only happen if she had some money.

What Mae didn't realise was that as the months went by, she was turning into a very beautiful young woman, and Sandy was glad that her friend was locked up. She knew that men could be ruthless in the presence of such beauty as Mae possessed. A wicked man wouldn't hesitate to abuse Mae and thus extinguish the innocence and light in her eyes.

Sandy herself had also stopped grumbling about living in this terrible household, because she was making extra money from the hankies she sold for Mae. She also had dreams of going to London and finding work in a better household, and she was saving up for that time. Her greatest desire was to take her mother and two sisters away from the painful life they lived with her drunkard father. While she knew that her mother might never leave her father, Sandy was determined that when she had enough money, she would take her sisters away. They were growing up very fast, and she didn't want them falling prey to worthless men in the village who would make them age faster than their years. Her own mother was still young and attractive, but years of abuse by her father and weakness due to illness had turned her into a shadow of herself.

Sandy was determined not to accept the suit of any man unless she was sure that he loved her and also that he would provide for her family. For the time being, she was contented being a maid in this household, which also provided safety to her person. Apart from overworking her, no one had ever harassed her, and especially not the men who worked in Mr. Lester's stables. She readily admitted that Mae, though a prisoner in her uncle's attic, was much safer being locked up her than out there in the world on her own.

A FRIEND IN NEED

No matter how many days turned into weeks and then months, the one thing Mae never forgot was her birthday. That's because it fell on Christmas Day, and things changed in the household around the Christmas season. She had counted three birthdays since being shut up in the attic and the fourth was coming up in a few days' time, when she would be turning eighteen. She had a tidy nest egg hidden in the trunk of the old musty clothing, one she knew no one would ever look into.

Sandy had remained faithful all through, and even shared her dreams with Mae. The maid was only sad that her own savings weren't growing.

"I feel like for every step I take forward in my life, I'm dragged backwards five more," the maid told Mae. "I told Mama about the hankies that I've been selling and even gave her money to keep for me." Sandy had told

Mae one day. "But she told my father, and he took all the money away from her. So, I have to still work hard for a few more years before I can truly be free."

"You'll get there," Mae had soothed. "I'll try to increase the number that I've been making so you can get some more money. In fact, I think I've saved sufficient money for myself, so keep everything that we sell from today for yourself."

"You would do that for me?" Sandy seemed surprised.

"Sandy, you've done so much for me in the past four years and made my imprisonment easier to bear. I know that God has blinded my uncle and his family from knowing whatever is going on, because if they knew they would easily get rid of you, just to make me suffer."

"And I'll never forget this kindness."

Their friendship grew, and the two young women became very comfortable with each other. The only topic they never discussed was Herbert Patterson, for Sandy wouldn't let Mae ask her questions about the man. And Mae didn't want to alienate her friend, so she stopped asking altogether.

But each night, she would reach for the locket and touch it, thinking about the man who had given it to her. He would be twenty-three now, and she wondered if he lived with his mother on the estate, or if he'd gone to London to find other prospects for himself.

On Christmas Day, the day she turned eighteen, Mae woke up early and sat in the darkness, wondering if anything would change at all. She felt that she had enough money now to leave her uncle's house, but she was closely watched by her aunt and cousins, and escaping would take a lot of planning. She needed Sandy for this, but so far, the young woman also steered clear of the topic of helping Mae to escape.

For four years, she'd lived out of sight of people, including the new cook in the house. Sandy had informed her that she was the only remaining maid in the house, the others having been let go. According to Sandy, it seemed as if Uncle John's fortunes had changed for the worse, and there was much strain in the household. Even her cousins no longer went out to buy clothes, hats, and shoes as before, and Mae wondered what could have happened.

She heard someone on the stairs on that early morning, and she waited to see who it was, for she was sure that it wasn't Sandy. It was Cousin Bella. The woman walked into the room, her nose in the air as usual. She was carrying a pile of dresses under her arm, and she tossed them at Mae.

"See that you repair these for me as soon as possible. We'll be visiting some family friends from tomorrow until the New Year, and I don't want to look odd in last year's garments."

"Yes, Cousin Bella," Mae said. As soon as Bella had left, Sandy came in. Mae mentioned the dresses, pointing them out to her friend.

"I'm surprised that Cousin Bella is going to wear these used dresses. She would never have done that before."

"I told you that your uncle seems to be in trouble, for I heard him and your aunt quarrelling. She wanted him to purchase new clothes for your cousins, but he was angry and told her that there was no more money for such frivolities."

"Cousin Bella told me that they will be visiting friends from tomorrow until the New Year."

Sandy scoffed, "Your cousins are searching for husbands, and there's no secret about that. They probably hope to find some wealthy young men, now that their father can't provide for them as before."

"Bella and Ida are very beautiful, and I hope they get good husbands," Mae said without malice.

Sandy gave her a strange look. "You're too good to be true. After the way those two have treated you over the years, and here you are, still wishing them well."

"It doesn't matter what they have done, they deserve to find good men who will appreciate their beauty."

"Dear girl, true beauty is not what's on the outside but what's inside a person's heart. Your cousins have the ugliest hearts that I've ever seen in such young woman.

Else they would never have rejoiced about their parents keeping you locked up in here as if you were a dangerous lunatic in an asylum. I'm just glad that I won't have to see them again after the New Year."

"Why? What's going to happen to you?" Mae looked at Sandy with dread. "I hope I haven't gotten you into trouble."

Sandy grinned. "Nothing like that. I met someone who lives in Manchester. His name is Owen. He's asked me to marry him, and I said yes."

"I'm so happy for you, and I pray that he treats you well."

"Owen is a good man. He's a cobbler and has his own store in Manchester. We met a few months ago when he came to bury his Mama, and I thought he would forget all about me. But he has returned and asked me to move to Manchester, where I'll help him with his business. He has also agreed that my sisters can come and live with us." She looked sad for a moment. "I just wish Mama would agree to come too. Owen says there are many jobs in the factories in Manchester and Ma can earn a good living. But Mama won't leave my father."

"She loves him and is a good woman who is faithful and true to her husband."

"I just wish my father would realise how much my mother has given up for him. One thing I know is that as soon as we get to Manchester, I'll find work so as to help my husband out, so we won't have to struggle too much. And when my sisters are old enough, I'll make sure they also get to work. In that way we can send Mama money for upkeep."

"Won't your father take it all away and drink it?"

"Mama is wiser now. I know that she won't be able to stop him from drinking, but at least she'll be careful to hide some of the money from him."

Mae was really happy for her friend. If anyone deserved happiness and blessings, it was Sandy, for in a way she'd been Mae's bulwark in this unfriendly and hostile house. "May you be blessed and be happy all the days of your life," Mae said, though her heart was sad now that she would be losing a valuable ally. She had no idea what would happen to her after Sandy's departure.

"Well, I have to go downstairs and prepare breakfast for the family," Sandy said. "But I'll still be here until a few days after the New Year because I need to get all my wages paid by your aunt. She promised to settle my final accounts after returning from this visit they're making tomorrow. Merry Christmas and happy birthday Mae. I'll make sure that I bring you some cake."

"Thank you, now go before you get into trouble."

Mae had just finished dressing and was standing at the window staring outside at the snow as it fell when she heard heavy footsteps coming up the stairs. The door was unbolted and suddenly her uncle stood in the doorway.

She couldn't say that she'd seen much of him in the past four years, but he seemed to have aged so much, it shocked her. His hair was greyer around the temples and his shoulders were stooped. The clothes that used to fit him very well now hung like rags on his stooping form.

Uncle and niece stared at each other silently for a while before the former cleared his throat. Uncle John seemed surprised that Mae wasn't screaming or crying over his ill treatment of her. She had decided that she would never show such kind of weakness to her tormentors, for they only revelled in punishing her more. She stood there staring at her uncle, who seemed ill at ease.

"What are you doing?" He asked and Mae stared at him wordlessly. "There's something I have to tell you." He stepped further into the room and Mae retreated to the back of the attic. His stance wasn't menacing at all, but Mae remembered Sandy warning her to always be careful around any man who was older than she was.

"Never trust a man and don't ever turn your back to him for it will make you vulnerable to sudden attack," the maid had told her. *"My friend Emma who lived down the road and worked for Mr. Gribble thought that because he was lame in one leg, he was harmless. She learned the hard way that a man is just as strong whether he has only one leg or both of them. Emma was lucky that one of the stable boys was in the house on that day when Mr. Gribble attacked her or else she would have been in a lot of trouble. As it is, she ran away and now I don't know where she is. Mae, never think that just because a man looks harmless that he can't hurt you.'*

So, with that warning in mind, Mae made sure she kept a safe distance from her uncle. If he tried to lunge at her, there were a few broken items that she would use as weapons to defend herself. For once she was glad that there were some broken pieces of furniture in the attic. Before he got a chance to harm her, she would have also done quite some damage to him, she thought.

"I brought you to this house when you had nothing, after picking you from the streets," her uncle said. "Over the years I've provided you with food, clothing, and shelter and now you've come of age. I happen to know that today is your eighteenth birthday, and so my obligation towards you comes to an end. You see, I made a promise to your mother that if anything happened to her and your father, I would take you in if you were still a child." He smiled but Mae, staring at him in stony silence, didn't respond,. "But that promise ceases on your eighteenth birthday, because from today you're no longer a child, but rather a mature and grown woman."

"I know you see me as a wicked man and think that I've been unjustly cruel to you by keeping you locked up these past four years. But you were very vulnerable and trusting of those who might have taken advantage of you. Mae, I had to protect you in the only way I knew how," he paused as if expecting her to say something, but she remained silent. "It's my duty as your only living relative to make sure that you have a good future. I was afraid that some village lout would entice you away, deceive you, and ruin your life and dignity. All this I did for your own good."

"So now that I've come of age, Uncle John, are you sending me away from your home?" Mae could barely contain her excitement.

"In a manner of speaking, yes, but I have made some arrangements for you." His words sounded ominous, and Mae frowned. What kind of arrangements had her uncle made for her?

"I don't understand," she said.

"Mae, you've grown into a beautiful young woman, and the last thing I want is for you to end up in trouble when you leave this house. So as your uncle and guardian, I'm happy to tell you that I've found you a suitable husband."

Uncle John seemed slightly disappointed when Mae did nothing more than give him a slight nod as if encouraging him to continue talking.

"Mr. Watson is our neighbour, but you don't know him because he and his wife have always been reserved and don't attend too many functions. But he lost his wife last year and she left him four children. Being a man of means, he has promised that you'll be well taken care of as his wife and mother to his children. You see, it's time that you returned my goodness to me."

"By marrying an old widower?" Mae burst out. "I won't agree to marry that old man, never!"

At her outburst, her uncle's countenance changed. "You're nothing but an ingrate who thinks only about herself. Do you think it was easy for me to take care of you and provide for all your needs? It cost me money, and now you have to repay my kindness to you. Mr. Watson is willing to settle a good sum of money on you, and you owe me. Things haven't been going well for me, and this is your chance to show gratitude for all that we've done for you."

Mae's lips tightened. She knew that arguing with her uncle was just a waste of time. She bowed her head and fell silent once again.

"Prepare yourself, because on the fifth day of the New Year, you and Mr. Watson will be getting married.

Make no mistake, you'll do as I say, or there will be trouble for you."

Mae held herself together and listened for the next few minutes as her uncle pleaded, cajoled, and even threatened, but she said nothing. In the end, he walked out angrily, slammed the door and forcefully pushed the bolt home. That was when she collapsed on the floor and burst into tears.

.

THROUGH THE CRACKS

As if listening to her uncle's evil plans for her future wasn't enough, the door was unbolted again in the middle of the morning. This time it was Bella who pranced in, dressed to the nines, and she looked very beautiful. The expression on her face told Mae that her cousin was here to taunt her yet again.

"Have you come to your senses now?" Bella asked, her nose wrinkling in disgust as she looked at Mae. "It's your birthday today, and you're still a prisoner in this attic. Kneel down and beg me for your freedom and perhaps I'll feel pity and put in a good word with Papa, so he'll let you go."

Mae didn't respond.

"And there's something else you need to know." Mae decided that the best way to deal with Bella and whatever she had to say was to ignore her. "Herbert is back, and he's become very handsome in the years that he's been away." Mae jerked like one who'd been struck, and her cousin noticed that she'd turned pale. Bella burst into mocking laughter, "Oh, you poor thing, I know you were besotted with the man, but he only ever felt sorry for you. You see, you're nothing but a penniless beggar and of no worth to anyone."

"Herbert was my friend," Mae said defensively, fighting back the tears.

"You said it yourself, he was just a mere friend, but only because you wouldn't stop pestering the poor man with your foolish stories. He was too polite a gentleman to tell you that you were nothing but a bother to him. That's how well brought up men behave even if they have to endure the unwanted presence of people who bother them."

Bella's words cut deep into her heart, but Mae refused to show any more emotions, because her cousin's taunts would only get worse. She refused to give Cousin Bella the satisfaction of humiliating her again.

Her uncle had said it, that she was now of age, and so it was up to her to start taking care of herself. For one, the New Year wasn't going to find her still living in this household. There's no way that she was going to allow anyone to force her into marriage with an old man who had four children. Even though she had no idea who Mr. Watson was, the fact that he had four children meant that he was of considerable age.

She had made a promise to herself that she would never betray Herbert. If what Bella was saying was true, then it meant that he was home again, and her heart yearned for him.

"There's something I need to let you know," Bella went on. "My marriage to Herbert has been approved of by my parents and his mother. We're getting married very soon, and that should tell you that you've never been of any importance to him." Bella strutted around the small room, and Mae was careful to stay out of her way. "When I become Mrs. Herbert Patterson, I'll wear furs and jewels that will make every woman in this country green with envy. And the house." Bella's eyes glowed., "That beautiful manor will become my new home and I'll be mistress of it. Mrs. Patterson, his mother of course, will move to the smaller house and leave the larger one to us. Can you just imagine the balls and social gatherings that I'll hold in my new home?" She paused. "My life will be on the same level as Queen Victoria's. I heard Papa telling Mama that when Mrs. Patterson dies, Herbert will inherit all that wealth. I'll be so rich that money and jewels will be dripping from my fingers like droplets of water." She wriggled her long fingers.

"I don't hear you mentioning anything about love," Mae said quietly.

"Love?" Bella scoffed. "Only fools marry for love. Herbert is a handsome man, but that doesn't matter, because if he were poor then I wouldn't touch him." She grimaced. "It's what he possesses that counts for me. A beautiful woman like me expects to be decked in the finest muslins, furs, and jewellery. After I give him an heir and a spare, I'll allow him to have his indiscretions because everything he owns will belong to me and my sons."

Mae thought she would gag at Bella's callous words. It was very clear that her cousin was only interested in prestige and would never love Herbert. It was up to her to stop him from making such a terrible mistake that would ruin his life forever. But in order to do that she needed to get out of this house, and she knew just what to do.

"Oh!" She doubled up and clutched her stomach.

"What?" Bella asked rudely, clearly annoyed that her ranting wasn't making Mae angry or weepy.

"My stomach," Mae hissed as if in pain and fell to her knees. She then rolled on the floor, still clutching her stomach. "The pain is killing me."

Bella took one look and fled, locking Mae inside the attic. Mae giggled, and when she was sure her cousin was gone, she jumped to her feet and rushed to the old trunk where she retrieved the small purse that she'd made for herself and which contained all her money. She slipped it under her clothes and sat to wait.

Sandy came in through the door in a hurry, "What's going on, Mae? Bella rushed downstairs and I heard her telling her mother that you're unwell. But there are guests downstairs for Christmas luncheon, and Mrs. Lester sent me up here to check on you. Your uncle has been complaining that there's no money to waste, and yet he's gone on to host a very grand luncheon today. Do you know that he even brought in extra maids to help?"

"Sandy!" Mae knew that if she didn't stop her friend from chatting, she would soon forget the reason why she was here.

"I'm sorry, are you ill?"

"Sandy I'm not ill but you've got to help me."

"How? What's going on?"

Mae quickly told her friend all that her uncle had told her and his wicked plans for her life, and then what Bella had also revealed. "I have to leave this house, or Uncle John will force me to marry that man who is older than my grandfather."

"Yes, I know Mr. Watson, and as you say, he's a very old man," Sandy said. She frowned slightly. "Wait here." She left the room, and Mae felt like crying. It seemed as if

Sandy wasn't willing to help her, and so she had to find another way.

But then her friend returned a few minutes later. "Here, put these on quickly." She handed her a maid's uniform and large bonnet. "Hurry up so we don't get caught."

Once Mae was dressed like one of the maids and her long thick hair folded into the bonnet, Sandy managed to get her downstairs and pushed a basket into her hands. In a loud voice Sandy then 'ordered' the new maid to hurry up and bring some eggs from the chicken coop. The kitchen was bustling with activity, and no one paid any attention to the 'maid' who slipped out through the back door.

Mae's heart was thumping, and she forced herself to look like she was going towards the chicken coop. She was praying that the hole in the hedge would still be there for her to slip through and get to the other side. It was, and she tossed the basket aside, darted into the hedge, all the while praying that she would find Herbert in the arbour. Four years had gone by since she'd last seen him, and she hoped that his habits hadn't changed.

DON'T WEEP FOR ME

Herbert had escaped from the house where his mother had some people over for Christmas Day lunch. At least today they hadn't been invited over to Mr. Lester's house, for he would have firmly and politely declined to attend the luncheon. He wasn't in any mood for celebrating, because his heart was heavy. As he sat in the arbour wondering if Mae was still alive, he thought he heard rustling in the undergrowth. The next thing he saw was a maid emerging from the bushes, and he frowned because the uniform indicated that she wasn't one of theirs.

Then he did a double take when the young woman drew closer. It was his Mae, but she looked so different. The last time he'd seen her she'd been a gangly teenager with spots on her face. The woman walking towards him was so beautiful that he felt his throat closing up with emotion.

"Mae." His voice sounded weak in his own ears. The tightness pulled across his chest, leaving him unsettled.

Four good years had gone by since he'd last seen her, and the changes in her physical appearance were vast. The first thing he noticed when she was much closer was that her skin was very pale, as if she hadn't been in the sun for a long time. Her eyes carried deep sadness that tore at his heart. Gone was the cheerful girl he'd known, and in her place was a woman who looked like she'd been through a terrible ordeal.

Herbert drew a steady breath. "Mae, where have you been all these years? I searched everywhere for you, but in vain. What happened to you?"

Mae smiled sadly at her friend. "You never came to look for me." He saw the tears in her eyes. "Every night I prayed that you would find me, but you never came. It was as if you went away and forgot all about me. I counted days and Christmases, but you never came."

Herbert knew that words wouldn't be sufficient to comfort Mae, so he drew back his right sleeve. Mae gasped when she saw the long, ugly gash on his forearm. Then he raised his trouser over his right leg and she saw another long scar. Finally, he turned his head to the right and she saw the scar running from his ear to the back of his neck.

"What happened to you?" Mae cried out. "Who did this to you?" Her tears started falling unchecked.

Herbert sighed. "Two years ago, when I returned home, I thought I would find you. You had disappeared on Christmas Day, and I never saw you before I had to report to the military academy. After being in the academy for six months, I was to be posted abroad, but first I asked for permission to come home and see my family. When I got here and asked about you, I was told that you had gone back to Ravenscroft to live with your relatives. At the time I didn't have much time because my unit had to report for the mission, so I went away but had every intention of travelling to Ravenscroft to find you."

Mae stared at him as if he was speaking Greek and not English. "Ravenscroft, where is that?"

"It's a village in Pembroke, Wales."

"I've never been there," Mae said, wiping her eyes.

Herbert smiled tenderly at her. "You've been there before, but you were very small then, when your parents took you to visit your relatives. But I'm getting ahead of myself," he said. "I wanted to immediately follow you to Pembroke but then I was recalled to the army. and it would be another full year before I returned to the shores of England."

"Where did you go?"

"Overseas to the colonies. My unit was stationed first in Egypt and then we moved to the Gold Coast. But as soon as I returned to England, I resigned my commission from the army."

"Why?"

"Because I needed to find you, Mae. So, I went to Ravenscroft and met your Aunt Morgan, who is such a wonderful woman. She told me that she'd only seen you once when you were a baby."

"I have an aunt in Wales?"

"Yes, your mother's cousin. When I told Aunt Morgan that I was searching for you because you were missing, the poor woman wept so much that I was afraid she would be ill. She made me promise to find you and take you to her."

"I'd like that," Mae fell silent for a brief moment. It was exciting to know that she had another living relative who wanted her. But then her face fell. She recalled how excited she'd been to come to live with her uncle many years ago when Mr. Davenport snatched her from the streets. She'd expected to find a warm and welcoming home, to be embraced by a loving family, and to be treated as one of them. Instead, she'd only known pain for the past eleven years, four of them locked up like a lunatic in an asylum. But she needed Herbert to tell her more. "What happened when you left Pembroke?" she asked him.

"I returned to London, thinking that maybe you had gone back to the streets where you lived with that old woman." He looked sorrowful. "I thought that you might have run away to the streets, and as I was searching for you, I saw someone who looked like you. It was a young girl, and from behind I believed that it was you so I followed her. She led me to an alley, where her accomplices were waiting."

Mae started crying again when she thought about what had happened to Herbert.

"That girl and her three gang members set upon me, stabbed my hand and leg and took all my valuables then left me for dead. But for the mercy of God, I would be dead and long buried," his voice carried weariness. "Even after I recovered, I never stopped searching for you. I've been working in London these past two years, and every chance I got, I roamed the streets of London searching for you." He held her by the shoulders. She'd grown slightly taller but was still a head shorter than him. "My lovely Mae, what happened to you? Where did you go?"

Mae's body went slack, and she wiped her tears away. "Do you recall that last Christmas Day that we were together?"

Herbert nodded, "Four years ago, yes I recall."

"Do you remember me telling you that I felt as if someone was hiding in the bushes and watching us?"

Dread filled Herbert's heart at the words, but he merely nodded. "It was Bella. She went and reported me to my uncle. When I got back to the house, he was waiting for me."

"Did he hit you?" Herbert growled menacingly.

"No, but he locked me up in the attic for five days while he and his family went to visit some people. They didn't give me any food," she sobbed. "Mrs. Brown found me on the day before the New Year. I nearly died, but they saved me and because of her kind act, Mrs. Brown lost her position in the house and had to move away. The other servant was warned to never let me out of the house except for twice a day to use the outhouse. My uncle kept me locked up in the attic like a prisoner for four years, until today."

"Oh, Mae, I'm so sorry." He looked her over. "Are you alright? How did you manage to escape?"

"Sandy the maid helped me. I knew that I had to come and warn you not to marry Bella. She doesn't love you and will never be good for you."

He frowned. "I have no intentions of ever marrying Bella. Mae, I've been waiting for you to grow up so I can take you away from this place. We'll get married, and I'll always keep you safe."

His words sounded so good, and Mae thought she was dreaming. Then her heart fell. "But what about your mother? She'll never accept me as your wife because I'm nobody. You and I are from different worlds."

"Leave my mother out of this." He tugged at the chain that was around his neck. "I've kept this for four years and never took it off," he said. "I think it's time for me to give this to you, now that we're going to be together forever." He handed the chain over to Mae, and she clasped it in her palm. "This is how much I love you and believe that we're soul mates. Do you still have the locket that this chain belongs to?"

Mae's response was to smile and reach for the string around her neck. But before she could take it off and show the locket to Herbert, they heard angry footsteps coming their way.

"So, this is where you're hiding!" Mrs. Patterson looked enraged. She was holding a newspaper in her hand. "What do you think you're doing standing here with this worthless girl? Don't you know that you have obligations to our visitors?"

"Mother, please." Herbert stood in front of Mae as if to defend her. "Stop shouting."

"When the servant told me that he'd seen you in the arbour with a maid from next door, I realized that something was afoot. But I didn't expect that the person trespassing on my estate would be this worthless girl. I won't let you throw your life and dignity away on some worthless creature. Bella Lester is a beautiful woman and very suitable to be your wife. She comes from a good family, and I have approved her to be your wife." Mrs. Patterson fixed her gaze on Mae. "I don't know what you hoped to achieve by coming back to cause trouble for my son. Your uncle told me that you had fled to London and were living like a vagabond out there on the streets. I know that you're a ruined woman, a soiled dove, and as such I won't let you destroy my son's future. Who knows how many diseases that worthless body of yours is carrying?" She thrust the newspaper she was holding at Mae. "See for yourself. Herbert and Bella have already announced their engagement and will soon be getting married."

Mae slowly unfolded the newspaper and read the notice of engagement. Then she raised stricken eyes to Herbert. He saw the look of hopelessness and despair in them.

"Mae, don't believe any of that nonsense. I'm not part of it."

Mae's heart broke in that moment. When it had been Bella gloating to her, everything had seemed false, but the notice in one of the widely read newspapers in England meant that this was a done deal. The man she now acknowledged that she loved with her whole heart would be marrying her cousin soon. There was no future for her with Herbert.

"This changes everything," she whispered, holding on to the newspaper.

"It changes nothing, Mae." Herbert turned and held her by the shoulders. "Mae, please listen to me." He felt desperate, and it was as if a wall had gone up between them. "The fact that my mother put this notice in the newspaper doesn't mean that I sanctioned or agreed to her plans with your uncle and cousin."

Mrs. Patterson hissed, "You're nothing but a troublemaker, Mae, and if you don't leave my son alone, I'll make your life a living hell. You're nothing but a gold digger and someone who wants to bring shame to my family. I won't allow my son's dignity to be dragged into the mud."

Mae shook herself free of Herbert and stepped back. "I can never hope to overcome your family and mine," she said.

"I'll protect you, Mae. Don't listen to my mother's ugly and untrue words." But Mae was shaking her head.

"There can never be a future for us," she said. She loved Herbert very much, but she wasn't going to be the reason that he became the laughingstock of Sheffield. And in any case, even if she was to agree to what he was saying, life would be made very difficult for them, especially for her. His mother detested her, and her uncle would see to it that she never had any peace. It would mean living a life of trouble and torment from the two families. "Don't cry for me, Herbert." Her voice broke as she reached out a hand and wiped the tears from his face. "It's for the best that we never see each other again. This is goodbye forever," she sniffed.

"Good!" Mrs. Patterson interjected. "Go back home and stay there. I'll tell your uncle to deal with you so you can never bother my son again. In fact, didn't I hear that you're getting married to Mr. Watson?"

Mae wanted to scream at the woman to shut up.

"What's that?" Herbert looked at his mother and then back to Mae.

"Oh, she didn't tell you?" The woman laughed scornfully. "Little Miss Butter Won't Melt In her Mouth has accepted to be Mr. Watson's second wife."

"That's not true," Mae shouted.

"You weren't going to tell my son the truth about the betrothal. Tell him how you've been living in that man's house ever since his wife died. Wasn't that where you've been all this time, after your uncle found you on the streets of London and dragged you back here? The man felt pity for you, and to save you from shame, he allowed you to live in his house. Everyone in Patterson Village knows that you've been living in sin with a man old enough to be your grandfather. And now you want to confuse my son."

Mae saw the look on Herbert's face and knew that he was listening to his mother. The woman was lying, but it seemed as if he was set to believe her. It was the end for them, and without a further word Mae turned to walk away.

"Yes, leave right now. Go, and never come back. Return to your old lover and leave my son alone."

Herbert was rooted to the ground in shock. Who was telling the truth? Should he believe Mae's words that she'd been locked up by her uncle for four years or should he believe his mother? Was it possible for someone to be kept locked up for all that time without attempting to escape, or had Mae been trying to pull the wool over his eyes?

He was staring at Mae as she walked away and failed to see the triumphant look in his mother's eyes. When Mrs. Patterson saw the confused look on her son's face, she gloated inwardly. She had him doubting the young woman, and that was a good sign. It would be very easy to get him to obey her now and marry Bella Lester, a woman she wholly approved of. The usurper was gone from their lives forever.

"Come, Herbert." Her voice became gentle and soothing. "I'm sorry that you had to find out about Mae this way."

"I can't believe that Mae would betray our love like this," Herbert murmured as he allowed his mother to lead him back to the house.

PART IV
OVERRULED

THE BRIGHT ROAD TO FEAR

Once he got to the house, Herbert pulled away from his mother. His emotions were raw, and he needed to be alone so his mind could process the shocking information he'd just received.

"Herbert?" He'd never heard his mother's voice being so soft, and it irritated him because he felt as if she was patronizing him.

"Ma, I want to be alone for now," he said in a quiet voice.

"But we haven't finished Christmas Day lunch, and we have visitors waiting in the dining room."

"Give them my apologies," he said and turned to walk to his bedchamber. He climbed the stairs to the first floor like an old man and never once turned back to see if his mother was still down below.

Elaine Patterson wanted to call her son back, but she restrained herself. She was a shrewd woman, and she knew when to retreat. She'd pushed him, and he was at his breaking point.

A cold and calculating look entered her eyes. She had sowed the seed of doubt in his mind, and now she had to let it take root and grow. If she pushed Herbert too much, he would push back, and then everything she'd worked so hard to achieve would unravel.

No, she had to give her son his space or else she might ruin everything.

"Patience, Elaine," she murmured to herself. She would be patient and steer her son in the direction she wanted him to go. Once he was malleable, it would be easy to make him see that marrying Bella Lester was the right thing to do.

Of course, she knew that Bella didn't love Herbert. But Bella loved Patterson Estate and the prestige it would bring her, and when the time came, she would make a good mistress. Bella was just like her, and this estate needed a woman who was tough enough to run it.

Herbert was weak like his father, putting his emotions before sensibility, and that made for a poor manager. Elaine hadn't given her life for this estate only for it to slip out of her hands. Her cousin Roger had never given up hope of one day becoming the master of this estate. And worse, he had two sons who were about

Herbert's age who considered themselves as being entitled to this estate.

But that would never happen, not while Elaine was alive. Herbert would marry Bella and beget children, and her progeny would inherit and own this land forever.

Then she remembered that John Lester had informed her that the family would be leaving home on the morrow to visit some friends and would return in the New Year.

Elaine frowned. She had to impress it upon them not to leave because they were now very close to winning the prize. Bella had to stay behind so that they could begin making wedding plans as soon as possible.

After hastily dismissing her Christmas lunch guests, Elaine walked next door to put her plans in motion. The undesirable element was gone, and it was time to move forward with her remaining plans.

Darkness rolled over him in waves as he lay immobile on his bed. Herbert didn't know what day it was because he'd lost his mind when his mother told him that Mae was betrothed to another man.

His heart was crushed, and he'd locked himself inside his bedchamber, refusing to let anyone inside at all. No amount of begging on his mother's part had gotten him to open the door.

Then, as if from afar, he heard his dead father's gentle voice.

"You, my son, have a gentle heart like mine. I pray that it will remain tender always."

Herbert had been fourteen at the time, and his father had started showing signs of weakness from the illness that would eventually kill him three years later. At the time, Herbert hadn't even known that his father was ill, even though he'd lost weight. On that particular day, they were seated in the arbour, his father's favourite spot all year round.

It was Edwin who had planted the beautiful roses in the garden and constructed a greenhouse. He spent nearly all his waking hours in the greenhouse just to escape from the coldness in his house. Edwin had worked hard to grow the beautiful roses that adorned their home all year round.

"One day, all this will belong to you, and you'll be a very wealthy man," his father had told him. "Be careful to keep your soul pure and your heart tender towards everyone, my son. Don't ever let anyone influence you into becoming so hard inside that you don't feel the pain of others."

Herbert sighed and turned over in his bed. He dearly missed his father, and his death had devastated him. Even now, nearly six years later, he felt the pain as if his pa had just recently died. Herbert knew that if his father were still alive, he would never have allowed his mother to dictate to him the terms of his life.

When he was younger, Herbert had thought that his father was a weak man, for his mother had said it often enough. But after serving in the army and sharing his life with hundreds of other soldiers on the other side of the world, Herbert had learnt to respect the man that his father had been. It was very sad that he'd only come to that knowledge after his father was gone.

"Oh, Pa, you were a peacemaker and a very gentle man, but everyone thought you were weak," Herbert murmured.

It was also while serving in the army that Herbert had learnt that meekness wasn't weakness. If anything, a meek person was stronger than all the bullies because he knew he was strong but kept himself under control.

"I promise that here and now I'll strive to be a better man," he whispered as he got out of bed and wrinkled his nose in disgust. Now that he was back to his senses, he felt ashamed of how unkempt his person and his bedchamber was.

One of the virtues that had been drilled into him and his brother officers in the military was the need for cleanliness.

"*Cleanliness is next to godliness,*" was the favourite quote of one of their superiors, and the man had made sure that whether the unit was in the barracks or on a field mission, their quarters were kept spic and span.

Herbert drew back the drapes and opened the long windows to let fresh air in. A blast of cold air hit him and he shivered, but he didn't shut the window. He wanted the foul smell gone from his bedchamber.

"That's much better," he murmured as he walked to the door and turned the key and opened it. A servant was waiting outside, and Herbert knew that his mother had put the young man of about eighteen up to it. He stood attentively and waited for instructions.

"Please get me some hot water for my bath," Herbert instructed in a mild voice. "Where is my mother?"

"Mrs. Patterson told me to inform you, if you asked, that she's over at Mr. Lester's house to continue with preparations for your wedding with Miss Bella," the young man said innocently. "Master Herbert, shall I instruct the cook to prepare something for you to eat?"

Herbert nodded. "Thank you. That would be nice."

Once he was clean and replenished, Herbert felt much better. He needed to find Mae and make things right with her. Now that he'd had time to think things over, he realised that no matter what she had done, he loved her deeply, and he was willing to overlook all her faults. She could be redeemed, and he refused to give up on their love. It didn't matter if she was ruined. He loved her and was willing to do anything to make her his wife. His mother would have to understand that he wasn't going to be pushed around.

He was whistling as he passed through the small gate that separated their two estates. He ran into a servant girl who was coming out of the kitchen coop and called out to her.

"Miss, would you be so kind as to find Miss Mae and tell her that I'd like to see her, please?"

The young maid gave him a nervous look. She was carrying a basket of eggs and he feared that she would drop it, so he reached out and took it from her hands.

"What is it, Miss? Why do you look so scared? I'm not here to cause you any trouble. Please, just go into the house and tell Mae that Herbert wants to see her."

"Mae isn't here," the maid blurted out.

"Where is she?" Herbert felt despair welling up within him. "Has she gone back to Mr. Watson's house? Is that where she is?"

"What?" The girl scowled fiercely.

"I understand that Miss Mae was living in Mr. Watson's house since his wife died last year. Is that where she is?"

Herbert was surprised when the young woman gave him an indignant look. "I don't know what you've been hearing, but Miss Mae is a proper and virtuous lady. I'll not stand here and have you besmirching her good name with falsehoods like that."

"I'm sorry, but my mother told me that Miss Mae is engaged to be married to Mr. Watson, and she's been living with him for a while now."

"She'd like that now, wouldn't she," the maid hissed. "For your information, Miss Mae was kept locked up in her uncle's attic for the past four years, and I should know. I was the one who was instructed to attend to her, and much as it displeased me, I was allowed to only give her one meal a day. On Christmas Day, Mr. Lester told Mae that he wanted her to be married to Mr. Watson because the man has money. Mae is a good woman and she said that she would rather die than betray the man she loved." The maid paused and took a deep breath. "Mae showed me the locket that her soul mate gave her." Herbert's heart skipped a beat. "Mae said that only death would make her give up hope on her beloved. I was the one who helped her escape from the attic, and if Mr. Lester or his wife or those nasty daughters of theirs find out, it will be the end for me."

"You must be Sandy then," Herbert said. "Mae told me that you had helped her to get out of the house." He smiled but her face remained stoic. "I promise you that I won't tell anyone what you share with me. But why didn't Mae try to escape before? And why did she do it now?"

"Mae has no other relatives in the world and kept hoping that her beloved would one day return and save her. Then that hoity toity Miss Bella taunted her by telling her that she was getting married." Sandy frowned as if remembering something. "You're that Master Herbert, aren't you? Why didn't you ever come to save Mae?"

"Because I didn't know that she was still in the house and locked up in the attic. Her uncle told me that she had run away from home." He didn't want to get into too many details.

Sandy snorted. "Locked up is what Mae was, and for four good years. I find it hard to believe that such a sweet woman as Mae could be related to that brood of vipers."

Herbert still couldn't get over the shock of what he was hearing. "So, are you trying to tell me that Miss Mae never once left this house?"

"I'm telling you that Miss Mae has been her uncle's prisoner for these past four years. She convinced me to help her escape so she could come and warn you not to marry Miss Bella."

"She didn't come back to the house after she left my place on Christmas Day?"

Sandy shook her head. "The last time I saw Mae was three days ago, on Christmas Day, when I gave her the maid's uniform and helped her to escape from the house."

"Thank you," Herbert said as he handed her back the basket of eggs. He then retraced his steps back home and to his bedchamber, where he sat at his dressing table for a long while. Then he began to reflect on all the things his mother had told him about Mae.

Why had he allowed her to sow a seed of doubt in his mind? Why had he let her evil words sink into his heart three days ago? By now, Mae could be anywhere and in trouble. Three days was a long time, but then he realised that servants could also speak falsehoods. Sandy might be defending Mae because she was her friend. He needed to find out the truth once and for all.

It was Mr. Watson himself who confirmed to Herbert that he'd never set his eyes on Mae. He didn't even know what she looked like. It took some cunning and stealth on Herbert's part because he didn't want the man to become suspicious of his motives for asking about Mae.

Mr. Watson had been his father's acquaintance, and on the pretence of looking in on him to offer his condolences on the passing of his wife a year ago,

Herbert made his way to the man's house. He even had a bouquet of flowers to lay on the dead woman's grave, and he handed these to his host.

"Thank you. These are very beautiful." Mr. Watson received the flowers and placed them on a table in the hallway. "Your father was my friend," Mr. Watson said. He was middle aged and had a pot belly and receding hairline. "Edwin taught me how to grow flowers, but I'm afraid mine don't come out as beautiful as these ones." He pointed at the bouquet Herbert had brought him. "Would you like to see my garden? I don't have a greenhouse, but a few of the plants are still in bloom regardless of the snow. There's nothing as uplifting to the soul as a garden full of flowers in the spring. My garden just bursts with colour and sweet scent in spring, and I have your father to thank for that."

Herbert agreed to be given a tour of the garden because the inside of Mr. Watson's house was depressing. It didn't matter that the air outside was chilly. Herbert didn't relish the thought of sitting in the musty house.

Even though his mansion was large and the man was very wealthy, there was dust everywhere in the living room. Added to that were the four children ranging from three to ten years old running all around the house. It seemed to Herbert that the children were ill behaved, and nobody was taking good care of them. The harassed looking servant who was running after them looked like she was at her wits end. But Mr.

Watson merely looked on indulgently, not once rebuking his offspring for their bad behaviour.

Herbert recalled that Mr. Watson had been married in his youth, but after twenty years of a childless marriage, his first wife had died. Then he'd remarried and begotten four children with his second wife. She'd died during childbirth last year, and the baby with her, else there would have been five children in the house.

"I miss the days when your father would come over and give me some gardening tips." The two men stood on the veranda and looked out at the garden. Just as the man had said, there were one or two rose bushes with drooping flowers on them, the light stems weighed down by snowflakes.

"My first wife Brigitte used to love sitting in the garden during spring. And because your father was a very generous man, he would bring her some flowers every day when she fell ill and couldn't leave the house. Those flowers cheered her up very much."

"I'm very sorry for your double loss."

"Well, death is part of life, and those of us who are still alive must carry on living," Mr. Watson grinned. "In fact, soon I'll be taking another wife. I'm told she's young and very beautiful and will bear me many children. You might be knowing the girl." He looked enquiringly at Herbert, who shook his head. "Well, her uncle is Mr. Lester, who I believe is your neighbour."

"Mr. Lester is our neighbour, but I can't say that I know his niece. You see, I've been serving in the army and working in London. I only just got back recently because I've been thinking about settling down myself."

"Oh, yes." Mr. Watson scratched his chin. "I remember reading a notice in the newspaper about your own upcoming nuptials to Miss Bella Lester."

"Yes, Sir." Herbert grinned. He wanted to soften the man so he could find out more information and get to the truth.

"Congratulations are in order then."

Herbert gave a slight bow. "Thank you, Sir."

"Good, good." Mr. Watson rubbed his hands together. "Which reminds me, I need to place a notice in the newspapers about my upcoming marriage to the delightful Miss Mae." Then he frowned. "Though I find it strange that I've never once set my eyes on my intended bride. It's on her uncle's word that I know that she's beautiful. It's a pity you don't know the girl, or I would ask you more about her."

Herbert nodded slowly. "It's strange indeed, but why haven't you ever met your intended bride? Even I get to see my betrothed once a day, and when I was away, we used to send each other sweet letters."

"Well, I trust my good friend, John Lester. He promised me that he would get the girl to agree to a marriage between us. You see, John and I have an agreement. He's been having trouble lately, and things are looking bleak for him financially. I know it's because that wife of his and his daughters spend money like there's no tomorrow. I told him that he should have borrowed a leaf from me. I don't overindulge my wives, and that's why I'm a very wealthy man. It's a terrible thing to work so hard for my money and then have some woman come in and spend it as if she helped me acquire it." Herbert hid his distaste of the man. "When John came up with the idea of marrying off his niece to me, I agree to pay him the sum of …" The man named a figure that made Herbert want to throttle him. "We agreed that as soon as I marry the girl, I will pay him that money, and then she'll become my wife and take care of my children."

"You must have at least seen the girl when you visited Mr. Lester," Herbert insisted. "What man commits to marrying a woman he's never once set his eyes on?"

The man scratched his chin thoughtfully. "Believe me, I've been over to John's house on a number of occasions for social gatherings, but not once did he bring the girl so I could see her. Once, when I insisted on meeting my intended bride, I was informed that she'd travelled to Pembroke to visit her mother's relatives. But John made a strong promise to me that by the fifth day of the New Year, I will be marrying Mae Chester."

When Herbert left Mr. Watson's house after declining an offer of refreshments, he knew that he'd been deceived by his mother. Mae had been ill treated by her relatives, who had wanted to benefit from her. Her uncle had intended to sell her off against her wishes and he, Herbert, had made it easier for Mae to continue suffering. He hadn't protected his love and now she was out there in the world all alone and very vulnerable.

"They will pay," he hissed through clenched teeth as he made his way back home. And the very first person he would confront would be his mother.

PLANS FOR VENGEANCE

Herbert's mother hadn't returned home by the time he got back from Mr. Watson's house, and he knew that she was still next door at Mr. Lester's house.

It was time for Mae to be avenged, but first he needed to hear what those wicked people had to say, what other lies they would spew out.

He found his mother seated with her hosts in the living room of their house.

"There you are," she called out happily once the same maid he'd met before led him into the living room. "I told the servant to let you know where I was so you could join us when you finally woke up." Mrs. Patterson turned to her hosts. "Herbert has been working so hard as an aide for one of the commanders in the army. That's why he's been resting all these days. But since he's here now, why don't we carry on?"

He glanced around him with displeasure but then decided not to show his hand yet. Once all niceties were dispensed with, he was invited to sit. Mr. and Mrs. Lester were present, as well as Bella and his mother. He briefly wondered where the other Lester girl was, then dismissed her out of his mind. She wasn't important to him at all.

"This seems like an interesting gathering," Herbert said. "Why are we here?" His tone was still mild. "Mother, what's going on?"

"Herbert, let's not start again," Mrs. Patterson said in exasperation. There was something about her son that troubled her. He wasn't the same confused man he'd been three days ago.

Herbert decided that this lot didn't deserve any more courtesy from him. "Well, I think I know why this coven has gathered," he said, and everyone gasped at the insult. "If anyone dares to mention the nonsense that was printed in the newspapers, there'll be trouble for sure."

His eyes moved around the room, and no one could look at him. They stayed longer on Bella, and she decided to give him a demure look. She sat there looking very innocent and harmless, but he knew how cunning and manipulative she was. She actually reminded him of his mother, and he grimaced. The woman probably thought that, in the presence of her parents and his mother, she could manipulate him.

Doubtless she thought that they all had him cornered and that he would be complaisant to their whims. His eyes narrowed, and he nearly laughed out loud at how ridiculous their plans were. They had no idea that they'd made a huge mistake. His was not a complaisant nature, especially not after serving in the military for a number of years.

He'd left home a grieving, scared, and timid boy, but a courageous and bold man had returned in that scared lad's place. Over the years, he'd seen how his mother had manipulated his father and made his life miserable.

Looking at Bella and how she reminded him of his mother made him shudder visibly. The woman rated herself very highly. He admitted that she was beautiful, sophisticated, and well educated, and she clearly considered these attributes to be enough to win his heart and love.

He wanted to tell her that no amount of beauty or sophistication would ever make him forget his first and only true love, Mae. There was a slight sneer on his face as he turned to look at his mother. She was whispering something to Mr. Lester and paused midsentence when she noticed his gaze on her.

His mother was obsessed with the idea of him marrying a girl from a good family, one who would bolster his social standing and present her with a grandson and heir to the vast wealth left by his grandfather. Her constant nagging only exasperated him, and her craftiness was coming to an end today. He was here to tell them, once and for all, that he wasn't the least bit interested in the beautiful Miss Bella Lester, even if she was served to him on a golden platter. And knowing what he did now, about how these people had treated Mae, he was going to be very ruthless.

"Well?" He demanded from no one in particular. "Why isn't anyone saying anything?"

Mr. Lester cleared his throat. "Son, I'm glad that you decided to join us, even though I don't have good news for you."

Herbert wanted to scream at the man and tell him not to call him 'son.' He had a father whom he loved very much, even if he'd been dead for nearly six years.

"What news?" Herbert's voice was very polite, though he was bristling inside.

"It's about my niece." Mr. Lester looked slightly uncomfortable.

"Well, what about your niece?"

"She's dead," Mr. Lester blurted out, and Herbert felt as if someone had kicked him hard in the stomach, as if someone had torn his heart out of his chest. No, it couldn't be true. He refused to believe that his lovely Mae was dead. It took him a few minutes to calm down, and he hoped that no one had noted his reaction to the dreadful news.

"What happened to Mae?" His voice was hoarse, and he cleared his throat. "How and when did she die?"

It was his mother who responded to the question. "Son, I told you that the girl was good for nothing. Like every other ingrate who had ever walked this earth, that girl chose to bite the hands that fed her. For years, Mr. Lester fed and clothed the girl, but what did she do in return?"

"What did she do, Mother?" His eyes were fixed on Mr. Lester, who was looking very sanctimonious. "Mr. Lester, what is Mae supposed to have done now?"

"Son, don't be taken in by that girl's innocent looks. She was a schemer and very cunning. Can you believe that she stole my wife's expensive jewellery and clothes and ran away to London on Christmas Day?" Mr. Lester shook his head. "And as if that wasn't enough, she had the audacity to try and use my name to get herself employed by a good family. Before they could even write to me to confirm, she stole from them but was arrested and taken to Newgate Prison."

Herbert's heart skipped a beat.

"She was hanged for her crimes," his mother put in. "And I say good riddance to such vermin. At least the world now has one less criminal walking its streets."

Herbert bowed his head and remained silent for a long while. The story sounded all made up because the one thing he knew deep within his heart was that his Mae wasn't guilty of the horrible things they were accusing her of. While it was true that she might have changed in the four years since he'd last seen her, he refused to believe that her character had become degraded to the point where she became a thief.

He raised his head and took a deep breath. These people, all of them, were guilty of Mae's death if at all that was true. They had tormented her and led her into this.

"So what you're trying to tell me is that within three days Mae reached London, robbed a family, and was tried and hanged?" The story sounded ridiculous to his own ears, and from the way they all fidgeted in their chairs, he knew he had them.

"I want you to all listen to me very carefully." His voice was very quiet and calm. "My Mae is no thief, and that story you're telling me sounds like a fable. And if perchance it's true and she ended up in prison and dead, it's because you wicked people sent her there. The Mae I know would never do any of the terrible things you're accusing her of. Even if she took Mrs. Lester's jewellery, don't you think that counts as payment for the enslavement she suffered at your hands for all these years? She is supposed to be your relative, but you treated her worse than a servant and never paid her at all. So, if she took what you claim she did, good for her then, for it's just payment for labour given."

Mrs. Lester gasped but he ignored her. His mother held out a hand.

"Herbert," she pleaded. "The Mae you knew four years ago was a different person. By the time you saw her on Christmas Day, she was rotten to the core."

"Stop!" Herbert roared, startling his mother. "Don't you dare to open your mouth and say another false word about Mae. Watch your words, or so help me, there's going to be trouble in this house."

"Son, please listen to us. I know she presented herself to you as an innocent person, but she wasn't."

"The last time I listened to you people, three and a half years ago, you told me that Mae had gone back to Pembroke. You knew that I was going overseas to serve in the army and so wouldn't have the chance and time to check up on your story. Well, two years ago when I returned to England, I travelled to Pembroke and met your cousin Morgan." He saw Mr. Lester turn pale. "Cousin Morgan confirmed what I had suspected all along. Mae wasn't there; she'd never been there. When I finally saw her three days ago, on Christmas Day, she told me that you," he pointed at Mr. Lester, "had kept her imprisoned in your attic for four years. Now you've seen that I know that truth and have decided to come up with another cock and bull story."

"She was lying." Mr. Lester was sweating, no doubt as he saw his testimony falling apart. "That girl was nothing but a troublemaker and the bane of our lives. She ran away when she was fourteen, and we paid someone to find and bring her back home. She was a danger to herself and others."

"Ran away, you said?" Herbert stared at the man incredulously. "First you said she had gone to live with her relatives in Pembroke. Then my mother said she's been living with Mr. Watson in sin. Now the story has changed again, and you say that she ran away." His lips tightened. "That makes me know for sure that everything you've ever told me about Mae is a lie. And I won't sit here and listen to you spewing out lies against the woman that I love. If it's true that she's dead, then all of you are to blame. All of you, without exception, are criminals. And believe me, for as long as I have breath in my body, I'm going to search for the truth and clear Mae's name. I'll bring all your crimes against Mae to light, and we'll see if you'll still maintain your respectability."

He then turned to Bella, who shrank at the vehemence in his eyes. He pointed an accusing finger at her. "I'm giving you a final warning. Don't ever cross my path or so help me, I won't be responsible for my actions. Just as you went around spreading lies and rumours that you and I are engaged, you better retract those falsehoods and clear me from this sham, or I'll be forced to sue you for defamation."

He stood there glaring at them, and no one could meet his eyes.

"Be sure of one thing. I'll find Mae, whether she's dead or alive, and on the day that I do, there will be trouble such as has never been seen in Sheffield, or even the whole of England. You all better pray that I find Mae alive, because if she's dead, all of you," and he pointed at each one of them including his mother. "You're all to blame for Mae's misfortunes and I'll send you to your graves with much trouble upon your heads." He clenched his fists and then struck the glass table hard so that it shattered into thousands of pieces, startling everyone. Then he marched out of the house.

When he got home, he couldn't settle down because of the rage within him. Mae wasn't dead. She couldn't be. He entered the living room with clenched fists, and with a loud roar, picked up a vase that his mother had received from someone as a gift and hurled it with great force across the room, where it crashed against the wall and splintered into hundreds of pieces. Next to go was the glass topped coffee table, and by the time the servants came to check on what was happening, the living and dining rooms were a mess of glass and splintered wood.

One servant was to remark later that he'd never seen a man look as wild as Master Herbert did at that moment.

Herbert noticed the servants standing in the doorway leading to the kitchen and growled at them. "What are you looking at?" They all fled because no one wanted to confront him with the way that he looked.

Still fuming, he made his way to the study and opened the safe, pulling out two pistols that had belonged to his father. Herbert knew that he looked like a madman as he rushed out of the house, waving the pistols in the air. Anyone who saw him coming scampered to safety. When he burst into Mr. Lester's house again, he wasn't thinking clearly.

"You'll pay, all of you!" He pointed one pistol at his mother and the other at Mr. Lester.

"Son…" His mother looked terrified.

"Shut up and listen to me, all of you." He sniffed. "I want Mae. Bring Mae back or you can start digging your graves, for I'll not hesitate to end your lives. It you don't bring Mae to me, then I'll shoot all of you, and once you're all dead, I'll burn these houses to the ground. That's my warning to you. I'm going back home, Mother. Make sure that you bring Mae to me, or else don't come back home." Once again he turned his eyes to Bella, who shrank back at the pure loathing in them. "And as for you, I don't know where you ever got the idea that I could be interested in marrying you. I love Mae, who is worth thousands of you. If you don't retract that notice from the newspapers, I'll make you regret ever knowing me, and no man in England will ever want to marry you."

And with those harsh words Herbert left, but not before he had brought a few pictures on Mr. Lester's wall crashing down. He arrived home and entered his bedchamber, where once again he locked himself inside.

THE WOUNDED SOUL

It was while she was on the midday train to London that Mae realized that her hand was clutching something. Mercifully, the third-class coach, for that was all she could afford, was half empty. Apparently not many people used the midday train on Christmas Day. She had easily found a seat next to the window where she could look out if she didn't want to speak to the person next to her. The seat beside her remained empty and she was glad, because the last thing she needed was someone trying to make conversation with her.

Heavily, wearily, Mae leaned her head against the wall. Her eyes were full of tears. She wiped them away, but more kept coming. She felt completely shattered, torn up, and ripped apart.

Could a wounded heart ever heal, she wondered? She'd spent the last four years dreaming about Herbert and how he would march up the house like a knight in shining armour, demanding to know where her uncle was holding her captive. If he wasn't told, he would force his way through and enter the house. He would then break down all the doors until he found her and carry her to safety, where they would be together forever.

"Imbecile," she silently berated herself. A man like Herbert could never be with a woman like her. Even though he'd declared his love for her and willingness to rescue her, he'd quickly turned his back on her when his mother spewed out her lies. He'd chosen to believe that she was the kind of woman who would live with a man without being married to him. That told her just how low he thought of her.

Her empty hand went to the string around her neck, and she touched the locket nestled in her chest. But unlike other times, when the piece of jewellery had given her comfort, this time it seemed to mock her. Her fingers squeezed around the chain which Herbert had given her. Now she had the full set and knew that it was a very costly piece of jewellery. One mind had her thinking about selling it.

Though she had some money which she and Sandy had shared after selling the handkerchiefs over the years, it wouldn't last her long. She really needed to find work to do once she got to London, or else she would end up on the streets, where terrible dangers lurked, especially in the dark.

Mae smiled through her tears as she once again spread on her lap the newspaper that Mrs. Patterson had handed her. Ignoring the pages filled with personal notices of births, deaths, engagements, and marriages, she searched through the employment vacancies.

Much as Mae had hated living in her uncle's house because of the way she'd been treated, she was grateful for the few allies she'd made while there.

Her uncle and aunt had strictly forbidden their daughters' governess from teaching Mae anything. Mae would sneak to the schoolroom and listen at the doorway, but if her aunt found her, she earned herself a sound beating. Mrs. Brown had done her best to ensure that Mae didn't remain illiterate. It was because of the woman who herself had had very little formal education that Mae knew how to read and write. Mrs. Brown had also taught Mae how to sew and embroider, which was what had kept the young woman sane in her days of bondage. As Mae's eyes perused the newspaper, she saw many advertisements for various occupations, from leech collectors to mud larks, but none of them appealed to her. She was searching for a position that would come with board, since she knew that as a young woman alone on the streets of London, she would be very vulnerable and easy prey for unscrupulous and wicked people.

Putting all thoughts of Herbert and Bella and their upcoming nuptials aside, she buried her face in the advertisements. By the time the train rolled into Paddington Station, she'd memorized a few street names. It was late in the afternoon and Mae knew that she wouldn't get anything accomplished in the short hours of the day that were left. Being a holiday, she doubted that many places that might provide work for her would be open anyway.

Besides, she needed to find herself lodgings in a safe place. Mae was pushed and jostled by people hurrying in all directions, and she clutched her thin shawl close to her body, remembering that she was still dressed in the maid's uniform that Sandy had given her. Her destination was the residential area on Paddington Street where she'd lived with her parents. Though she'd only been four years old when she lost her parents, Mae could recall the road they'd taken every Sunday after church to the railway station.

Being very poor, and with no extra money for treats and comforts, her father would hoist her up on his shoulders and hold her there with one hand while the other went around her mother's waist. Then he would bring them to Paddington Station, where they would watch the trains coming and going in different directions. Once in a while, when he had an extra shilling or two, he would buy them some roasted corn on the cob or soft candy.

Mae noticed that London had changed in the eleven years that she'd been away, and she wondered if she would find anyone who remembered her as a child. Probably not, and she wasn't sure that their old neighbours would even still be living in the same place. She wasn't sure if the slum dwelling that she and her parents had lived in would even still be there, not with the reforms that were being done to change the face of London. She'd read something of the sort in the newspaper which was still clutched in her hand.

As she trudged along, she caught sight of a large notice stuck on the window of an old but respectable looking building. 'Room to let,' the sign said.

Gathering all her courage, she walked up to the front door and knocked. It was immediately opened by a shabbily dressed woman with jaded brown eyes. The woman was anywhere between thirty to forty years old.

"Yes?" She asked tiredly, and Mae noticed that she was missing her two front lower teeth.

"I need a room," Mae said. "I saw the notice on the window and came to ask if the room is still available."

"There are rooms available," Mae was told, and her heart lifted up in a silent song. "Four shillings per week for bed and breakfast only."

"May I please come in?" Mae could smell onions being fried, and her stomach rumbled, reminding her that the last meal she'd taken was yesterday's ration in her uncle's house. It was hard to believe that it was still Christmas Day and her birthday. She also didn't want to remain standing on the doorstep, for her presence was attracting the wrong kind of attention.

"Come in then." The woman stepped aside, and Mae entered into what seemed to be a small parlour. It was dusty, and she immediately sneezed.

"Don't you have any luggage?" The woman looked at her suspiciously.

"I first came to find a place to stay, and then I'll go back to the railway station to bring my luggage. You see, I just arrived from Sheffield and didn't want to haul my luggage around without first knowing where I was going." Mae silently begged for forgiveness for the lie she was telling, but she couldn't risk being tossed out again. Though this house wasn't too clean, she felt that she could trust the woman standing before her.

"I run a clean and respectable house here and won't be accepting anyone looking or acting suspicious. Also, I won't accept you bringing any visitors to your room."

"I promise you that I'm a respectable person, Ma'am," Mae said. Her pleading eyes must have touched something in the woman's heart, for she locked the front door and motioned for Mae to follow her. They walked down a long corridor with rooms on either side, but the doors were locked. They entered the kitchen, which was at the far end of the corridor, and Mae felt her mouth begin to water when she smelled the aroma wafting in the air.

"Breakfast is served at seven in the morning without fail. If you're late, you'll miss it. I expect you to keep your room tidy, and I'll show you where to empty your chamber pot each morning. I lock the doors strictly at six o'clock every evening. Though this is one of the better neighbourhoods in downtown London, I have to be careful not to let in any riffraff. That's the reason every room has a chamber pot, since no one can open these doors until six in the morning."

On and on the instructions went, but Mae's mind was fixated on the bubbling pot over the large open fireplace. There was a table in the middle of the kitchen.

"This is where all my lodgers take their meals. Are you hungry? Supper is one shilling, and I don't serve lunch because I expect my boarders to be out there earning a living and not lazing around the house."

"Should I pay you now for the week's board and today's supper?"

"That will be five shillings." The woman held out a hand as if expecting Mae to make some excuse for not having the money. Mae pulled out a hanky from her inner pocket and untied one of the edges. She counted out five shillings from the seven she had and placed them in the woman's hand.

"Thank you," Mae said, and the woman looked at her in surprise.

"Why are you thanking me? I should be the one doing it," she said as she tucked the money away into her bosom.

Mae smiled. "For opening your door to me. I promise that I won't give you any trouble."

"And what is your name, Child?"

"Mae Chester."

"Welcome to London, Mae Chester. You can call me Sabine Walker or simply Sabine."

For the next two days, Mae woke up very early, and after cleaning her room that was on the first floor she went down and cleaned the parlour and kitchen as well. She washed all the dishes, pots, and pans that had been used the previous night.

Mrs. Walker had told her that there were five other lodgers in the house, and she'd heard them coming and going at various times, but everyone was usually home by six and the doors were locked tight. In the two days that she'd been here, Mae had met a couple of them along the corridors, but for the most part she was careful to stay out of sight, since they were men. She never once forgot Sandy's warning to be careful around adult men.

Once she was done with the cleaning and had taken the simple breakfast offered, a cup of black tea and a thick slice of bread with a thin slice of cheese, she would leave the house in search of work.

On the third day, as she finished cleaning the kitchen, Mrs. Walker came in. The woman smiled at her. "I've had this lodging house for the past three years after my husband and his mother passed away. But no one has ever helped me in this way. I do all the cooking and cleaning by myself. You're a good and kind person, Miss Mae Chester."

Mae had since told her host a little bit about her life and that she didn't have any more luggage, save for what she was dressed in. The woman said she understood and accepted her as she was, even giving her two old frocks, which were still in good condition. They had belonged to Mrs. Walker's mother-in-law, and though they were ill fitting, it was better than nothing.

"Keeping our home clean is the least I can do, considering how kind you've been to me."

"I just wish I was making enough money to offer you full time work here as a housekeeper, so you wouldn't have to go out on the streets, where it's not safe for one like you. I worry a lot when you're gone, and I pray for you every day."

Her kind words touched Mae's heart. "Thank you so much for your kindness to me, and I promise that I'll always be careful when I'm out there."

The next few days passed swiftly for Mae, and her life was busy and fulfilling. Because she helped a lot around the lodging house, Mrs. Walker provided her with supper for free. That meant that Mae was able to save whatever little money she made from the casual jobs she picked up every day. Her desire was to find a more permanent position so she could earn more money.

But no matter how much she worked and kept herself busy, it wasn't enough to fill the emptiness that had taken residence inside her. The feelings of loneliness and despair often caught up with her late at night when she was in her small room. She would reflect on what her life might have been if she and Herbert had ended up together. If he'd kept his promise to protect and care for her, she would probably be in a very different place.

With each passing day, Mae felt emptier, even though she always had a smile fixed on her face. She lived in dread of the day that she would find out through the newspapers that Herbert and Bella were finally married and starting a new life together.

One of the lodgers, Mr. Plank, brought in a newspaper every day, and he left this in the parlour for anyone who wished to read it. Mae only checked the vacancies section, steering clear of the personals.

Mae knew that for as long as she lived, no other man would ever come close to measuring up to Herbert in her mind and heart. She accepted that she would never belong to another man, and she would keep her heart closed because she couldn't bear suffering such deep anguish and pain again.

Deep sorrow swept over her as the sadness lodged inside her. It was time to forget about Herbert, because she clearly wasn't in any of his thoughts, probably never had been. She wondered how she could possibly still love him after all that had happened.

A few days later, Mae left the house after bidding Mrs. Walker and Mr. Plank farewell. The house looked so much better, and her hostess was happier than when Mae had first come to live in the lodging house. The young woman knew that some of the happiness had to do with having someone to help with the daily chores, but most was because of Mr. Plank, who was a widower and an old soldier.

Through their evening talks, Mae had found out that Mrs. Walker had lost her teeth when her drunk husband had knocked them out. She and Mr. Walker had been married for ten years but never had any children. He'd started drinking heavily and lost his good position as a supervisor in one of the textile mills in Manchester. They were then forced to move back to London to live with his mother in this house.

Sabine Walker had put up with the verbal and physical abuse because she had nowhere to go, being an orphan with no living relatives. Then her husband fell ill, and his mother followed. Within days, both of them were dead. That's when she'd started taking in lodgers, six of them at a time, and Mr. Plank was her most regular one.

"He started coming here three years ago after I lost my husband and mother-in-law. He had lost his wife and needed to get away from his home in Kent. He usually stays for a few months and then returns to take care of his business in Kent."

From her tone, Mae deduced that the woman had a deep fondness for her lodger, and Mae had seen Mr. Plank looking at Sabine Walker adoringly. She wished the two of them would stop being shy and admit that they had feelings for each other, but that wasn't her business. She prayed that they wouldn't break each other's hearts.

Mae was walking past the London Metropolitan Hospital when she felt something, or rather someone, slam hard into her from the back. Irritated, she turned to scold the person, but then realised that it was a small elderly woman. Her blue eyes looked wild, and she was twitching nervously.

"My shawl!" The woman grabbed Mae's red shawl. "You stole my shawl."

People stopped to watch and see what Mae would do as the woman screamed at the top of her voice. At first Mae was shocked by the attack, which was unwarranted, but she quickly realised that the woman wasn't well. The hospital clothes she was garbed in told a story of their own.

Instead of fighting back, as the onlookers expected her to do, Mae started singing softly, praying that her soothing voice would calm the woman down. Then a surprising thing happened! The little woman stopped screaming and struggling and drew closer to Mae like a little child seeking shelter from its mother. Mae continued singing, and when the woman was close enough, she put an arm around her and held her in a gentle embrace. She covered the woman's thin shoulders with her shawl.

The woman sagged against her, and Mae knew that the poor thing was exhausted. She gently moved to the side and out of the path where people were passing. When they were at the wall of the hospital, Mae lowered them both until they were seated on the ground, their feet stretched out before them. She still held onto the woman.

Mae didn't stop singing until she heard the woman's soft snores. People stared at her in disbelief, for her actions were completely unexpected. As they walked away, a few tossed coins at her feet, and she smiled while thanking them. But even as she sat there on the cold ground with the tiny woman in her arms, Mae wondered at human character and the strange desire to look upon the sufferings of others without lifting a hand to help. She was sure that if the tiny old lady had started hitting her, no one in the crowd would have rescued her.

Suddenly, two agitated nurses burst through the small crowd and came to a standstill. They stared at Mae as if seeing an apparition.

"How?" One of the nurses, a blond woman with bright blue eyes, asked in a whisper. She was stockily built, and she wrung her plump hands nervously. "How did you get Mrs. Halliday to calm down enough to fall asleep?"

Mae merely smiled at the nurse.

"Thank you, dear girl," the second nurse said. "Mrs. Halliday hasn't slept a wink since her children brought her to the hospital two weeks ago. She prowls around the corridors of the hospital while screaming and snatching things from people. We've even tried to administer laudanum so she will settle down, but it hasn't worked. You truly are a miracle girl, Miss," the nurse told her.

"She's really cold," Mae said, accepting the hand that reached down to lift her. Mrs. Halliday opened her eyes and looked around her wildly. She opened her mouth to start screaming again, but then she caught sight of Mae, and her face broke into a smile.

"Well, I never!" the first nurse said.

"I want to stay with you." Mrs. Halliday latched onto Mae's right arm. "Susie, please don't leave me," the woman whimpered.

"I won't leave you," Mae murmured soothingly even as she stared helplessly at the nurses.

"Susie, if you leave me again, I'll die," the sick woman said.

"You'll have to come with us," the first nurse pleaded. "Or else we won't get Mrs. Halliday to settle down."

"I was on my way to look for work," Mae said.

"Mrs. Halliday's family is wealthy, and when they hear that you've been able to calm their mother down, you can be sure that they will hire you to be her care giver."

Mae agreed to accompany the nurses as they took Mrs. Halliday back into the hospital. And even if she wanted to, she couldn't have left because the poor woman refused to let go of her hand. One of the nurses gathered the few coins on the ground and pushed them in Mae's pocket. "You earned them," she said when Mae tried to protest.

The two nurses led the way to the private wing of the hospital, and Mae was surprised when they stepped into one of the rooms. It looked like a room from a luxurious hotel.

There was a large bed at one end of the room and a smaller cot on the opposite side. "Can you please get Mrs. Halliday to sleep?" the second nurse asked, and Mae nodded.

"Mrs. Halliday…"

"Susie!" The woman slapped Mae's cheek gently. "You cheeky girl, call me Grandma, as you've always done." Mae looked at the nurses, who nodded. They seemed eager and ready to do anything that would keep the woman calm.

"Grandma, I want you to get into your bed so you can rest. It's getting chilly, and I don't want you to catch cold."

"Susie, will you stay with me as I sleep?" The woman's eyes filled with tears. "Don't leave me here alone."

"I'll be right here where you wake up, Grandma."

The woman allowed Mae to put her to bed. She grabbed hold of Mae's hand. "Stay with me and sing me a song."

"Yes, Grandma." Mae sang a few of the hymns that she knew until the woman's breath slowed down in sleep.

"My dear girl, you're a miracle worker," the plump nurse said. "What's your name?"

"Mae Chester."

"I'm Hilda, and my colleague here is Emily. You don't know how grateful we are to you for what you've done. No one, not even her own children, have been able to calm Mrs. Halliday down. In the past two weeks, her children have brought in about seven care givers, and all of them left after only a few hours of taking care of the poor woman."

"Who is Susie, and why does Mrs. Halliday think that I'm her?"

Hilda and Emily looked at each other, and Mae thought they weren't going to respond to her question. Then Hilda shrugged. "We might as well tell you, so you can understand this poor woman and why she's acting in this manner." At Emily's nod, she went on. "Susie is Mrs. Halliday's granddaughter, or should I say was. Susie passed away a month ago, and Mrs. Halliday hasn't been the same since. According to what Susie's father told us, he's Mrs. Halliday's son, the two of them were very close right from when the girl was born."

"How old was Susie at the time of her death?"

"Eighteen years old. She drowned when her fiancé took her sailing and their boat capsized."

"Oh no, poor woman." Mae looked down at the sleeping woman, resisting the urge to gently stroke her hair. "That's really terrible."

"Mrs. Halliday was inconsolable and became so very ill that her children despaired for her life. This is the first time she's accepted anyone to get close to her without fighting them off. We've had a very difficult time trying to keep her to stay calm."

"But I can't stay here forever." Mae thought about Mrs. Walker. "My landlady will be worried if I don't return home."

"We'll go there if need be and explain to her the situation here, but please, Mae, don't leave Mrs. Halliday's side."

It came as no surprise to everyone when the hospital offered Mae a position as a nurses' assistant so she could take care of patients. In the few days that she was in the hospital, she was able to handle Mrs. Halliday and two other elderly women who were ill. She would sing to them, brush out their hair, and spend most of the time calming them down. She spent the nights in Mrs. Halliday's room, and the woman slept like a baby through the night, much to everyone's relief.

When Mrs. Halliday's family came to visit her the next Saturday, for they came once a week, Mae got to meet them. The two sons and their wives, as well as Mrs. Halliday's two married daughters, were happy to see their mother looking very calm. They all stared at Mae in wonder when the nurses told them how she'd been the only one who had managed to keep their mother calm.

They were even more surprised when their mother remained lucid throughout the visit, though her eyes kept searching for Mae, who hung around the room. At some point, the two men were called to the doctor's office, and they returned, their faces quite grim.

When one of the wives would have asked what news they bore, Mae shook her head because Mrs. Halliday was still wide awake. Finally, she yawned and started nodding off.

"Grandma, we need to take our nap," Mae said gently. "Here, let me help you lie down so you can get some rest."

"Tell these people to go away," Mrs. Halliday said. "But I want you to stay with me."

"Yes, Grandma."

"Susie, you're too good to me," Mrs. Halliday murmured as she drifted off to sleep. The nurses no longer had to sedate her so she could sleep.

"You're a godsend," Marjory, Mrs. Halliday's eldest daughter, told Mae. "We despaired of Mama ever getting her senses back."

"I'm sorry that you heard her calling me Susie." One of the wives bit back a sob at Mae's words. "The nurses told me what happened to Susie. Please accept my deepest condolences on the death of your daughter," Mae spoke in a low voice.

"Mother has been inconsolable," Thomas Halliday said. "Ever since our daughter died, she hasn't had a calm moment. Mama went berserk and even tried to harm herself because of her deep grief. We didn't know what else to do, so we brought her to the hospital. But the doctor says that they've done all they can for our mother. Physically she's healthy, but it's her mental health that has us worried. We've been advised to take her to an asylum which they've recommended, where Mama will receive better care to manage her condition."

"I'll miss her so much." Mae smiled as she looked down at the sleeping woman. It was hard to believe that she'd been here for only a week. It felt like a lifetime! But she also suddenly realised that she'd been very busy and barely had time to think about Herbert. "Mrs. Halliday is such a lovely woman."

"We'd like to propose something to you," Burke, the second son, said, and his brother nodded. "We'd like to hire your services so you can be Mama's private care giver. The doctors and nurses can't stop praising you enough for what you've done for her these past few days."

"What?" Mae couldn't believe what she was hearing.

"Yes," Thomas interjected. "We're ready to pay you twice the wages that you've been receiving while working here. The doctor told us that though the hospital had offered you a position here, they can only pay you little wages. We'll take good care of you as you've taken care of our mother."

"But where will I stay? It's been easy taking care of your mother here in the hospital because a bed," she pointed at her cot in the corner, "was provided for me."

"The institution recommended by the doctor is a private asylum with very good facilities. You and Mama will share a room, as you're doing now."

Mae smiled broadly as she nodded her acceptance.

DARK HOUR BEFORE DAWN

Much as his mother knocked on his door, Herbert refused to open up for her. He put his hands over his ears as if to shut the sound out.

"Herbert, please open this door," she pleaded. "I don't want you doing anything foolish. I'm worried about you because you haven't returned your father's pistols to the safe. They're loaded, and you might hurt yourself"

"Go away, Mother."

"I'm very worried. Please open the door so we can talk and clear all misunderstandings. I didn't mean to hurt you."

"It's not a misunderstanding, Mother. You blatantly lied to me, and I won't open this door until you bring Mae back and I see her with my two eyes."

"Herbert, please." He heard someone sniffing. To his knowledge, he'd never seen his mother shedding a single tear. She didn't cry when his grandfather died and certainly not when his own Pa passed away.

"Mother, stop crying and go away. I don't want to hear anything you have to say."

"How do you expect me to go away when my only child is in danger? I don't want to lose you because you're all I've got, Herbert. Please open the door so we can talk, and I'll do whatever you ask of me."

"No," Herbert shouted. "Just go away and leave me alone."

"I'll be right here if you need me."

Herbert lay on the bed and turned his face away from the door. He didn't want to talk to anyone, least of all his mother. He covered himself with the thick quilt and immediately fell asleep.

When he woke up several hours later, the room was shrouded in darkness and the drapes were still wide open. It was a moonless night, but as his eyes got accustomed to the darkness, he could make out the items of furniture in his room. He felt something poking his side, and when he reached out his hand, he discovered that he'd been lying on his father's pistols.

Carefully rising up from the bed, he picked them up and gently placed them under his bed. Back in the army, the soldiers had always been warned never to sleep with their loaded weapons in their beds or even under their pillows. The weapons could easily discharge their bullets and cause fatalities when a person accidentally rolled on them if the trigger wasn't secure.

His head was throbbing as his stomach growled. It had been a while since his last meal, and he knew that he had to eat if he was to keep his strength up. The house was silent, and he knew that his mother was probably in bed by now. Since all the servants lived away from the manor, he was sure that it was empty.

Grimacing at how dry his mouth was, he tiptoed to the door, unbolted it, and listened to hear if anything would stir. Because the hinges were always well oiled, the door made no sound as he opened it further. Just as he'd expected, the corridor was empty, and the lanterns placed along the wall bathed the whole place in soft light,

He looked towards his mother's chamber, which was two rooms down the corridor from his, and noticed the light under the door. She was still awake!

Easing from his room, his bare feet made no sound as he walked to the staircase and stood on the top landing. There was another lantern in the lobby downstairs, but the house remained silent. He slowly took the stairs, expecting someone to jump out of the shadows, but nothing of the sort happened. Everything was still.

The kitchen was warm, and he could see the fire burning low in the grate. A large cauldron sat on the fire. He could hear it bubbling, the aroma attracting him. He knew that the cook was boiling bones for stock, as she did every night.

His mouth watered as he reached for a bowl from the cabinet, walked over to the boiling pot, and scooped up some soup. The steam hurt his fingers, and he nearly dropped the bowl into the boiling pot, but he managed to save and carry it to the table. He raised the wick on the kitchen lamp and entered the pantry to get himself some bread. He found cured ham, cheese, and a loaf of fresh whole wheat bread.

Once his collection was complete, Herbert made himself a thick sandwich, which he ate with the soup, and he washed everything down with a mug of cold milk. Up until the time he'd joined the army, Herbert had never once set foot in the kitchen to prepare anything for himself. His father had tried to get him to learn how to take care of himself, but his mother had nearly raised the roof with her rage.

"That's what servants are for," she'd screamed. "I don't want my son doing menial tasks like a simpleton. He's the Patterson heir, not some common village lout."

But when he joined the army and got posted abroad, he'd learned the hard way that being independent doesn't make one weak. If anything, it strengthens a person.

After he was replete, he washed whatever dishes he'd used and cleaned the kitchen counter, leaving it as clean as he'd found it. Then he continued to sit at the table, holding his head in his hands. His life had fallen apart, and he felt very weary. All through his time in the army, he'd lived for the moment when Mae would turn eighteen so he could return home, propose, and marry her. He'd dreamed of Mae for four years, during which time she'd grown up into a very beautiful woman. The spots on her face had cleared, leaving her face smooth and soft, but she was very pale, and it was all because she'd been locked up by her uncle for all that time.

After his conversation with Mr. Watson, Herbert thought he knew why Mr. Lester had kept Mae locked up. It was evident that Mr. Lester had hoped to force Mae into marriage with the older man for his own benefit. He must have felt that if Mae continued being free, she would run away from all the mistreatment. Mr. Watson had mentioned that Mae's uncle was doing very badly financially, and so had made arrangements to be paid for her. That was probably why Bella was being pushed at him in the name of securing his future. The thought angered Herbert because he was in charge of his own future, not his mother or anyone else.

He would make them tell him where his Mae was, because he refused to believe that she was dead, as they had said.

✳

For the next few weeks Herbert played a cat and mouse game with his mother. He behaved as if he was a soldier out in enemy territory, so he stocked his room with everything he thought he would need during a siege.

He couldn't do it all on his own, so he took the young servant Miles into his confidence. He made Miles promise not to betray him to his mother.

"I know that you've always dreamed of going to London," he told the younger man. "If you help me in this, I'll pay you enough money to keep you going for a full year until you find your feet while in London."

"Master Herbert, what would you have me do?"

"Water is crucial for me," Herbert told the young man. "Find a way of bringing me water for my bath every single day and emptying my chamber pot. Also, whenever I run out of any supplies, I'll let you know then you can replenish my stock."

"What if your mother finds out that I'm helping you? I'll get into a lot of trouble, for sure."

"No, no, no," Herbert sought to reassure his servant. "If we're careful and you keep your mouth shut, my mother will never find out what we're doing. Don't trust anyone, not even your family, for everyone is terrified of my mother, and if she threatens them, they'll have no choice but to tell her everything. Ignorance is bliss, and the less anyone knows the better for them."

"I, too, am terrified of Mrs. Patterson," Miles said dryly. "If she ever singles me out and asks me, I might not be able to keep anything from her."

"Then make sure you stay out of her way. Work with the horses and stay out in the fields. As my personal servant now, you can always tell Ma that you need to exercise my fine set of horses, and that will keep you out of her way. When evening comes and Ma is busy with other things, you can return and see to my needs."

Miles frowned while shaking his head. He looked scared, "Master Herbert, I don't know if I can pull this off."

"I won't blame you if you want to walk away, but all I'm asking you is that you try and help me. This is very important to me. Also, keep an ear out for any information about the neighbours. I'd like to know what they are up to."

The young man gave him a confused look. "Sir, I don't understand."

Much as Herbert needed his servant's help and cooperation, he was also cautious about divulging too much information to the young man. The less Miles knew, the harder it would be for anyone to coerce any information out of him.

Herbert laughed. "I believe you're aware the Miss Bella and I are engaged to be married."

"But everyone knows that you rejected her," Miles was brave enough to say. "So why should I then watch the neighbours?"

"Just so I can know about any plans they may be having with regards to the engagement."

"This is all about Miss Mae, isn't it, Sir? We've heard whispers about the young woman who was kept a prisoner in her uncle's house, and your mother has warned all of us to inform her if we ever spot Miss Mae around this place."

Herbert nodded., "But don't ever let anyone know that I'm searching for her. Find out all you can from the stable boys who work for Mr. Lester, for I'm sure that gossip is rife. They might just reveal something that will help me know where Miss Mae is."

Miles was a good accomplice, and for several days they were able to hide their actions from Mrs. Patterson, but eventually their luck ran out when one of the other servants threatened to betray Miles to the mistress of the manor.

"Master Herbert, I'm afraid that someone has found out what I've been doing and is now blackmailing me. He says that if I don't give him money, then he'll reveal everything to Mrs. Patterson."

Herbert was silent for a moment. He felt terrible about putting the young man on the spot. Knowing how vicious his mother could be if she felt that she was crossed, he didn't want the man getting into any trouble.

"Who do you live with?" he asked Miles.

"I live alone because my uncle who used to work for your mother died last year, and his wife and children moved away. I took over his cottage and have been living there ever since."

"Good! Now this is what you'll do." Herbert reached into his drawer and pulled out a thick wad of notes. "There's enough money here to get you to London, where you can get the fresh start that you've always longed for. Do you have any relatives living in London?"

"Yes, Sir, my mother's sister, though she's elderly, but I know she'll receive me well. I lived with her for a while after my parents died but had to leave because her husband didn't want me there. Still, Aunt Vera did all she could to protect me. Last year, after my uncle died, Aunt Vera wanted me to go and live with her in London. You see, her daughters, three of them, are married and gone from home, and now she's all alone. It's time for me to take care of her."

"What happened to her husband?"

"He died about two years before Uncle David. At the time, Aunt Vera asked Uncle David if I could go and live with her, but he decided that I needed to first learn how to earn my own living. Also, I like my position, but with all that's happening around here, I believe the time has come for me to leave."

"Don't go back to the cottage to collect anything. From this room, just leave and take the first train out of Sheffield. I don't trust that person not to have already reported you to my mother." Miles nodded. "Do you have anything of importance of sentimental value back at the cottage?"

Miles shook his head. "No Sir, I can easily replace whatever I've left in the cottage because they're just simple clothes."

"Good," Herbert reached into the drawer again and added a few more notes to the first lot. Then he handed all the money to Miles. "Take good care of yourself and stay out of trouble. If you ever need me, just send me a message through the vicar, and I'll do whatever I can to help."

"Thank you, Sir, and I promise to stay out of trouble."

With Miles gone, Herbert began to feel that the walls were closing in on him. His one regret was that he still had no information about Mae's whereabouts. What if she was in trouble and he couldn't reach her? What if she'd ended up in wrong hands and fallen into harlotry just to survive? Herbert knew that he would never forgive himself if something terrible ever happened to Mae. He blamed himself for allowing his mother to get into his head and turn him against Mae, even briefly.

Two days later, as Herbert was sleeping, he was woken up abruptly when his door splintered, and four hefty men bore down on him. He had no time to reach for the pistols that were under still his bed. The men restrained him in a straitjacket, such as was used for dangerous lunatics.

"Let me go," Herbert screamed wildly. Ever since barricading himself in his bedchamber, and with Miles' exit from his life, he hadn't groomed himself, so his hair was unkempt, and his beard had grown longer. "Release me at once!" He tried to struggle, but the restraints were too strong for him.

"Son, I'm doing this for you." His mother stood aside as the men carried him from his bedchamber and took him outside.

"Where are they taking me?"

"To a place where you'll be well looked after." Herbert thought he saw a sheen in his mother's eyes but then told himself that his eyes must be deceiving him. His mother never showed any emotions at all.

"Ma, please stop them."

"I don't want you to hurt yourself and living like a recluse isn't healthy. You're all I have, and once you're cured of your insanity over that worthless girl, then I'll allow you to return home and live a normal life."

Herbert realised that his mother had chosen this dark hour of night to carry out her ambush on him because there were no servants in the house. He knew that struggling would only make the restraints tighter. He also knew that the only way to get out of this situation was by pretending to be subdued, and when he got the chance, he would then fight for his freedom.

PART V
OVERCOMING

BAREFACED DISGUISE

Mae's fingers played with the chain around her neck, touching the locket and rubbing it between two fingers. She'd often thought of visiting a pawn shop or two to get rid of the chain and locket which reminded her of Herbert and brought her nothing but pain. It was only the fact that she couldn't be away from Mrs. Halliday for long that prevented her from getting rid of the items. She also admitted to herself that deep down, she didn't want to get rid of her last and only connection with the love of her life.

It was mid-February now, two months since she'd last seen Herbert, and she was sure that he and Bella were married at last. The thought gave her pain, and sometimes she thought her heart would explode. She also avoided reading newspapers because she didn't want to come face to face with her loss.

Even though Mrs. Halliday's children had paid for subscriptions, so newspapers and magazines were delivered to the asylum every few days, Mae mostly ignored them, but her charge liked to look at the colourful pictures in the magazines, and Mae indulged her without getting too involved. Mrs. Halliday's children wanted her to be well informed and kept up to date on the happenings in the world, hence the reading materials they provided. St. Agatha's Rest and Rejuvenation Home was a very expensive facility, and Mae enjoyed all the luxuries extended to her.

The room they'd been allocated had its own bath and privy, something Mae had never seen before. She was used to outhouses and had never known that indoor plumbing worked in this way. There was plenty of water, both hot and cold, gushing out from the taps, and to Mae it felt as if they were living in a luxurious hotel instead of an asylum.

They were provided with five meals a day, all very delicious and in such large quantities that she started feeling as if she was gaining a lot of weight.

With each passing day, Mae was sad as she noticed that her elderly charge was withdrawing into herself. She had stopped screaming and yelling from the moment Mae became her full care giver, and the bond between them was strong. Mae never stopped thanking God for bringing Mrs. Halliday into her life, for she'd been saved from a terrible life on the streets.

Just last week, when Mrs. Halliday's daughters had come to visit her, Mae had requested for permission to leave the hospital for a short while. She explained to them about Mrs. Walker and how she needed to let the woman know that she was alright.

But when Mae got to the lodging house, she found a large 'For Sale' sign standing on the front porch. The place was boarded up, and she knocked at the next door to ask what had happened to her friend.

A middle-aged woman opened the door, "I hope you're not some salesperson wanting to sell me something," the woman said.

"No, Ma'am, I lived next door with Mrs. Walker but went to work somewhere else. I came to visit her, but there's a sign that says the place is for sale."

The woman smiled. "Sabine finally got a good break in life," the woman laughed softly. "That lodger of hers, Mr. Plank, proposed marriage and refused to take no for an answer. They were married just two weeks ago, and she's gone to live in Kent with him." The woman's eyes were glowing. "I used to see the shabbily dressed man but didn't know that he comes from fine stock. According to Sabine, he's a very wealthy man, and she's set for life now."

"Thank you," Mae said, feeling very happy for her friend. She prayed that Mr. Plank would treat her friend well.

Mae returned to the asylum, feeling at peace.

She was cleaning the room while Mrs. Halliday took a midmorning nap, which had become more frequent lately. The door opened, and a tall man entered the room.

This must be the new doctor, Mae told herself as he moved to the bed where the patient lay, two nurses flanking him. She'd never seen him before today, but she had heard a few nurses giggling about the new handsome doctor who had joined the institution.

"How is Mrs. Halliday today?" he asked her. "Is she doing better than yesterday?"

"No, Sir, I noticed that Mrs. Halliday's breathing is becoming laboured, and I informed the night nurses," Mae said. "They called in Dr. Phillips, and he gave her some medication to settle her down."

The doctor grunted, then assisted by the two nurses, they skilfully but gently examined the elderly woman without disturbing her nap.

"I don't like the sound of her chest," the doctor said, putting his stethoscope back around his neck. "She seems to have contracted pneumonia." His gaze was sharp on Mae. "Have you been keeping Mrs. Halliday warm all the time? I hope you haven't been feeding her cold food and drinks."

Mae opened her mouth to respond to the doctor's query, but one of the nurses beat her to it.

"Dr, Osborne, you'll find no better care giver in this institution than Mae here. She takes very good care of Mrs. Halliday, and no one has ever complained about her. I was here when Mrs. Halliday was first admitted, and Dr. Phillips expressed his concern about the state of her chest. This is something that has been eating her up for a long while. Dr. Phillips prescribed medication for her condition, but it seems as if it's not working. It's not Mae's fault."

The doctor nodded and gave Mae a brief smile. He then left instructions for the nurses to check in on the elderly woman every hour without fail and report any changes to her health condition to him. He also instructed Mae to be extra vigilant and especially at night.

"It's clear that Mrs. Halliday is fading away." His eyes, when they rested on Mae, were filled with compassion. "We'll do our best to treat the pneumonia, but from what I can see, these are Mrs. Halliday's final days. So, we'll make her as comfortable as possible."

Mae didn't want to believe what the doctor was saying because she couldn't imagine losing Mrs. Halliday. She'd grown very fond of the woman.

That evening, Mrs. Halliday woke up and requested to be helped to sit up. She smiled tenderly at Mae. "What's your name, dearie?" she asked after taking some warm broth. "I've been calling you Susie, but I know that it's not your name." She sounded very lucid, and Mae was happy. Mrs. Halliday was getting better, and if this continued, she would be out of here in no time. Mae refused to believe that her friend was at death's door.

"My name is Mae Chester."

"Dear Mae, you've been so good to me, and I'm sorry for all the times that I've been a difficult patient." She held out her right hand and Mae took it. "I see a lot of sadness in your eyes, the kind that comes from a heart that has been wounded and even broken many times."

Mae felt the tears prickling at the back of her eyes at the tenderness she saw in her charge's eyes. Only one other person had looked at her in that way recently, and a sob broke out from her lips.

"There, there," Mrs. Halliday said as she patted her hand. "You're too young and beautiful to be allowed to remain sad for so long. My oldest grandson is a good fellow, and I know you would make a suitable wife for him. I'll tell his mother to ask him to come and visit me so the two of you can get acquainted." Mae shook her head. "What is it?"

"Mrs. Halliday, I can never love another man the way I love Herbert. From the first time I met him when I was twelve, my heart belonged to him. But he's married to someone else now, and my heart is broken." She sniffed. "I don't think I ever want to go through such deep pain again."

Mrs. Halliday looked at her with eyes full of compassion. "Mae, I know that you don't want to hear this, but please listen to me. Love hurts, but it's a beautiful thing, and if allowed to, it can grow again. Take my own story, for example." She smiled in fond remembrance. "I got married to the love of my life, my soul mate, when I was only sixteen. William was the best thing that had ever happened to me. He came from a very wealthy family, and I was just the simple governess to his brother's children, but from the first moment our eyes met, there was never anyone else for either one of us. His family would never have allowed their beloved son to marry a simple governess, so we eloped and ran away to America." The woman paused and seemed lost in her thoughts for a while. "That was before Napoleon invaded Europe and proclaimed himself the ruler of all mankind." The woman's tone was sarcastic, and Mae found herself giggling. "We lived in America for twenty years, and our lives were so beautiful. My William was a very shrewd businessman. We owned a steel plant, and there was great demand for our products as expansion of the railways began in earnest. Our two daughters were born there." Mrs. Halliday bowed her head. "But then William fell ill, and he begged me to bring him back home to England. As soon as we got here and he saw his family again, he died. My beloved William had been ill for a while but hid it from me and the girls. He held onto his life long enough to return home. My heart was broken, and I just wanted to die after I lost him."

"I'm so sorry," Mae murmured, her own tears forgotten for the moment.

"I neglected myself and my daughters." Mrs. Halliday wiped her eyes with the edge of her sheet. "There's no grief so deep like that of one who has lost their soul mate. When you bury your soul mate, it feels as if you're also burying your heart with the person. It hurts so deeply that getting over that takes the grace of God and His strength."

There was silence for a while, and the woman leaned back against the pillows, closing her eyes. She was still for so long that Mae thought she had fallen asleep. In the two months that Mae had been caring for Mrs. Halliday, the woman hadn't been this lucid. Just as Mae was about to rise and straighten her charge's beddings, she opened her eyes.

"I mourned for my William for ten years, and I thank God every day for his solicitor who invested our money wisely, so we had enough money to live on. You see, even after we returned from America, his family still refused to accept me and my children, and we had to fend for ourselves. But my husband had made provision for us and we never struggled," she sighed. "But then ten years later I met Mr. Halliday. He was a widower and a soldier and didn't have any children of his own. He taught me to love again, and our two sons were born in the next two years. The man loved me so much, and what made me open up to him was that he never felt threatened by William's presence in my life. He kept my first husband's memory alive for our daughters, and I respected him to his dying day. The good Lord gave us forty years together. Mr. Halliday died just two months before Susie, and that broke my heart all over again."

"I'm so sorry." Mae didn't know what else to say.

Mrs. Halliday gave her a tearful smile, "Child, a heart can be broken many times, but when love comes knocking again it will heal. There will be scars, of course, but with time these stop hurting so badly." She looked at Mae with clear piercing eyes. "No man or woman, for that matter, lives forever. There's a time to be born and a time to die, as the good book says. A time to laugh and a time to mourn. You're still very young, and life will teach you to expect the unexpected, and you have to learn to live with it. Also, it's important to know that people come into our lives for different reasons. Some are there for a brief moment so we can learn something from them, but when the time comes for them to leave, let them go. Let fellows go and don't hold onto them longer than you should. Forgive those who have wounded you and live a humble and meek life, striving for peace with all men." The woman smiled. "And some folks come into our lives and stay longer. Learn to appreciate them and the time that the Lord gives you with them. But no matter how long they stay, one day they will leave again. That's the cycle of life and you have to understand it. I'm eighty-six years old and have outlived all my peers by over two decades. My two husbands taught me to forgive others and live peaceably with all mankind. And now that I'm about to rest and go the way of the earth, my heart is clean towards all, and free from every anger, pain and offence. Do that and you'll live as long as I have or perhaps even longer. Forgive and let folks go, don't hold them in your heart."

Mae pondered the woman's words the whole night, which happened to be her last of consciousness. Mrs. Halliday never spoke a single word to anyone again, because the next day she slipped into a coma, from which she never woke up again. Two days later, she died while surrounded by her four children and six grandchildren, a peaceful smile on her face.

Mae was praying that Mrs. Halliday's children would remember how well she had taken care of their mother and perhaps offer her a position in one of their households. But apart from the oldest daughter pressing her wages into her hand, none of the others spoke to her. That same afternoon, they took away Mrs. Halliday's body to prepare it for burial, and no one even bid her farewell. It was as if she didn't exist to them.

"Forgive," Mae chanted to herself as she stripped the bedding off Mrs. Halliday's bed. "Don't hold folks in your heart," she murmured. She was surprised to find an envelope addressed to her under the mattress when she lifted it, intending to carry it outside for airing. She quickly slipped the envelope into her pocket when she heard someone coming. It was the ward matron, Mrs. Dell. The woman had been very kind to Mae in all the time that she'd been here.

"Oh Mae, I'm glad that you're still here. I thought Mrs. Halliday's children would take you with them."

Mae shook her head without saying a word, not trusting herself to speak lest she burst into tears of disappointment. Once again, she was back to being alone, and she didn't know where she would go.

"Thank you for stripping and cleaning the room because we need it for a new patient who'll be brought in tomorrow morning." Mrs. Dell walked around the room, touching the few things that Mrs. Halliday's family had left behind, like the mug and plate she used, and the pile of magazines she'd loved perusing through. "Mrs. Halliday was an ideal patient and will be greatly missed." She looked at Mae. "I don't understand why her children didn't take you with them. Or maybe they intend to return for you after burying their mother."

Mae didn't think so. "No, Ma'am."

Had Mrs. Walker still been around, Mae would have returned to her lodging house to rent a room from her once again. Now she had to find somewhere else to live and work to do, and the thought was quite daunting.

"Mmh!" The matron sighed. "Do you have anywhere to stay for today?"

"No, Ma'am."

"Then do this, stay here for tonight and if anyone asks, I'll tell them that you're cleaning the room. But you must leave first thing tomorrow morning, or else I could get into trouble."

"Thank you." Mae felt slightly relieved. At least for today she had somewhere to sleep. Tomorrow would take care of itself.

"It's a pity that our new patient is a man, or else I would have recommended you to be his care giver."

"I'll be alright from tomorrow."

Mrs. Dell smiled at Mae. "I have faith that something good will happen for you after the way you tirelessly and selflessly took care of Mrs. Halliday. She died very peacefully and happily, and that means she left you a great blessing. Good times are coming in your life, Mae Chester."

"Amen," the young woman whispered, praying that the prophecy would be fulfilled soon. "Also have no worries about your meals for today. I'll send someone to bring you something to eat as usual. Just make sure you don't go roaming along the corridors and attracting attention to yourself. Lock yourself in the room as soon as your dinner tray is brought to you."

"Thank you."

Mae spent a quiet night sleeping on her small cot. Even though the bed that Mrs. Halliday had occupied was now empty, she couldn't bring herself to lie in it. She would miss the old lady. Sometime in the early hours of the morning she woke up and remembered the letter that Mrs. Halliday had left for her.

She drew the envelope out of her pocket, and being careful to keep the lamp burning low so as not to attract any attention, she tore it open. The last thing Mae wanted was for someone to come checking on the room that was supposed to be empty. She was surprised to find two twenty-pound notes in the envelope, and a letter.

"Dear Mae,

This is my last gift to you because you've been a wonderful care giver and companion in my final days on this earth. It will surprise you that I found the time to write when everyone thought that I was deranged and out of my senses. I had my moments of lucidity and took advantage of that.

Mae, I have a feeling that once I'm gone, my children will ignore you. It's a sad thing that all of them are so self-absorbed in their own lives that they don't consider other people. Please don't hold anything against them. I know that they will settle what is due to you and maybe not even give you anything extra. So, this is my own way of saying thank you for what you did for me.

Be a good girl always and remember that God loves and cares very much about you. Whenever I was well, I prayed for you, and I know that one day all your pain will be gone.

Remember me with fondness when I'm gone, even though I know that I was at times a very difficult patient. Don't mourn for too long. These last two months have been very comfortable, and I leave you my blessings that you'll have a very long, happy, and prosperous life. God will take care of you for me because I have prayed for you.

I remain always in your debt.

Margaret Halliday.

PS: Use five shillings out of my gift to you to buy yourself a hat and wear it on your wedding day. Consider it a special blessing for you on that great day when you'll be getting married to your soul mate."

Mae folded the letter and wept for a very long time as she thought about the kindness of a stranger.

Moving to a small windowless stuffy room after the luxury of her previous quarters didn't daunt Mae at all. She'd been careful not to let her good fortune these past few weeks go to her head. If anything, she was grateful for the room which was hers alone. It had a small cot and wash basin, but for other needs, she had to use the outhouse like her peers.

The room was in one of the oldest buildings of the institution and was subdivided into numerous small cubicles. This hostel was the designated quarters for the junior nurses and other female subordinate staff. The men lived on the other side of the large institution, and the only time Mae saw them was during working hours. Otherwise, they weren't allowed to interact unless it had to do with work, which suited Mae fine. The last thing she wanted was for some man to try and woo her. She was done with love forever!

It was Mrs. Dell who had recommended Mae for her new position, and she would forever be grateful to the woman.

The old building in which she lived was behind the newest wing of the asylum, and the two buildings were separated by a high wall, as if to tuck the old one out of sight. Though the accommodations were very basic, and Mae had to work very long and tiring hours in the laundry room and sometimes cleaning the wards, she did it with cheerful spirits and a smile on her face.

She was able to eat good food because she also helped out in the kitchen, unlike her peers, who never lifted a finger to go over and above the duties specifically allocated to them.

One afternoon, as she was cleaning the corridor of their hostel, which the junior nurses referred to as 'Purgatory,' she became aware of the presence of two nurses. Because she was out of sight, and at this time most of the other staff were out of the hostel and attending to their duties, the young woman believed that they were alone.

Mae would have ignored them and carried on with her work but for the words that reached her ears.

"Have you heard about St. Agatha's newest inmate? He's a very handsome fellow but a complete lunatic, and I doubt that there's any cure or hope for him in this world," one nurse said.

"Poor fellow," her colleague murmured. "Yes, I heard about him from Mrs. Dell."

"When he was brought in, his mother warned the doctors that he has cannibalistic tendencies and is completely insane. Because of how wild he is, the fellow has to be kept restrained at all times, and even his mouth has to be bridled so he won't bite anyone. Even the biggest and meanest orderlies are afraid of entering his room. After all, who wants to leave the room of a raving lunatic without an ear or fingers?"

"Yes, I heard about that too," the second nurse said. "And it is said that he has been attacking anyone who tries to get too close to him."

The two women fell silent, and Mae prepared to move away because she thought they were done. In any case, she didn't want to be caught eavesdropping by the nurses who were very unkind to those subordinates they felt were beneath them.

Footsteps sounded, "What are the two of you doing here?" A third person joined the two nurses. Mae paused and waited to hear what else was going on.

"I was just telling Tryphosa here about that new lunatic in the isolation ward."

The newcomer laughed. "Oh, so you've also heard about him! He keeps screaming for someone called May whenever the bridle is removed from his mouth, and he won't shut up. Initially he was supposed to have been put in the private room that the other old woman used to occupy."

"You mean Mrs. Halliday's room? But how can a man be put in a women's ward?"

"Lack of space is the cause of all these problems. All the male private rooms are filled with wealthy lunatics." The three women laughed heartily. Mae frowned, feeling badly that people would dare to poke fun at the sufferings of others.

"Anyway," the newcomer continued, "Matron has instructed the orderlies to simply pass the handsome lunatic's food through the slots at the bottom of the door. None of the cleaners will even go near that room, and I wonder how long the man will be kept in there before the room turns into something worse than the sewers. He's been admitted here because he comes from a very wealthy family, and you all know that this place is about making as much money from those lunatics as possible."

Mae quickly finished cleaning the corridor and went to unhang and fold the laundry. One good thing about working in this place, even if the wages were very low on account of her not being properly educated, was that she didn't have to do the laundry by hand. There were large machines for that purpose.

Over the next two days, Mae found herself thinking about the patient in the isolation ward. Only the completely insane were dumped there, those who were considered to be very dangerous, not only to themselves, but to others as well. Twice a week, an industrial washer would come in and clean the rooms as well as wash the patients.

Mae had once heard an orderly describing how the isolation wards and patients in them were cleaned, and she found it very inhumane. It was very cruel treatment towards people who, through no fault of theirs most of the time, had lost their minds.

According to the orderly, the industrial washer would use a hose and direct the flow of water towards the patient. As the patient struggled to stay alive, given the force of water directed at him or her, two orderlies wearing protective gear would rush in and strip him or her, tying the person to the restraints on the wall, and then would scrub them with hard brushes. Thereafter, the dirt would be vacuumed out, and after the patient was dressed and placed once more in the straitjacket, they would be left alone for three or four days, when the washing would be repeated. She imagined that the poor inmates had to crawl on their bellies in order to eat their food, for with their hands bound by the straitjackets and nobody willing to help them, there was nothing else they could do. It pained Mae to think of humanity being reduced to living like wild animals, and every time she got a moment, she went to the chapel to pray for the poor suffering souls.

"Poor man." Mae thought of the newest inmate as she lay in bed. But something nagged at her mind. She had no idea why the new patient's plight bothered her, but she knew that she needed to go and see him, if for nothing else but to speak a kind word to him. Of course, she would be sure not to get close to him, but she had found that her singing calmed the mad men and women she'd often come into contact with.

Early the next morning, as soon as she was done hanging out the laundry in the inner room, because it was raining hard, she made her way to the isolation ward on the pretext of collecting the laundry after the industrial washer had left.

The ward was silent, very quiet, and Mae paused at the main door, feeling too scared to proceed further.

"This is not a good idea," she thought to herself. In any case, what was she doing here? She decided to return to her normal duties, but something stopped her. Suddenly there was a loud noise, which startled her, as if someone was screaming for help. It was the voice that had haunted her dreams and thoughts for weeks.

"It can't be," she murmured, forgetting all her initial fears. The doors to the rooms in the isolation ward were made of reinforced steel because wooden ones could easily be compromised if one of the inmates was strong enough. Mae felt a little bit safe because none of the inmates could jump out and attack her. She could hear someone crying in one of the rooms at the end of the corridor, and she approached it slowly and cautiously.

"My beautiful darling Mae," the person was lamenting. "Are you dead or still alive? Where are you, my beloved? How will I ever find you in this cruel world?"

Mae was momentarily struck dumb. It sounded like Herbert, but maybe she was mistaken. The doors were never locked with keys, but only bolted from the outside. She stood outside the door and listened for a little bit longer as the man wept and lamented. Then she threw all caution to the wind and decided to enter the room and see this handsome lunatic for herself. If those nurses were to be believed, the man was restrained in a straitjacket and posed no threat.

She furtively unbolted the door and stepped inside the brightly lit room. The man, who was standing at the window that was reinforced with thick bars, slowly turned around and Mae gave a small cry as she ran to him and threw her arms around him.

"Oh, my Herbert, what have they done to you?" The tears came. She untied the restraints as she sobbed. "Who put you in here like an animal?"

Mae realised that Herbert was struggling to let himself free from her arms. "Who are you?" His eyes were wild and full of suspicion. She knew that mere words wouldn't reach him in his current state. She dropped her arms from around him and reached for the chain around her neck, drew out the locket, and opened it. She then pulled out the small, folded piece of paper that had lain there for six years.

"M and H together forever," she read out softly. "Mae and Herbert together forever."

"Mae?" Herbert blinked rapidly, not believing what his eyes were showing him. He thought he was seeing an apparition. "Mae, is it really you?"

"Yes, my darling," Mae laughed happily and removed the last of the restraints. "It's really me."

"How?" Herbert touched her face with his freed hands and turned her head from side to side to make sure that she was real.

"It's a long story, but I'm here now and will rescue you."

Herbert sighed. "My mother will never let me out of this place. She has people watching me all the time."

"I promise you that if it's the last thing that I'll ever do, I will find a way of getting you out of this place. You're not a lunatic, and I'm so sorry that you've been treated so badly. Stay strong, my darling."

"Mae, are you real?" Herbert touched her face again. "Please don't be cruel and break my heart. I can't live again if all this is just a dream. I don't want to wake up if this is a mere dream. If you have any mercy, kill me before I wake up so I can die with sweet memories of having seen my beloved Mae as the last thing I'll have on this earth."

"Herbert," she said as she touched his cheek with a trembling hand. "It's really me, your Mae."

Tears shone in his eyes, "They told me that you had died."

"They all lied to you." Mae looked towards the slightly open door. "I have to go, but I promise you that I'll be back. If I'm found here and the report reaches your mother, there will be much trouble for sure."

Herbert nodded, understanding that what Mae was saying was true. He didn't want to let her out of his sight ever again, but they had to be careful. "Go now, my love, and be safe." He hugged her for a long moment and then released her. "Come back to me."

"I promise that I will." She kissed his cheek, and then loosely retied the straitjacket. "This is just in case anyone comes in to check on you. Let them think that you're still all tied up."

Herbert smiled. "My darling, I'll be counting the minutes until I can see you again."

Mae quickly slipped out of the room and bolted the door once again. She heard voices coming from down the corridor and rushed to the large bin at the other end, where she found a heap of laundry. She turned her back and pretended to be busy piling the laundry up.

It was two young doctors, and they barely noticed her presence. Mae had realised that many doctors and nurses barely paid attention to the subordinate staff. It was as if they didn't exist at all, and she was glad because that was now working in her favour.

"The lunatic in room three is the worst of them all," one of the doctors was saying. "His mother insists that he should always be restrained because he's a danger not only to himself, but to others as well."

Mae frowned because the two worthless doctors were discussing her beloved. She watched them until they disappeared out of her sight. Even if it killed her, she would find a way of getting Herbert out of this hellhole that his mother had sunk him in.

THE PROMISED LAND

When Herbert remained silent in his room for two days in a row, the doctors grew quite concerned. Everyone had gotten used to his ranting and raving, day and night, and the silence made them fear that he might be dead.

What no one knew was that Mae had visited him again and urged him to remain silent so his mother would be requested to visit.

"Let everyone see that you're back to your senses and feel that the treatment they administered to you has worked."

"Very well then."

When the wary doctors came to check on him, four orderlies accompanied them just in case he turned and attacked them.

But Herbert remained calm. "I'm not going to hurt anyone," he said. "Please, can someone give me a haircut and help me shave my beard off? It's very itchy and irritating, and I can't even sleep."

A barber was quickly brought in, and he groomed Herbert. Clean clothes were brought for him, and the doctors congratulated each other for having brought back this particular patient from lunacy.

"Mr. Patterson, we're so happy that you're well."

"I'm thankful that you've all taken good care of me and made me well again. But I wish to go home and continue with my life."

"We've sent a telegram to your mother, and she'll be here tomorrow," Herbert was informed by the doctor who came to check on him in the evening. "Let's see what she says about your recovery."

"Thank you, doctor."

Mae was eager to know what was happening with Herbert, but she forced herself to remain calm and patient. They were very close to victory, and she could actually taste it. The last thing she was going to do was rouse any suspicions at all and jeopardise their plans.

When she'd visited Herbert the last time, he'd begged her to stay away because his mother would be visiting him in a day or two.

"If my mother even has an inkling that you're in this place, she'll cause trouble for you and have me taken away to another place where I'll never see you again."

Because of this, Mae made sure that on the day Mrs. Patterson was visiting her son, she was on the other side of the asylum where no one was likely to see her and send her in Herbert's direction. Now that he was considered sane and sober, the cleaners were able to visit his room. She didn't want to be one of those sent there because she might run into Mrs. Patterson.

Even as she worked, she was praying that nothing would go wrong, for Herbert had told her that as soon as his mother declared him fit to be discharged, he would find her, and they would leave this place together and never be parted again.

"Lord, please remember us," Mae prayed.

Herbert softened his expression when his mother entered his room. She was the last person he wanted to see, but for now she controlled his life. He was also careful not to overdo things, because by nature, his mother was a very suspicious person. She would see through any acts of unusual affection.

"Oh, Herbert!" Mrs. Patterson entered the room. "I'm so happy to see that you're well again. You can't imagine my joy when I received the telegram from the doctors telling me that you were well and asking for me." But she made no move to draw closer or hug him, for which he was glad, because that kind of hypocrisy was too much for him. He sat on the bed and smiled at her. "At first, I was suspicious, but I can see that you're back to your normal self. And you look very handsome, just like your grandfather."

Herbert knew that he looked nothing like his grandfather, but he let his mother have this. He smiled. "It feels good to be well again." He ran a hand through his now short hair. "It was a really dark time in my life, and I'm very sorry to have put you through so much pain, Mama."

"My joy is that you're well again, and all is forgiven. But you know that everything I did was for your own good. People asked about you, and I told them that you had returned to serve overseas, so no one will ever know that you were in this asylum and behaving like a lunatic." Herbert nodded. "I was afraid that that worthless, good for nothing girl had bewitched you or something, and that's why you had turned into a lunatic."

"Mama, you don't have to worry about that anymore. The treatment worked and I'm whole again." His tone was mild, though he was inwardly seething at his mother's continued insults towards Mae. "Being locked up in this place, away from any disturbances, has given me enough time to think. You've done so much for me, and so you deserve my full loyalty and obedience."

"Oh, Herbert!" His mother clapped her hands happily.

"I know that everything you did was meant for my good, and that's why I now realise that I ought to do as you desire, Ma." Herbert bowed his head as if suddenly shy.

"Do you really mean that?" There was a catch in his mother's voice. "Are you ready to accept that all the plans I've made for your life are good for you?"

"Yes, Ma. You chose Miss Bella to be my bride, and now I acknowledge that I didn't do right by her. I pray that she will forgive me and give me another chance to be the husband she needs."

"Bella has nothing against you, and she has no idea that you're in this place. I thought about telling her so she could accompany me, but I don't want her to reject you because of your condition." And for that Herbert was silently glad. "Like everyone else, she believes that you're back serving in the army, and seeing you again will make her very happy."

Herbert nodded. "And thank you for defending me to her, Ma. Miss Bella is a very beautiful and intelligent woman, the right kind of a wife for me."

"What about that other girl?" And his mother's lip curled in scorn.

"Ma," Herbert looked up. "That's all in the past now, and besides, I now believe that she's dead, or else wouldn't she have returned to her uncle's place by now?" He sighed. "I have to move on with my life and make better choices. I want to make you happy, so Miss Bella and I will get married and give you grandchildren. That's the least I can do, seeing as you've been very patient with me."

"Oh, Herbert, you don't know how happy that makes me feel. We'll get home and immediately begin making wedding preparations."

"I'd really like that, Ma. I'm now ready to marry whoever you and God have decided for me. And I'll do my best to be a good husband to Miss Bella." Then he thought of something. "Ma, would you find me the best designer, so that I can gift Miss Bella with a wedding gown that's out of this world?"

"My son is back," Mrs. Patterson beamed. "Leave all arrangements to me now, and I'll do my very best to give you the kind of wedding that people will still be talking about decades from now."

"Ma, thank you for bringing me to this place. Everyone here has been so kind to me. They took good care of me, and that's why I'm well again."

"Only the best for my son. I need to get you discharged immediately so we can return home, where you belong."

"Thank you, Ma." He gave her an uncertain smile.

"What is it, Herbert?"

"Ma, before we go, I'd like to say thank you to all the doctors, nurses, and orderlies who took such good care of me. Without them, this place wouldn't have been comfortable at all."

"That's a very good idea. Shall we go to the office so I can get you discharged?" Herbert nodded. "Then you can ask to see all those who played a part in your recovery."

"I'd like to reward them also. Nothing much, but small cash tokens, to say thank you."

"Yes, of course. I have enough money for all that."

"Thank you, Ma."

Because Herbert didn't know the layout of the asylum compound, he and Mae had agreed that once he was free from his mother, he would ask to be shown where the chapel was, since it was open to patients, staff, and even visitors.

His only prayer was that his mother wouldn't insist on coming along, and that Mae would be alone, and no one would question their being together. He stopped an orderly that he met on the way and asked for directions to the chapel.

His mother had brought him fine clothes, and he knew that he looked dashing, nothing like the lunatic who had been locked up in the isolation ward for the past three weeks. He knew that no one could recognize him, and even if they did, his excuse was that he was going to the chapel to give thanks to God for his speedy recovery.

Once he got to the chapel, he slipped into one of the back pews, glad that the place wasn't too brightly lit. He'd practically run there because he wanted to get Mae out of this place today, and to safety, but he'd forgotten that he was still weak from days of not receiving proper nourishment, so he had to catch his breath for a few minutes. The thick wad of notes his mother had given him felt heavy in the breast pocket of his jacket.

When he was once again breathing normally, he raised his head and noticed the person kneeling at the altar. It was Mae, and since there was no one else in the chapel, he rose to his feet and slowly approached her, but he was still careful not to get too close to her. He knelt down within speaking distance from her without the need for them to shout to be heard.

"Mae, I've been discharged, and my mother thinks that I'm going around saying my farewells and rewarding those who took care of me. I need to get you out of here as soon as possible before anyone becomes suspicious. Is there any other entrance apart from the front door?"

Mae nodded. "There's the side entrance that is usually used by vendors and suppliers as well as those staff members who don't live on the compound."

"Do you have to go back for anything?

"No, but you need this." She reached to the side and picked up a white coat such as doctors wear. "Put this on."

"You lead the way, and I'll follow behind. But don't walk too fast because I'm still not strong enough to hurry."

They left the chapel, Mae walking in front of Herbert. She was praying that Mrs. Patterson wouldn't get it into her head to come in search of her son.

They got to the side gate without any incident. It was well guarded because the administration had to be careful that no patient slipped out unnoticed. The guard was dozing, and Mae's heart was pounding as she approached him. Since she was dressed in her normal cleaner's uniform, he barely gave her a second glance and let her step outside. She was relieved and knew that the guard had acted dismissively because he no doubt assumed that she was running an errand for one of the doctors or nurses, which wasn't unusual at all.

The man sat up straight when Herbert approached him, but since the man confidently walked towards him in a white coat, he assumed that he was one of the doctors going off duty, and he even saluted him.

Mae didn't breathe until Herbert was standing next to her outside the asylum.

"There's my mother's carriage." Herbert pointed at the vehicle that was parked at the front door. "I told her to go ahead, and I would find her when I was done saying goodbye to my friends, if I can call them that."

"Then we have to use the back alley," Mae said, moving in the opposite direction from Mrs. Patterson's carriage, and Herbert quickly followed her. They slipped into the alley, and Mae was glad that Herbert was with her. All staff, and especially the women had been warned severally to never use the alley, especially if they were alone. It was a long alley and they met no one, but it was a relief when they emerged on Oxford Street.

"We can't stop now." Herbert looked at Mae's ugly cleaner's tunic. "Here, put his on to cover yourself. I'll buy you better clothes when we get to a place where it's safe."

"Where are we headed?" Mae ignored the looks that they were getting from passers-by as she pulled on the white coat.

"King's Cross Station," Herbert said. "We'll catch a train out of London and head to the north."

Mae only started breathing again when they were settled in the first-class compartment that Herbert had paid for out of the money his mother had given him. It was quite a tidy sum, and if they were frugal and careful, it would last them for a while until he was well enough to contact his father's solicitor and obtain the money he'd left him. Herbert also had his soldier's pension, and all they had to do was settle down in a little town and work hard.

Once they entered the compartment, Herbert shut the door and held out his hands, and Mae walked into them.

They stood in that position for a long while, neither of them wishing to move away from the other, as if afraid that if they did so, something might separate them again.

It was the ticket examiner's knock that separated them, and Mae sat down as Herbert got the door.

"Tickets, please!"

"Yes, Sir," Herbert produced their tickets. The man glanced at them then looked at Mae and back to Herbert."

"Where to?"

"Gretna Green," Herbert said with a straight face and the man gave him a sly wink.

"Aah!" He winked again. "You won't be disturbed by anyone, and if you like, I can send a porter to take care of your needs until you get to your destination."

"We'd like that very much, Sir." Herbert tipped the man generously. He tipped his hat at them and closed the door. They heard him whistling as he moved to the next compartment to check their tickets.

Herbert sighed. "Mae, I've ruined your good name."

She shrugged. "We've done nothing wrong, so there's nothing to feel guilty about. Besides, I don't care what anyone says because I'm here with you."

Herbert sat down next to her. "Maybe I'm being presumptuous, but have you ever heard of Gretna Green?" Mae blushed, and he chuckled softly. "I can see that you have, and do you know why people go there?"

"To get married in haste."

"Oh, dear girl, yes, we're in haste." He raised her chin. "This is probably not the way you ever imagined getting married, but it's the only way I can keep you safe from your uncle and anyone else who would wish to put you in bondage again."

When Herbert mentioned her uncle, Mae's face turned white, and Herbert saw the terror in her eyes.

"Mae, listen to me. No one will ever hurt you again, not while I live and breathe."

"But where will we live after we get married? We can't go back to your mother's house, for she will do everything in her power to separate us again."

"I'll take you to Ravenscroft, but that will be after our honeymoon. Aunt Morgan is a good woman and will keep you safe. The last time I saw her, I told her how badly your uncle was treating you, and she wept."

"If she was so concerned about me then why didn't she ever come looking for me?" Mae asked sullenly.

Herbert touched her cheek. "Because for many years, Aunt Morgan has suffered ill health and has been bedridden most of the time. She has no husband nor children, and she told me that she's the last of your mother's living relatives, well, apart from Mr. Lester. Your father also has no living relatives left, so you're the last of his lineage."

Mae still wasn't convinced that she would be safe with her mother's relative. "Are you sure Aunt Morgan won't write to Uncle John and tell him to come and get me? Years ago, when that man snatched me from Mrs.

Brittle and took me to live with my uncle, I was so excited and happy because I believed that I would find love and acceptance in his home. How wrong I was!" She turned her face away and looked at the passing scenery. The train was heading out of London now and had picked up speed.

"Mae, you never have to fear again or worry. And to further reassure you, no one will ever find us because they'll be searching for Herbert Patterson. I'm changing my name and taking up my father's real name."

"Oh!"

THE LIGHT OF DAY

"All I have to offer you is faith, love, and hope," Mae whispered as her husband's arms went around her from behind. "And the promise that I'll never willingly, knowingly, or consciously do anything to hurt you. And when I do, I'll be the first to ask for your forgiveness, for I love you so much, Herbert. I don't have a good name from a good family, or even a dowry. All I have is myself and my heart."

Herbert's heart was bursting with love and joy over his new bride's words. He still couldn't believe that they were finally married. "And the name I give you is my own," Herbert paused. "Mae, my miracle bride, I give you my name, Herbert Alexander Cameron."

Mae frowned slightly. "I don't understand." She turned around in his arms until they were facing each other. "Your surname is Patterson, isn't it?"

He gently brushed his lips against hers. "Mae, on the day we travelled to this place, don't you remember me telling you that I was changing my name and taking up my father's surname?"

She blushed. "I think I was too busy with my head in the clouds to pay much attention then. All I was thinking of at the time was becoming your wife at last."

"Well, the reason I'm reverting back to my father's name is because it has never been Patterson. When Pa married my mother thirty years ago, he had to change his name. My grandfather and Mama made that one of the stipulations of the agreement they had in place at the time. Papa's surname changed to Patterson, even though his name was Cameron."

"That's really odd that your mother refused to give up her surname and take your father's."

"I found out that my paternal grandfather had died while heavily in debt, and my grandmother was about to lose her home. She might have ended up living on the streets or in a workhouse." His face was grim. "And on the other side of it, my great grandfather had died, and according to his will, the only way Ma could inherit the estate was if she married and bore an heir, or else the inheritance would have gone to her distant cousin. That's when Ma convinced my poor simple father to be her husband while she paid off all his debts. So, my rightful name is Cameron, and I want all our children to bear that name and be proud of their heritage."

"And I'll carry that name with pride and honour." Mae leaned against her husband's chest.

"Don't you care that the Cameron name has no wealth, fame, or prestige attached to it? I have nothing to my name save the skills I acquired while I was in the army, my little pension, and a few pounds that my father left me, which I have yet to receive from his solicitor."

"And that simple man holds my heart forever. I wouldn't give up my life with you for anything in the world, not for all the gold or spices in the new world. My prayer is that you and I will have many years together, living our lives very simply and bringing up our children to love and honour God and treat others with kindness and respect."

"Will you still feel that way when the going gets very tough because we don't have any money?"

A shadow crossed Mae's face, but she quickly dispelled it and smiled. "When life becomes tough, we'll hold on to the promises we've made to each other and have faith that God will see us through. I was a small child, but when my parents were alive, we didn't have much. Yet the love they had for each other and for me made our little cottage a little heaven on earth. That's what I always held onto when things got really bad. That one day I would be with the one who loved and accepted me just as I am." She smiled through her tears. "My darling Herbert, it has taken six years for us to be together, but finally God did it for us."

"I love you so much, Mrs. Cameron," Herbert said quite emotionally and kissed her soundly on the lips.

"I love you, too," Mae managed to gasp when he finally let her up for some air.

"I feel like I want to hold on to this moment and never let go," Herbert murmured.

"We'll have many more in the years to come." She was grinning from ear to ear. "If anyone had told me a few weeks ago that I would be this happy, I would have thought that the person was teasing me," she said. Yet it was now unfolding and finally she was with the man she loved with her whole heart.

"This is not a dream but the truth, my dearest."

A few days later, Herbert looked at his wife with a heavy heart, knowing that what he was about to tell her would dim the light in her eyes. But it had to be done.

"We're leaving for Ravenscroft tomorrow," he told her. "When we get there, we'll live with Aunt Morgan until we can find a place of our own."

"I'd like that very much." Mae thought about a little cottage with a picket fence and a cat or two, her idea of bliss.

"But then I have to travel to Sheffield for a few days." Mae raised her head sharply at his words. He looked into her eyes, and as he'd feared, the joy went out of them. "Please don't look at me like that."

"Why are you going back to Sheffield? Or do you intend to keep me hidden in Ravenscroft while you go on with your life on your grandfather's estate?" She pulled away from him and moved to the other side of the room, wrapping her arms around her stomach. A coldness descended into her heart.

"Mae, how can you even think that? I need to go and wrap up some business in Sheffield with my father's solicitor, and also to see my mother and tell her that all her plans against us failed."

Mae shook her head, feeling very frightened. What if Herbert returned home and his mother convinced him to stay there? After all, she was his mother, and he loved her very much. Mrs. Patterson had a way of making Herbert submit to her every decision. What if her marriage was over in just two weeks?

They travelled to Ravenscroft, and all through the journey, Mae sat silently beside her husband. Gone was her cheerfulness, and Herbert nearly changed his mind about leaving her. But this was something he had to do, sort of tying up loose ends, because he never wanted anything to come up and interfere with their marriage.

"You'll be safe here with Aunt Morgan," Herbert told her as they walked up to the door, which was immediately flung open, and Mae found herself engulfed in a strong and warm embrace.

"My Ashley's little girl!" Mae found herself being held by the shoulders and observed with green eyes just like her mother's and hers. "I despaired of ever seeing you, but I see that your young man has kept the promises he made to an old woman two years ago."

Herbert laughed as he followed the two women into the house. "Aunt Morgan, I try as much as possible to keep all my promises." He dropped their two small suitcases on the floor.

"And I'm so happy to see my little one." Aunt Morgan made Mae feel warm inside. It was the same feeling she'd had years ago as a child when her parents were still alive. It was the same one she'd felt when Peter and Simeon Ashton's parents had taken her into their home. And it was also the same feeling that she'd been having for the past two weeks in the arms of her husband.

She was loved, she was accepted, and she belonged.

"You look a little sad, child." Aunt Morgan sat down on her battered couch and patted the space beside her. Mae joined her. "Your young man came here about two years ago and did extensive repairs on this house that is now your home too. The house is now steadier and sounder than ever before, and there hasn't been a single leak ever since."

"I was very happy to be of service to you, Ma'am," Herbert tipped his hat at her.

Aunt Morgan turned to Mae. "Don't you like it here?" Mae saw a fleeting shadow on her aunt's face and felt bad about being moody and sullen on such a happy day.

"Aunt Morgan," Herbert said slowly, observing his wife's downcast head. "I need to travel back to Sheffield for a few days."

"Aah!" The woman nodded in understanding. She gently patted Mae's hands, which were on her lap. "Dearie, this seems important to your husband, and he needs to do it. There's no need to have that gloomy face when he'll be back before you even realise that he's been gone."

"But what if he doesn't come back?" Mae burst out, and to her consternation, the tears started flowing. "Mrs. Patterson has always been determined to keep us apart. What if she succeeds in doing that and I never see Herbert again? Does he want me to die?"

"Mae." Herbert crouched before her and held her hands in his. "No one and nothing will ever keep us apart again. We've been friends for the past six years, and so much has happened to us in that time. It was as if every evil and wicked thing was determined to keep us apart, but they didn't succeed. Our love is stronger than any opposition, challenges, or obstacles that have tried to stand in our way."

"Your mother had you locked up in an asylum and lied to everyone so they wouldn't listen to you and help you. What makes you think that she won't do the same thing again? I know that you love your mother very much like any good son should, and you're her only child. She'll do anything to keep you by her side and make you do as she desires, including locking you up in an asylum so that I never see you again."

Aunt Morgan frowned and turned her gaze to Herbert. "Mae is right, and her fears are valid, Herbert. It's not safe for you to travel to Sheffield on your own. You'll be alone, and your mother will have people who have served her and are loyal to her all around her. You won't stand a chance against such strong foes, and your life could be in danger once again."

"Aunt Morgan, my darling Mae, you don't have to worry. I'll never set foot on Mama's estate on my own because I know what she's capable of," he smiled. "I love my mother and believe me, being her son for twenty-three years has made me know that she's capable of doing much harm just to get her own way. I'm not blind to my mother's faults at all, so you don't have to be afraid. I promise that I'll be very careful."

Herbert first travelled back to London because he needed to see his friends and tell them about his plans. Peter and Simeon were really happy to see him.

"It's been a while, Captain, and you look very happy and contented. The last time we saw you was when you'd been attacked by those vagabonds and looked like death in that hospital bed. What has changed since we last saw each other?" Simeon asked as the three of them entered the Gentleman's Club on Bond Street. It was an old but still very respectable establishment that was owned by an elderly soldier.

They sat down at a table in a corner. "Well, tell us, because something big seems to have happened to you, and recently," Peter urged, raising his hand to catch an attendant's attention. The man came over, and Herbert waited for his friends to place their orders. Being teetotallers, all three of them asked for ginger ale.

"I got married two weeks ago," Herbert said, and Simeon cheered as Peter slapped him heavily on the back.

"Congratulations! We saw the notice in the newspaper and were hoping to receive an invitation to the wedding of the year as advertised. Or did our invitations get lost in the mail?" Peter winked at his brother.

Herbert smiled and shook his head. "I didn't marry Miss Bella Lester, for that's whose name was coupled with mine in that advertisement."

His two friends gave him incredulous looks, then Simeon spoke up. "You broke off your engagement and married another woman instead?"

"Miss Lester and I were never engaged. It was all my mother and the young woman's parents who arranged it all. I've always been in love with someone else." He sighed and sat back in the plush sofa seat. "We've been through so much, and I can say that our love has been tested by fire. Mae especially has lived such a tough life."

"Your bride's name is May?"

"No, Mae Chester, though now she's Mae Cameron.," Herbert was shocked when his friends both turned very pale and looked as if they'd heard from the other side of life. "Did I say something wrong?"

"Mae Chester, you said. She should be eighteen, her birthday falls on Christmas Day, and she has the most expressive and innocent green eyes," Peter said. "Is that the Mae Chester that you're referring to?"

It was Herbert's turn to stare at his friends, "How is it that you've described my bride so accurately?"

Simeon shook his head, and it was obvious that he was still in shock. "You won't believe us if we told you, but perhaps you'll believe it when you hear everything from our parents' lips."

And that was how Herbert found himself seated in Peter and Simeon's parents' warm parlour telling them all about Mae and the kind of life she'd lived ever since he met her for the first time six years ago.

"She was the most delightful child," Mrs. Ashton said. She was gripping her husband's hand and her knuckles were white. "We loved her so much because she was the little girl that we'd always wanted." Her voice broke. "When Mae was so cruelly taken away from us, it nearly broke us completely."

Herbert leaned forward, elbows on his knees. "What happened?"

Peter took up the story. "We found her wandering alone in the park. She was about four or five years old at the time. She was all alone, and so Simeon and I brought her to Ma. When no one came forward to claim her many weeks later, Ma and Pa decided to adopt her. I was eight and Simeon was six. Yes, two years older than Mae, so she was four. She became our little sister and we loved her very much."

Simeon took over. "But then Ma and Pa had to travel to Bristol when our maternal grandmother took ill." He looked at his father, who gave him a slight nod. "Our paternal grandmother came to stay with us so she could take care of us. A few days later we received news that our parents had been killed in an accident in Bristol." Simeon shook his head, "Grandma Beth didn't waste a moment. She immediately ordered our governess to get rid of Mae, and we never saw her again."

"When we returned from Bristol, we searched all over for Mae." Mrs. Ashton was crying openly. "We never stopped praying and hoping that we would see our little girl again. It's hard to believe that our Little Mae is still alive and married to you. Do you think she blames us for abandoning her?"

"You didn't abandon Mae, and when she hears this story, she'll tell you the same thing. Mae has such a sweet disposition and a tender heart, and she doesn't hold any bitterness towards anyone. It's just not in her nature."

"When are you returning to Ravenscroft?" Mrs. Ashton asked. "We'd all like to come with you and see our little girl." The other three members of the family nodded.

"Well, first I have to go to Sheffield because I have some unfinished business with my father's solicitor. I'd also like to see my mother and tell her that I forgive her for the terrible things she did." He told them all about being locked up in that asylum by his own mother. "Mae and Aunt Morgan are afraid that Ma might get people to subdue me and take me to a place where I'll never be seen nor heard of again. And they're right. My mother never accepts defeat and always wants to have her own way. She'll do anything to make sure that Mae and I are separated forever."

"In that case," Mr. Ashton spoke up, "we'll all travel to Sheffield with you," and once more his family nodded.

It was hard to believe that he'd only been away from Patterson Estate for a few weeks. Herbert couldn't bring himself to call the place home, for it had ceased to be that a long time ago. It looked like years and not mere weeks had gone by since he was last on the estate.

His mother was at home, and incidentally, Mr. Lester and his whole family were present as well. The five of them stared in shock as Herbert and his four companions walked into the manor.

After exchanging greetings briefly, Herbert turned to his mother. "Ma, I won't take up much of your time, because I can see that you're busy with your visitors."

"Herbert, we've been searching all over for you and were afraid that something terrible had happened to you. After I discharged you from the hospital, I waited in the carriage, and everyone searched everywhere for you."

Herbert gave her a lopsided smile. "Ma, I'll have you know that I walked out of the asylum with my own two feet. Mae and I got married two weeks ago."

"What?" His mother spluttered.

"Yes, Ma. For some strange reason, the same asylum where you took me to get me locked up was the place where the one person you didn't want me to ever see again was to be found. Mae was working at St. Agatha's," he laughed. "Destiny is very strange indeed, for what were the chances of that ever happening? With your own two hands, Mother, you delivered me into the arms of the woman that I love more than anything else in this world." His mother paled. "You wanted me to forget the woman I love and were prepared to go to any lengths to see that we would never be together again." Herbert blinked rapidly, "I was treated worse than a leper, locked up and restrained like a wild animal until Mae saved my life, for I would surely have died in that place."

"Herbert, please." His mother held out her hands beseechingly. "I did it all to protect you. Please sit down so we can talk about this."

But Herbert shook his head. "Like I said, we don't want to take up much of your time, and we have a train to catch. Mother, the reason I'm here today is to let you know that I've made a decision to forfeit any claims to the Patterson estate, seeing as it isn't my birth right."

"No, you're my heir."

"No, Mother, I'm my father's heir and I'm going to legally take back his name. Henceforth, I'm just plain ordinary Herbert Cameron, as it should have been from the beginning. Mae and I will live in Pembroke for the rest of our lives as ordinary people. Aunt Morgan has given us a home, and that's where we'll live forever."

"I won't let my son throw his life away living like a homeless vagabond."

"Mother, Mr. Ashton is a barrister, and I've retained his services to represent me in every legal matter, including that of changing my name to my father's. Also, he's here to look out for my interests and protection. If you want to live in peace, then you'll do well to leave me and mine alone. I haven't come here to claim any part of your estate because it wasn't my father's. I came to tell you that in spite of all the things you did to me, I still love and forgive you. And I pray that one day you'll see that there's life beyond this estate that you've given up your life and humaneness for."

"Herbert, you can't do this to me. I've held everything in trust for you. This is your inheritance."

"And I don't need it. You made my father's life a living hell because of this estate and your wealth. Pa would have loved you and we would have been a good family, but you wouldn't give love and family a chance. All you did was for yourself. My father married you to save his mother from going to debtor's prison or ending up in a poor workhouse. He thought he would be free once you had what you wanted, namely a false marriage and an heir."

"You don't understand what you're saying. I did it all for you."

"Mother, in a strange way I do understand why you did the things that you did." His voice was gentle and the look he gave her was one of compassion. How he wished his mother would see that true happiness in life didn't lie behind one's possessions and station in life. "It's not too late for you to change, Mother. My father died of a broken heart because he eventually grew to love you, and that was the reason he stayed, not just because of me. Yet you never showed him even an iota of affection. Over the years you eroded his confidence and he stopped believing in himself. And for a time, you made me think that my father was a weak man. But Pa was humble and gentle, and he put up with you and your behaviours for all his adult life. I'm not like that, Mother." He smiled and his face glowed. "My love for Mae has made me strong, and I'll fight for us for the rest of our lives. She loves me for who I am and not what I can give her, like Miss Bella here." Bella looked down, her face flaming. "Because it's clear that you'll never accept my Mae, I'm leaving forever. I made a promise to my father that I would never marry a woman who didn't love, respect, and esteem me. He made me promise to never marry a woman I didn't love." Once again his eyes went to Bella. "It wouldn't be fair to either of us, and life is too short for me to go around bearing the guilt of knowing that I'm making someone very unhappy. Please forgive me, Miss Bella, if I ever gave you the impression that I was interested in marrying you. You're young and will find someone worthy of your love, but it isn't me." He turned to his mother. "Goodbye, Mother, and I forgive you. Also please forgive me for not being the kind of son you wanted, one you would manipulate and control to suit yourself."

"No, please," Mrs. Patterson burst out. "Herbert, please don't leave me. I'll change and do anything you want, including accepting that woman as your wife."

Herbert shook his head. "Mother, please don't make this harder for yourself. And that woman as you so scathingly refer to has a name and it's Mae. Mrs. Mae Cameron, beloved wife of Herbert Cameron."

Herbert was gone for a full week, and with each passing day, Mae saw her happiness slipping away. Aunt Morgan tried to comfort her, but she was inconsolable.

"You'll make yourself ill with much sorrow," Aunt Morgan told Mae on Sunday afternoon, one week since her husband had left. They had attended service at the local church, but Mae was too distraught and had barely listened to the sermon. Her heart was breaking as she imagined Mrs. Patterson holding on to Herbert and convincing him that he'd made a mistake in marrying her.

"Herbert will never come back," Mae moaned softly, holding her stomach. She refused to eat the simple meal that Aunt Morgan placed before her. Maybe someday she would be able to get past this pain, but for now she let it fester within her. There was a knock at the door, and since Aunt Morgan was closest to it, she opened it.

Mae had her back to the door and so she didn't see whoever it was that came into the house, and in any case, she wasn't interested in making small talk with the neighbours.

Then strong hands gripped her from behind and she gave a small scream. When she turned around and saw that it was her husband, she flew over the couch and landed in his arms, sobbing with deep relief. She couldn't believe that her Herbert was back.

"Now, my darling, if you can just calm down, I have a surprise for you," Herbert said softly when she finally stopped weeping. That was when Mae noticed that the house was full of strangers. They were all standing silently in the small parlour, and she gave them a cursory glance. Then something about the older woman made her take a second glance. She looked very familiar, and then the woman started singing softly.

"Mama?" Mae moved out of Herbert's arms and approached the visitors. Something clicked in her mind. "Papa? Peter? Simeon?" And then she was suddenly in Mrs. Ashton's arms, and they had a wonderful reunion as Herbert and Aunt Morgan looked on, beaming from ear to ear.

"Thank you," Mae said after a while, and she moved back into her husband's arms. "My life is getting better and better each day."

"And you deserve all the happiness that you're receiving."

Mae leaned closer and pressed her lips to his cheek. "You're a loving man, strong and kind, and have brought my family back to me. You've been good to Aunt Morgan even when you didn't have to be. Herbert, you've showed me that truly life can be good, and I love you so much. See how you gave up your name and your inheritance for me, and it humbles me very much because I don't deserve such a noble sacrifice."

"Mae." Herbert reached down and took her hands in his. "Nothing in this world is as important to me as loving you and being loved by you. I would give up the clothes on my back without a second thought, just to have you."

Mae squeezed her husband's hands then put them around her. She relaxed against him, contented and at peace with the world. In that moment her heart swelled with love and overflowed with forgiveness, and she felt as if she was flying.

Truly love sets one free, she thought. She was secure in Herbert's love, and it gave her the strength to face the world and whatever else would come.

She even felt generous enough to forgive her uncle and Herbert's mother and everyone who had ever hurt her.

She smiled and closed her eyes as she leaned on his chest, his strong arms around her and hers around him. Life was very beautiful.

EPILOGUE

Three Years Later

The love he and Mae shared never failed to amaze Herbert. Every single day, as he looked at his wife and twin sons, he counted his blessings. The boys, Edwin and Clive Cameron, had just turned two years old and were boisterous children, full of life, and they brought much happiness to their parents.

And then there was his beautiful little ten-month-old daughter named Morgan for her grand aunt who had died a year prior.

Their family was growing, and now they had a home to call their own, for Aunt Morgan had left them her house and four acres of land in her will. Never again would they see themselves as homeless vagabonds.

Three years before, Herbert had been shocked when his father's solicitor handed him quite a substantial amount of money.

"Your father saved his money and asked me to invest it for him, and these are the rewards of his investments."

Herbert had expected a paltry amount, so what he received as an inheritance from his father blew his mind. He and Morgan opened up a mercantile, and they lived a simple life on his pension and with their farming activities also. The sad thing was that his mother had died a year before, still filled with bitterness and anger at having been thwarted in her plans to hold onto the estate. His uncle Roger was now the estate owner and Herbert didn't begrudge him the inheritance. If anything, it was a relief to him that the estate no longer had any hold on him.

The last they'd heard about Uncle Lester and his wife was that they still lived on their estate, which was made possible when Ida had married the wealthy but old Mr. Watson. As for Bella, she now lived in Paris, though nobody knew what she was doing there.

The Ashtons were all the family that Herbert and Mae needed, and every mid-year they would travel to London to visit them. Peter and Simeon were still serving in the army and doing very well. Herbert didn't miss his old life at all because he had a new one with Mae and his beautiful children.

Thinking about all the blessings he'd received in abundance these past three years made Herbert smile. Seeing his wife and children sleeping so peacefully without a care in the world on this Christmas Day in the morning filled his soul with gladness. His life was good, no, it was wonderful.

An indistinct sound alerted the happy papa that one of his sons was waking up. It was probably Edwin, who was a very light sleeper like his mother. Clive, Mae loved to say, slept like a log, and nothing ever woke him up unless his sleep was over.

Quietly Herbert slipped out of bed and approached the large bassinet he'd lovingly fashioned for his sons. And just as he'd guessed, Edwin was awake and sitting up rubbing his eyes.

"Papa," the boy said as he raised both arms so his father could lift him up.

"Yes, my son?" Herbert bent down and scooped the child into his arms. "Sh! Don't make noise or you'll wake your mama and siblings up."

Edwin listened to his father with the seriousness of a firstborn child.

"Tree," Edwin said.

"You want to see our tree?" Herbert smiled as he carried his son out of the bedroom and to the living room. The fireplace glowed and the lantern that he'd left burning cast pretty shadows on the colourful tree standing in one corner of the room.

Edwin wriggled in his father's arms, and Herbert put him down, chuckling as he watched his oldest child toddle towards the Christmas tree they'd decorated together over the past few days.

Christmas Day in the Cameron household was celebrated with much joy, for it meant double blessings for the family. First, the memory of the Saviour who had come into the world to save mankind and bring redemption for all, and also it was Mama Cameron's birthday.

"What are you two doing up so early?" Mae's voice came to Herbert from the doorway. She held Morgan in her arms, while Clive clutched at her night robe, rubbing his eyes sleepily.

"Your son knows that today is Christmas Day and also his mother's birthday." Just then, the church bells began to toll in the distance. "I love Christmas Day," Herbert murmured as he watched Clive join his brother, and both boys sat around the tree rearranging the small gifts that their parents had placed there. Then he walked over to Mae and pulled her into his arms, baby and all.

"Merry Christmas, my darling." He kissed the top of her head. "And happy birthday to you, too."

"Merry Christmas to the best father and husband in the whole wide world," Mae murmured sleepily.

"Here, let me get you all back to bed, for it's still too early for us to be awake," Herbert said this as he watched his sons drooping. He carried them both to bed and then returned for his wife and Morgan, who was fast asleep in her mother's arms. He took her and placed her in the small cot that was hers alone.

After settling his family down, Herbert returned to the living room and stood before the fireplace.

"Dear Lord, thank You so much for all these wonderful blessings that You've bestowed on me. Thank You for the gift of our Lord Jesus Christ who was born on a special day like this one thousands of years ago. Thank You for my family and friends and for setting us free."

Herbert then returned to the bedroom and crawled into the large bed beside his wife. Though their house had two extra rooms, one of which was their nursery, for this season they had moved their children's cots back into their room so the family could be together.

Mae murmured sleepily, then settled down and cuddled close to him. As a log burst into flames in the grate in the next room, Herbert smiled. His father would be pleased with him for heeding his advice and marrying the woman of his dreams and his soul mate. Mae, his miracle.

"Thank you." He smiled, closed his eyes, and allowed sleep to take him over. Truly he was blessed.

THANK YOU FOR CHOOSING A PUREREAD BOOK!

We hope you enjoyed the story, and as a way to thank you for choosing PureRead we'd like to send you this free book, and other fun reader rewards…

Click here for your free copy of Whitechapel Waif
PureRead.com/victorian

AND THERE'S MORE...

We also want to bless you with a first chapter of Rosie Swan's brand new Christmas Victorian Romance, Workhouse Girl's Christmas Dream.

Turn the page and let's begin...

WORKHOUSE GIRL'S CHRISTMAS DREAM

PART 1 - CHRISTMAS STORMS

Christmas Day, Walsall County, England.

The storm that had been threatening for days reached the mining village of Walsall when least expected. Its violence was particularly felt in the old farmhouse that stood next to the village crossroads early in the morning on Christmas Day. A clap of thunder as loud as a blast from the dynamite used in the coal miles rumbled across the house, shaking its very foundations. A bolt of lightning sliced through the sky and struck a tree out in the yard, which immediately burst into flames. It seemed as if nature itself were sending out an ominous sign to the inhabitants of the old farmhouse that morning.

The flaming tree frightened the little girl whose face was pressed to the window as she watched nature in all her glory. She jumped back and crouched under the window sill like a scared rabbit, her eyes wide and filled with terror. In her whole life she'd never seen something as fascinating or as frightening as lightning striking a tree and causing it to burst into flames. That was the tree that she and her parents liked to sit under in the summer, sipping lemonade and watching as the villagers went past. Once in a while villagers would stop and be offered a glass of lemonade to refresh their thirsty throats. Now there would be no more reposing under the tree, and smoke from the burning tree filled the house, causing the child to choke.

For many years to come, eleven-year-old Amanda Jane Wood would always associate Christmas Day with terrible storms, fire, smoke and fear. First, fear of the terrible storm that was raging outside and then also the dark shadow of death that hovered in the three-roomed farmhouse. She coughed and tried to cover her face but in vain; the smoke was thick in the small living room.

Rain blew into the house through one of the cracked windows, soaking the child as she cowered under the windowsill. She rushed out of the living room and went to find her mother who was in her bedchamber. Mandy knew that when her parents' door was closed she wasn't supposed to open it without knocking first. And even then, she had to wait until she was bid to enter, so she stood there with her small hand raised as she prepared to knock. The storm made it impossible for her to hear whatever was going on and she knocked softly then waited.

Mrs. Edna Wood had just finished giving her husband a bed bath and dressing him in his best clothes as a way of preparing him for what was to come. Husband and wife both knew that this day wasn't going to end happily as most Christmas Days in the past had. That was the reason the twenty-nine-year-old man had held onto his wife's hand for a long while. The storm raged on outside, but in this small cosy room two souls were bidding farewell to each other, even though neither wanted to let go.

"Promise me that you'll always take care of Mandy," he whispered, his voice raspy even as his chest heaved. He was struggling to breathe, and she wished he would reserve his strength because talking was taking its toll on him. His once-ruddy skin was now sallow, and she could see the veins on his scrawny hands. Her once-virile man, the champion of her heart, was now nothing but skin and bones. Her heart was breaking, but she put on a brave smile. "And promise me that you'll also take good care of yourself."

"I promise," her voice was also a whisper as she fought back her tears. She had wept in private for many days, and this wasn't the time to do it openly. She had to be strong even though all she wanted to do was raise her head and scream, and ask why this was happening to her happy family. Why did death have to come to one so young when there were many old people in the village, she asked silently, then repented for her wicked thoughts. God was the giver of life and He chose who to preserve and who to take away. It wasn't up to her to decide because she was just a mere human being. But it hurt to know that this was the last time she was going to be with this man who held her heart.

"And always tell her that I love her so much but I have to leave. It's time for me to go, even though I wish I could stay with her, with you, my darling." And his shaking hand brought her palm to his cracked lips where he placed a soft kiss. His face was lined with the fatigue that comes to one who has been ailing for a while and whose body is giving up the fight. "It was so good with you, Edna," he whispered as he let her hand drop, his own too weak to continue holding it, and he closed his eyes. He opened his eyes briefly and smiled, "If I had to do it again, I would choose you over every other woman in the world. I would love you and be with you; always remember that."

The woman nodded, and when he fell asleep, she gazed at the face of the man she had loved for nearly twelve years, and tears coursed down her cheek. Why was death so cruel? And what would happen to her and Mandy when her beloved was gone?

She wiped her eyes because she didn't want Mandy to see her tears and rose up to go and empty the small basin. That's when she met with Mandy at the door of the bedchamber and the child looked terrified.

"Mandy, what's frightened you like this?" She looked toward the living room which was filled with smoke. "And why is there so much smoke in the house? Have you been burning things again?" Her voice was unusually harsh; then she toned it down. "Mandy you know that I've always told you to be careful with fire."

"Mama, the tree in the yard is burning and then the rain is pouring into the living room," Amanda was shivering but whether from the cold or fear or both wasn't clear. "The lightning struck the tree and it started burning."

"I'll fix the window later," Edna wiped the sweat off her forehead with the corner of her sleeve.

"How is Papa? May I go in and see him now? He promised that he would tell me the Christmas story today, Mama."

Edna gave her daughter a sad smile, "Not now, Mandy," she whispered. "Papa is tired and resting." She was normally a strong woman but taking care of her sick husband for the past one month had taken its toll on her. Slender and of average height, her blue eyes were troubled as they settled on her only child. She didn't want to frighten Mandy, but things weren't looking good for them, and their future was uncertain. She knew that Mr. Wood wasn't going to make it to the evening, and she didn't want to imagine what would happen to them after today. He had been her rock from the moment they had met and she felt like she was falling with no one to hold her.

"Mama today is Christmas Day and Mrs. Fount said we should celebrate it at her house with them. Will we be going there later, and will Papa come with us?" Mandy asked as she followed her mother into the third room of the house which served as both kitchen and Mandy's bedroom. Her mother had partitioned the room with a curtain to separate the child's sleeping area from the side they prepared meals on.

"Indeed it's Christmas Day," Mrs. Wood responded absentmindedly as she stroked the fire in the grate.

There was a pot of chicken bones on it from their dinner last evening. She was preparing some broth to feed her husband, even though he'd told her that he wasn't hungry any more.

Mandy looked around the kitchen and frowned slightly, wondering why her mother wasn't preparing the delicious pies that she always did when they were visiting their neighbours. In the past all the families in the village celebrated Christmas together and gathered at the home of anyone who chose to be the host for that particular year. This time it was Mrs. Fount who lived on the west side of them and whose house was much bigger than everyone else's in the village. Her husband was the village constable, and her two daughters Gillian and Alison, who were ten and eight respectively, were Mandy's best friends.

Christmas was always such a fun-filled and happy season, but Mandy had the strange feeling that it wasn't going to be like that this year.

"Ma?" Mandy saw the sadness on her mother's face.

"Yes my love?"

"You haven't baked anything to take to Mrs. Fount's house. Will we not have Christmas this year?"

Mrs. Wood sighed as she turned to her daughter. Now was the time for the truth which couldn't be hidden any longer.

"Mandy, you'll soon be twelve and are growing up, and I don't want to hide anything from you any longer."

Mandy felt fear but looked at her mother with wide eyes, hazel like her father's.

"You know that your father has been very ill this past one month and we were hoping he would get better. Sadly, that hasn't been the case, so all the money we had has been used up in getting him medicines. There's nothing left for me to buy even half a pound of ham to make pies, and we have no flour in the bin," She smiled and pulled Mandy close. "But I promise you that next year things will be better."

"So Papa will get better and then we'll have a good Christmas next year, Ma?"

"Oh Mandy," Edna had prayed for that miracle from the moment her husband had noticed the blood in his sputum when he coughed. That had been two months ago and she had done all she could, using all the traditional remedies she remembered her mother teaching her. From warm milk laced with honey, to boiled roots, there was nothing she hadn't tried. But the cough had only gotten worse and finally they had to accept the truth.

Mandy and her mother held each other for a while listening as the storm began to abate. As the storm died down, a heavy bout of coughing from the bedchamber made her mother immediately release her. She ran out of the kitchen.

Mandy wanted to follow her, but something held her back. She hated seeing her father suffering and especially when he tried to pretend he wasn't in pain. Her mother had told her that she shouldn't tire him by asking too many questions. She also didn't want to go back to the living room which was chilly and full of smoke. Her stomach rumbled with hunger and she wished her mother would serve her some of the broth that was bubbling merrily on the fire.

Mama would take care of things once she was done taking care of Papa, the child thought as she moved behind the curtain to her small cot. She climbed on it and curled up, feeling the warmth from her frayed blanket. Papa had promised to buy her a nice woollen one once he got better and she smiled at the thought.

Mandy never complained even when she went without a lot of the things that Jill and Ally possessed. She always believed that one day her father would buy her everything her heart desired, and so her life was filled with childish contentment.

Jill and Ally had a large bedroom in which they slept but Mandy loved her spot here in the kitchen. She always lay on her small bed and watched her mother cooking, most times falling asleep because of the warmth from the fire and having to be woken up to eat.

Her eyes felt heavy even as she listened to the murmuring voices in the other room. Her parents were probably talking about what to do for Christmas and she smiled as she closed her eyes. The little girl was soon asleep, unaware that life was about to change for them forever.

It was the wailing that roused Mandy from her deep sleep. At first she thought it was part of the dream she'd been having. But then she became aware of footsteps coming and going in the kitchen which had earlier been empty. And she could smell something besides the chicken broth that had been boiling on the fire. Pie and freshly baked bread!

The little girl's stomach growled again and she pushed the curtain aside and got off her narrow cot, wondering if her mother had been fibbing before. A smile broke out on her face as she saw the small kitchen table. It was loaded with many covered dishes emitting delicious aromas. Yes, Christmas Day was going to be a celebration and it was being held at their house.

"I must be dreaming," the child thought because just before she'd fallen asleep there had been nothing in the kitchen. Yet now the small table was groaning under the weight of all the dishes placed upon it. No one seemed to have noticed her yet so she reached out a hand to pick up a pie from the tray nearest to her bed. Mama wouldn't mind and besides, she was so hungry. She'd just taken the first bite out of the fruit pie when the loud wail came again and the small sweet pastry dropped from her hand to the floor.

"Mama," Mandy cried out, recognising the wailing voice and rushing out of the kitchen, brushing past neighbours who moved out of the way for her. Her mother was in her bedchamber and Mrs. Fount and Mrs. Wiser another neighbour were seated on the bed on either side of her mother.

Mandy frowned because this room was her parents' private domain and she couldn't recall any time that neighbours had been allowed inside. And yet here they were and she couldn't see any signs of her father who was supposed to be in the bed that her mother and the neighbours were sitting on.

"Ma?" Mandy stood at the doorway, too scared to go into her parents' bedchamber. That her mother was crying and wailing clearly meant that something bad had happened. The only other time she'd seen her mother this upset was years ago when she was about four and her grandmother and grandfather had died just days apart from each other. And on that day Mandy had seen her father wrapping his arms around her mother and comforting her. But if something bad had happened, where was her father to comfort her mother again?

"Oh, Mandy," her mother caught sight of her and held her arms out. Mandy ran to her mother and fell into her arms. "Oh, Mandy," she repeated, tears clogging her throat.

Mandy suddenly got the feeling that she was never going to see her father again. At eleven years of age the young girl knew about death after losing both sets of grandparents when she was of an age of reasoning. And also, they lived in a mining village where they had one or two funerals a week. Though she was still too young to comprehend the effects of coal mining on the lives of the miners, she knew that people who worked in the mines were always dying; then they were buried and their families mourned.

When her grandparents had died, she and her mother had been comforted by her father. But he wasn't here now, and she'd never once thought that she would be one of those children in the village who lost their fathers. A few of her friends had buried their fathers, but Mandy always thought that such a misfortune was far from her. Now a red cord would be stuck to the front of their door, signifying that the angel of death had visited them, as her father liked to say.

"Papa?" She asked softly and her mother heard her. This had to be a bad dream and she willed herself to wake up.

"Mandy, we have to be strong. Your father has gone and left us," Mrs. Wood broke into sobbing even as her arms tightened around her daughter. "What will I do now without you, Anthony," the woman wailed.

"We're here for you and your daughter," Mrs. Fount put her arms around Mandy and her mother. "My family will help in every way that we can," she made the promise, which Mandy was to remember at a later date.

"Death comes to all of us at one time or other," Mrs. Wiser said, confirming Mandy's fears. Her father was dead and she knew that he would soon be put in a hole in the ground like all the other dead people she'd seen; they would cover him with earth and she would never see him again.

Then Mandy felt something rising within her, from her stomach it moved to her chest then throat and forced its way out of her in a wail that many would later say had sent chills down their backs.

"No," she struggled to get free of her mother's arms. Mrs. Fount's arms dropped but her mother's held fast. She wanted to be set free so she could go and meet her father at the end of the bridge where she liked to wait for him as he returned from the mines which were about two miles from the village. What her childish mind refused to accept was that the coal mines had claimed yet another victim, and this time it was her father. Anthony Wood, loving husband and beloved father was no more.

"Pa is coming back," the child wailed. "Let me alone so I can go and wait for him at the bridge," she struggled to get free but her mother's arms only tightened around her small body.

"Mandy, you have to be strong," Mrs. Wiser said. "Your mama needs you right now. Stop that nonsense at once and accept what has happened. Denying it won't make your father come back."

But the child ignored the woman's harsh rebuke and continued to struggle in her mother's arms. Finally Mrs. Wood's hands were too weak and tired to continue holding the struggling child and she let go. Mandy rushed out of the room, ignoring calls from the neighbours who seemed to be everywhere. Their small house was filled with people, but she brushed them all aside when they tried to reach for her. She raced through the small living room where she saw Mr. Fount, the police constable who also acted as coroner whenever anyone died, and she also saw Reverend Jones, the vicar of their parish along with a few other male neighbours. They were standing around talking, but she didn't wait to hear what they had to say.

"Mandy," another voice called out as she tore out of the house through the front door, noticing the red cord hanging from the door. Her eyes were fixed on the road. It had stopped raining and the sun was even trying to break through the thick clouds. Mandy's focus was on getting to the bridge where she would wait for her father and skip beside him all the way home. Usually he left a little bit of whatever her mother had packed for his lunch and gave it to her as a present for waiting for him.

Come rain or sunshine, the child never missed a day waiting for her father at the bridge, unless she was sick and in bed.

There were few people on the road on account of the heavy storm that had passed. And also, it was early afternoon on Christmas Day and most folks were at home taking long lunches or early dinners. But none of Mandy's friends whose fathers also worked in the mines were outside as usual. That didn't even occur to her as she ran on, even though she soon found herself alone on the road.

Usually all the children of Walsall Village whose fathers worked in the coal mines would race each other to Old Walsall Bridge and play there among the rocks until the men arrived. Then each child would walk or dance back home with their father.

Today, however, it didn't occur to Mandy that the road leading to the bridge was empty. Her grief shrouded her in a world of her own, pushing her back into the past and she didn't even remember that it was

Christmas Day and the mines were shut down until after the holidays. All she wanted was her father.

Mandy got to the bridge, crossed it and sat down on one of the many little rocks that someone had once called the waiting station. One or two people passed by, giving her odd looks but the child's eyes were fixed on the path that her father usually took from the mines.

"Not my Pa," Mandy muttered as a man hurried toward the bridge and crossed it to the other side. "Not my Pa," she said of yet another, getting into the game she and her friends usually played as they waited. The game would go on until one of the children spotted his or her father. Thereafter, the lucky child would jump up and shout,

"My Pa is here, no more delays, no more waiting," and the others would giggle and continue with the game until the last man had returned. Sometimes when there was an explosion or a cave in at the mines, the children and their mothers would huddle together at the 'waiting station', each praying that their father and husband wasn't the latest victim to be claimed by the mines.

"Mandy," the soft voice broke through the child's continuous muttering and she looked up to find her mother crossing the bridge.

"Ma," she said, "I've been waiting for my Pa, but he isn't here yet. And I haven't seen the other men returning. Are they still working in the mines?" Mandy's eyes returned to the path leading to the mines.

"Oh Mandy," her mother walked slowly towards her. Mandy noted that she looked very tired and her eyes were red. Mrs. Wood had suffered five miscarriages, and when she'd given up hope of ever having a child, Mandy had been conceived.

It was clear to all that the little girl was the apple of her parents' eyes, but rather than become pampered and spoiled, she had such a sweet nature that everyone in the village liked her. The traders and store owners always had little treats for her whenever her parents sent her to get groceries.

"Mandy, today is Christmas Day and the mines are closed for the holidays," her mother reminded gently. She sat down on the same rock as her daughter and stretched out her shawl to cover them both.

Mandy raised stricken eyes to her mother. "Then where is my Pa?"

"Oh, Mandy," Mrs. Wood pulled her daughter close. "It's so cold out here and I need to get you home where it's warm. Besides, we have visitors and shouldn't leave them alone or they will think that we're being very poor hosts."

"But Pa…"

"Mandy!" Her mother's voice was gentle but firm. "For the past one month your father never went to the mines and you know the reason why, don't you? Remember that you haven't been out here to the bridge in all that time," Mrs. Wood raised her daughter's chin. "Your Pa was very sick and he was hurting terribly. You even saw that sometimes he would cough out blood and then wasn't able to breathe properly. He wanted to stay with us but the pain was too much for him to bear," Mrs. Wood's voice broke on a sob. "He begged me to let him go even when I didn't want to, and told me to tell you that he loves you so much and will be watching over you from heaven."

"But he didn't ask me before he left," Mandy cried out. "Why didn't he ask me? I wouldn't have let him go."

"Mandy, your father didn't want you to be sad so he didn't ask you."

"Ma, but why did he leave us? Didn't he love us anymore?" Mandy began to sob. "Why did he find it so easy to leave us?"

"Mandy, he didn't find it easy to leave us because he held on for as long as he could," Mrs. Wood said. Her husband, like many other miners before him, had suffered from black lung disease, which had only worsened as the days went by. "Your Pa loved us both so much but the pain became unbearable, and I let him rest," Mrs. Wood sobbed. The two held each other close and wept together for a long while.

They sat there at the 'waiting station' until the village lamplighter passed over the bridge, his ladder in his hand, on his way to light the gas streetlights.

"We have to get back home," Mandy heard her mother saying as if from a distance. "It's getting dark and we don't want to be out here until late." She rose to her feet and pulled Mandy up. Mother and daughter walked back home hand in hand, stopping every few steps to receive condolence messages from their neighbours.

And everyone had nice things to say about her father. Mandy heard them praising her father and saying that he was a good man who would be greatly missed. She wanted to shout and tell people not to talk about her father as if he wasn't there. Then she remembered that he was gone and actually wasn't there and fresh tears filled her eyes.

She would miss her Pa so much, and it was true: he'd been a very good man. Young as she was, Mandy understood what love was because she'd seen and experienced it in her home. And her father never stopped telling her and her mother that he loved them with his whole heart. Though they didn't have much, no one in need was ever turned away from their door.

"Even if there's nothing to eat in the house, make sure that everyone who comes to our door gets at least a simple glass of water," were her father's words to her so many times.

Mandy never understood why her father was so generous, sometimes causing her mother to complain that he was too kind. But Mr. Wood would simply laugh, ruffle Mandy's hair and kiss his wife's cheek.

"The Apostle Paul tells us to always open our homes to strangers for who knows, we may one day even welcome an angel into our humble abode," he would say. "And always remember that..."

"Angels are messengers who bring blessings from God to His people," Mandy and her mother would finish his sentence and they would all laugh.

It was because of her father's example that Mandy had learned to share everything she had with her friends. But sometimes they weren't as giving as she was, and she would then get upset and complain to her father.

"Mandy, don't always expect to be repaid for your kindness and generosity," he'd once told her when Jill and Ally refused to share their pastries with her. She had complained to him that her friends were very mean and yet she always shared everything with them. "Just do good, and one day it will find you when you need it most. God always rewards generosity even if it isn't immediately. What you hand out to someone through the front door returns to you through the back door."

Mrs. Wood paused at their small gate and Mandy looked up to see that someone had already lit the lanterns in the house and even placed two on the small porch. Their house was brighter than usual and she could see the red cord hanging on the open door. She wanted to rush up and tear it down.

Their small living room was filled with people and as soon as Mandy and her mother entered the house, the mourners parted to let them through. And that was when Mandy saw her father lying on the bier, covered up to his neck with a white sheet. He looked so peaceful and it was as if his lips were about to burst into a smile like they always did. Her Pa was such a happy man and she couldn't remember ever seeing him sad.

There was silence in the house as everyone watched to see what the child would do. They had seen her running out before and were worried that she wasn't in a very good frame of mind.

Mandy approached the bier, "My Pa looks like he's sleeping," she spoke to no one in particular. Mr. Anthony Wood looked peaceful in death, just as he had in life. "I wish he would open his eyes and wake up," she murmured.

She stood beside the bier for a long time, not feeling afraid of the dead body as was her usual practice. Even when a neighbour died and her parents took her to pay their respects to the family, Mandy would never get close to the bier.

Yet now she drew close without any fear, putting out a hand to touch her father's cold face. "Pa is cold," Mandy said, adjusting the bed sheet. A sob broke out among the mourners but Mandy ignored it. "I wish he was still here with us," she said sadly.

Then she turned to find her mother watching her. So she walked to where she was and put her arms around her.

"Ma, please don't ever go away like Pa and leave me alone."

Mrs. Wood choked up, "Oh, Mandy!"

"Now what will we do without my Pa," the child asked in a soft voice, sounding very lost.

What will happen to Mandy and her mother?

Workhouse Girl's Christmas Dream is a heartbreakingly beautiful Christmas story of rags to riches set in Victorian England. Mandy's story is one you will enjoy to the final happy ever after…

Continue Reading on Amazon

Continue Reading on Amazon

LOVE VICTORIAN ROMANCE?

If you enjoyed this story why not continue straight away
with other books in our PureRead Victorian Romance
library?

Read them all...

Orphan Christmas Miracle

An Orphan's Escape

The Lowly Maiden's Loyalty

Ruby of the Slums

The Dancing Orphan's Second Chance

Cotton Girl Orphan & The Stolen Man

Victorian Slum Girl's Dream

The Lost Orphan of Cheapside

Dora's Workhouse Child

Saltwick River Orphan

Workhouse Girl and The Veiled Lady

OUR GIFT TO YOU

AS A WAY TO SAY THANK YOU WE WOULD
LOVE TO SEND YOU THIS BEAUTIFUL
STORY FREE OF CHARGE.

Our Reader List is 100% FREE

Click here for your free copy of Whitechapel Waif

PureRead.com/victorian

At PureRead we publish books you can trust. Great tales
without smut or swearing, but with all of the mystery and
romance you expect from a great story.

Be the first to know when we release new books, take part in
our fun competitions, and get surprise free books in your
inbox by signing up to our Reader list.

As a thank you you'll receive an exclusive copy of Whitechapel Waif - a beautiful book available only to our subscribers...

Click here for your free copy of Whitechapel Waif

PureRead.com/victorian

Printed in Great Britain
by Amazon

24704164R00223